Two S

Alex Kane is a writer from Glasgow, specialising in gang-land crime and psychological thrillers. When not writing, Alex can be found relaxing at home reading, or drinking tea and/or gin (sometimes all of the above).

Also by Alex Kane

TWO SISTERS

ALEX KANE

hera

First published in the United Kingdom in 2024 by

Hera Books
Unit 9 (Canelo), 5th Floor
Cargo Works, 1-2 Hatfields
London SE1 9PG
United Kingdom

A CIP catalogue record for this book is available from the British Library.

Print ISBN 978 1 80436 041 5
Ebook ISBN 978 1 80436 930 2

Look for more great books at www.herabooks.com

Printed and bound in Great Britain by Clays Ltd, Elcograf S.p.A.

1

MIX
Paper | Supporting
responsible forestry
FSC® C018072

For my daughter and husband x

'Sooner or later, we all dance with the devil.'

Sherrilyn Kenyon

Prologue

Please, make it to the hostel, Molly Rose thought to herself as she ran faster than she thought possible. *I'll be safe at the hostel. Then I can phone the police.* She daren't speak out loud, or even whisper in case he heard her. It was bad enough that the grass beneath her feet rustled with every step she took.

Running uphill was hard at the best of times, but doing it while trying to navigate her way through the cover of darkness and avoid being taken out by low-hanging branches. But it was the only way she could get away from her attacker. When she'd made the connection between what she'd witnessed earlier and who was now following her, she knew she was in trouble if she didn't move fast.

Her legs burned so much she wasn't sure she was going to make it to the top of the hill but she pushed through the pain, all the while checking behind her to make sure there was enough of a gap between them that she could save herself.

Panic-stricken; Molly Rose felt herself begin to hyper-ventilate. *No,* she told herself. *Focus on survival.* But then she thought about the alternative. Pushing the horrors out of her head, she forced herself to keep moving through the trees. Soon, the top of the hostel building was visible. Lights warmed the windows and she tried to slow her breathing. Reaching into her pocket, she searched for her phone. But it wasn't there. It must have fallen out during her attempts to lose him. Glancing up again at the building that housed the hostel, Molly Rose decided she would make her way up slowly; going fast would make her panic, she could run out of energy or stumble over her own feet and he'd be more likely to catch her. *Breathe steadily*, she told herself.

Her eyes scanned the open grass around her. He could be there, hiding behind the tree right beside her and she wouldn't know.

Putting one foot in front of the other, Molly Rose climbed the rest of the hill, breathing in through her nose and out through her mouth. A half-brick sat at her feet and she picked it up. She rotated her body, holding the brick out in front of her. Wishing it was a loaded gun.

Reaching the wall at the top, it was a little higher than to her waist, but she used what little strength she had left to heave her body up and over it. She was now on the pavement, under the dim lights that lined the road. The hostel door was directly in front of her across the road. She stepped off the kerb and breathed a sigh of relief. She'd made it to safety.

Then she froze.

'Don't fucking move,' a voice came from behind her. *His* voice. 'Put the brick down. Now.'

Molly Rose felt something inside her die. She knew her time was up. She could swing her body around, strike him on the head. But would she be quick enough? With her size and weight, it was unlikely.

'I said, put the brick down. Unless you want to die right here?'

Molly Rose slowly lowered herself and placed the brick on the pavement before standing back up. Her entire body trembled. She scanned the street, desperately hoping someone would appear and come to her aid. No one else was around. Just her and him.

And then, she felt hands on her shoulders from behind. A rag stuffed into her mouth and bag quickly pulled over her head as she was bundled into a vehicle.

Hands quickly bound together as Molly Rose kicked and flailed as much as she could, the man breathed heavily as he fought against her attempts to get him off her.

But it was no use. The sound of an engine roared in her ears as he drove off with her in the boot. That, however, wasn't the thing that scared her the most. Molly Rose somehow managed to get the loose bag off by shaking her head.

It was dark, but not dark enough that she couldn't make out what she was lying next to. As Molly Rose blinked against the darkness and her eyes adjusted, she stared into the dead face of her best friend, Kassy.

FOURTH WOMAN GOES MISSING IN GLASGOW

Another prostitute has been reported missing in Glasgow – the fourth to have gone missing in a six-week period.

Kassandra Denholm, twenty-three, was reported to police as missing after she failed to return to her room at the Glasgow Hostel in the Park Circus area. Her friends are worried for her safety.

Police Scotland say they are looking for one suspect and are following up inquiries. No arrests have been made.

If you have any information on the whereabouts of Kassandra Denholm, Fearne McDermid, Tracy Finn or Julie Lindsay, get in touch with Police Scotland.

Chapter 1

THEN

Knocking gently on the door, Orla Hunter waited for the little shit to answer. She knew he'd be cheeky, a bit cocky. Lads his age always were. She already knew he was an arrogant little prick, but the idea of coming face to face with him and seeing it for herself made the anger bubble away inside her.

The sound of a chain coming undone on the other side of the door made her straighten her back. She needed to have a presence, a strong, not-to-be-fucked-with presence that would hopefully encourage him to back off.

The door opened slowly, as though he was cautious. Then, as he came into view in the doorway, he stared at her as if he was, one, relieved that it was her and not someone else; and, two, already bored with their meeting.

'What do you want?' he asked, looking her up and down.

'Do you know who I am?' Orla asked, already resisting the urge to punch him in the face.

Chewing on a piece of gum, he tucked it into the corner of his mouth and said: 'Aye. And what about it?'

'Then you'll know why I'm here,' she replied.

He played dumb, looked at her as if he had no idea what she was on about.

'She's fifteen, Dean.' His name felt like poison on her tongue. 'That means she's underage, if you're as stupid as you look, I'd imagine you'd need that explained to you.'

His brow furrowed and he stood up straight. 'Who do you think you're fucking talking too, ya old boot?'

She wasn't scared of him. He was just a little boy to her. He could only dream of being a real man.

'I'm talking to you, a *fucking paedophile*,' she replied, taking a step closer and jamming her foot in the door. He looked down and then back up at her. Shock crossed his face and she held back a smile. He was shaken.

'I'm no' a fucking paedo,' he replied.

'Oh really? So you're still fifteen yourself, are you?'

'I haven't fucking touched her,' he said. He glanced behind her and it seemed as though he was worried what people would think if they heard her accusation.

Narrowing her eyes, she replied: 'But the intention is there? I mean, why else would you give her money, buy her designer clothes? It has a name. It's called grooming. You'll go to prison for it. Do you know what they do to paedophiles in prison? *Do you?*'

He pulled the door open and squared up to her, pressing his forehead into hers, but without applying force, not enough to knock her off balance.

'If you want your precious little daughter to stop seeing me, then you're going to have to fucking kill me. Aren't ya?'

She stepped back and smiled at him. 'Bit far-fetched if you ask me,' she said, before leaning into his ear and whispering, 'But if you'd like, it could be arranged.'

They stared into each other's eyes, neither of them blinking. She wasn't going to let this go, even though she had no real intention of ever going that far. Of course she didn't. She wasn't a killer. She was the owner of an early year's franchise; she didn't have a bad bone in her body. But he didn't have to know that.

'And ya don't think I could have *you* done in?' he challenged. 'If ya knew who I was; who *we* are, then you wouldn't be standing here getting lippy with me.'

'Who's *we*?' Orla challenged. 'You and your mummy and daddy?'

Dean fell silent. By the flush of his cheeks, it was almost as though she'd embarrassed him. Good, she thought. A small price to pay for his actions.

Orla continued. 'I couldn't give a fuck who you are and you don't scare me, Dean. Not you or this "we" that you talk about. Just walk away from my daughter. I don't care how you do it. I don't care if you break her heart. If I find out that you haven't ended things in the next twenty-four hours, I'll make life very difficult for you. Trust me on that.'

He glared at her and she noticed how he swallowed. He tried to hide it, but she noticed.

Turning, she walked out of the building and down the street without looking back. She was serious: if Dean didn't end things with Molly Rose, the next knock at his door would be the police. She'd report him for statutory rape, and even if he was telling the truth and he hadn't touched Molly Rose, he'd be on the police's radar. It would be enough for Orla, for now. And she knew this was going to put a strain on her relationship with her daughter. But it was a risk she was willing to take to protect her.

Dean Davidson closed the door and leaned back against it.

'Are you fucking kidding?' his dad, Leo, asked.

'What do you mean?'

'You were supposed to keep your relationship with that wee lassie on the quiet, do things the proper way. She was our next big fucking target, and you go and bring her bloody ma to the door… scuppering the entire operation.'

Dean rolled his eyes and pushed himself off the door. 'I haven't. That's a bit dramatic, Dad.'

'Did you just backchat me?' Leo asked, his eyes boring into Dean's. 'Do you seriously think you're in a position to get lippy with me, Dean?'

'I'll sort it,' Dean said through gritted teeth.

'You fucking better, Dean. Because from where I'm standing, I might need to step in. And you know that—'

'Aye, I know,' Dean held his hands up. 'You don't get your hands dirty. You do the thinking, not the lifting. I get it.'

Leo grabbed Dean by the collar of his T-shirt and shoved him up against the door. 'It's not that I refuse to do the hard graft, Dean. I *literally* can't.'

Dean raised a brow. His dad could have gone into amateur dramatics the way he was going on.

'Don't you get it? I'm the one tasked with this operation. I've literally been given a list of instructions, descriptions. Like a fucking shopping list. I have to keep my name and face out of the limelight. If you fuck this up, you don't just fuck up *this* job. You fuck it all up. I've got bosses in Lithuania, Romania and Poland waiting on these girls. And you go and bring one of their fucking mammies to the door? Get a fucking grip of yourself, Dean, otherwise that woman will bring the police to us and they won't be our biggest problem. You have any idea what the bosses will do to us?'

Dean struggled under his dad's grip, but he was too weak against him.

'So, what the hell do you want me to do?' Dean shouted, before Leo let go.

Grabbing the back of Dean's head and pulling him close, he looked into his eyes and said: 'Do what she said. End it and get to work on the next girl. And make sure she's of fucking age, otherwise this will happen again. I swear to God, Dean, if you bring the police or another raging mammy to this door, the bosses will come after us and then we're all dead.'

Dean watched, full of rage and humiliation, as his dad walked along the hallway and slammed the home-office door shut behind him.

'Fucking pricks,' he muttered as he turned and moved through the flat and into the kitchen. Pulling a beer from the fridge, he placed the rim of the bottle cap on the edge of the counter and hit the top of it with the palm of his hand. He glugged greedily from the bottle, trying to calm his anger.

Who did she think she was? Turning up at his flat and speaking to him like he was a fucking child? Because of her and that stupid bitch of a daughter of hers, his dad thought he wasn't capable of getting the job done.

Dean imagined what it would be like to step out of the shadows of those older than him, the ones he worked for; including his dad. He'd do a better job than any of them put together, even those fuckers in Poland.

Molly Rose's face crept into his mind. This all stemmed back to her. If she'd just kept her fucking mouth shut about their relationship, kept it quiet, then she'd have been shipped off by now. He'd managed to get her on her own, stop her from having close relationships with others. Her mates had slowly faded out of the picture, but her mum? Nah, she was a different story.

Slamming the beer bottle onto the kitchen counter, Dean turned and placed his hands on the surface and stared out the window. He felt angrier with Molly Rose than anyone else right now. Stupid little bitch. He'd almost had her. He was so close.

He imagined her, on that flight to Poland, her pretty little face oblivious to what lay ahead of her and it made him smile, but just for a moment. Because it wasn't real. She'd fucked it up. Now, he was faced with having to undo all his hard work and starting from scratch with someone else.

Dean let out a roar and threw the bottle into the sink, beer and glass spraying everywhere as he tried to stem the anger. '*Fuck!*'

Chapter 2

2023

Charlie stood at the end of the drive of the house he owned; *used* to own and watched as the bailiffs pulled it apart from the inside out. The rage he felt was like nothing else and the only thing that could numb the pain of what he was witnessing was the bottle of vodka in his hand and the bottle of whisky in his rucksack. The only thing he had to his name now was the clothes on his back, along with the bag and the alcohol.

'Fucking scum!' he shouted, although his words slurred. 'D'ya fucking hear me? I said you're fucking scum!'

The men who cleared out what once was his mansion ignored him. He'd lost everything. Pissed it up a wall, snorted it up his nose; shagged away his money. The lot. That was a *lot* of alcohol, cocaine and girls. He'd had the money. He didn't think it would ever run out. And it wouldn't have if he hadn't acted like such an idiot with it. Now, he was homeless. There was only one person who could fix that. Who *should* fix that.

He'd kept an eye on her for a long time. Since as far back as when he'd been paid off. That inheritance was his, by right. Instead, his fuckwit of a stepdad had given it all to his daughter. A young girl who had no idea how to run things. How could she be expected to run things? She was a woman after all and had no place in that world. In fact, women were only good for one thing and even then they were a let-down. Every single last one of them. Charlie hated all women, including his mother. *Especially* his mother. Abandonment was something that had stayed with him since she'd left and, ever since, every female he'd ever come across had been the same: a self-centred, selfish bitch.

Charlie had been part of the Hallahan family as though he was blood, since he was just eight years old. But then, when it really came down to it, Finn had proven that, to him, blood really was thicker than water. It didn't matter to Finn that Charlie was far more capable of taking over. And now, here he was, some forty-odd years later, with nothing but a trail of destruction at his back and a path in front of him with no prospects. At the time he thought the money that Finn had given him would last forever. He didn't have to work – thank God for that, because it was never in his nature to work hard. He'd be happy to admit that. But when the money started to dwindle, he'd decided to start a little business of his own to keep the funds rolling in. Nothing major, just an off-the-back-of-a-lorry kind of thing. He'd brought in some younger lads, paid them a small cut of the sales and kept the rest. But then, the drink and the drugs got a hold of him, and he lost his touch when it came to robbery. In fact, he lost his touch with everything.

Charlie Hallahan adjusted the straps on his rucksack, making sure it was secure on his back. He opened the vodka bottle in his hand and slugged back a large mouthful. He looked up at the life he used to have within the walls of that house and realised that being homeless wasn't his only problem. It was imperative that he own that house again. He couldn't walk away from it. It contained too many secrets that could put an end to him.

He knew who could help him financially. It was *owed* to him, if not by blood but by principle. And he would get what he wanted. What he *deserved*.

Chapter 3

Janey Hallahan looked up at the flock of geese above her, heading across the North Channel and watched as they disappeared into the distance. The blue sky over Northern Ireland that morning, coupled with the calm air and warm sun made her feel more relaxed than she had in a long time.

'Love a spring morning, eh?' Ciaran said, appearing to her left with a mug of coffee in his hand. Taking it, Janey thanked him and sat down at the patio table. Their back garden overlooked the Northern Channel and, on days like this, Janey was so thankful for the view. It made the working life she led all worth it.

'Oh, I forgot to mention that Kristo called earlier. He's finalised the premises for the new salon in Glasgow and work begins next week on the refurb. Means I'll get things going on getting one of the girls in there soon and we can start putting money through there too,' Janey said.

'Good to know. I don't know what we'd do without Kristo,' Ciaran replied.

'I know. He makes Geo look like an apprentice, God rest his soul,' Janey said, lifting up her coffee mug and taking a sip. 'He was a good leader, Geo, and a good friend. But Kristo, I don't know... there's a loyalty there that I haven't seen in any of my other employees. It's like he's blood, or something. And in this business, that's all you can ever hope for. Someone who is going to run your business in your absence the exact way you want and need them to. Someone who has your back regardless of the risk. And he does it all with such integrity and grace. He doesn't draw attention to us at all, ever.'

Ciaran laughed. 'You're saying that if ever there was an award for best organised-crime leader, Kristo would win that?'

Janey smiled and shook her head at the ridiculousness of the idea. 'All I'm saying is, I thought Geo was irreplaceable.'

'Ooft, that's brutal even coming from you.' Ciaran raised a brow.

'You know what I mean. Geo McInroy was one of those employees that I couldn't fault.'

As much as business was on her mind, she couldn't fight the thoughts that were forcing their way in.

'Few boats headed out to Copeland Island this morning, by the looks of it,' Ciaran said, filling the silence as he sipped on his own coffee.

'Hmm,' Janey replied, far away in her head.

'I haven't forgotten what day it is, you know?' Ciaran said.

Janey glanced over at her husband, trying not to show on her face that she was suffering today.

'How old would the girls be now?'

She closed her eyes, as if in doing so, she would be able to block it all out. Of course, that was never the case. Every year, since she could remember, this day haunted her.

'They turn thirty-eight years old today,' Janey replied, turning her attention back to the water.

She watched as the geese fell away from sight. 'It only feels like a few weeks have passed since I gave birth to them. Fifteen, terrified of what the future would hold with and without them.'

Ciaran was quiet. That's what she loved about him. He always allowed her the time to speak. Never interrupting. Never judging.

'I know giving them up was the best thing for them. I wasn't ready to be a mother regardless of how I felt about them. I couldn't have given them what they needed, even with Finn's money at my back. But that doesn't mean I don't love them any less now than I did the day they were born.'

Janey got to her feet and pulled her woollen shawl tightly around her shoulders before leaving the patio area and heading down to the bottom of the garden. She reached the gate, unlatched it and walked out on to the private beach, shared by the two other houses on either side of her own. She was alone, thankfully. She needed to gather her thoughts.

She sat down on the dry sand and listened as the water lapped up onto the shore. She dug a small hole and placed her mug into it, before pulling out her cigarettes and lighting one.

Copeland Island stood out under the sun and she listened to every bird twitter, every lap of a wave, felt the grains of sand under her. But no matter what she focused on, she couldn't get her babies out of her head. The babies she gave up and the babies that she chose not to go on to have later in life with Ciaran. She didn't deserve to be a mother after abandoning her girls. And children didn't deserve to be a part of her world, where dirty money, drugs, guns and violence were ever-present. Building an empire was something Janey had thrown all her energy into once she'd taken the reins. Ciaran had been nothing but supportive about her decision not to go on to have other children. It just wasn't in her plans and Ciaran had been honest; it hadn't ever been in his either. In their thirty-three-year relationship, neither of them wavered on that.

She sighed deeply before taking a long draw on her cigarette. She missed the girls with every breath. And it hurt more with every passing year.

Ciaran sat down beside her and pulled her in to him. She welcomed the comfort.

'I often wonder if they ever think about me,' Janey said, trying her damnedest not to allow the tears to come.

'I bet they think about you every day. Not necessarily you, specifically, but the idea of you and who you might be,' Ciaran replied. 'Especially today.'

She placed the cigarette between her lips and took a long draw. 'I've never told you this and, to be honest, I don't know why. But I did contact them, once. Well, one of them anyway. It was a while ago. Last year, I think. She pretty much told me where to go. Do you think that'll ever change?'

'I'll not pretend to know the answer to that, sweetheart,' Ciaran replied. Janey exhaled and the smoke billowed up into the air.

'I don't know much about them, or what kind of life they've had. Sometimes I wonder if giving them up was the best or worst decision.'

Janey broke their embrace and lifted her coffee mug to take a sip.

'I suppose you'll never know the answer to those questions unless you decide to find out for yourself. And maybe you could. Maybe, you could use our contacts to find out how they're doing? You don't have to call them directly, but perhaps just knowing would set your mind at ease without having to deal with possible rejection?'

The cigarette between her fingers had burned down to the tip. She dunked it into the coffee mug and sighed.

'Yeah,' she said. 'Maybe.' The thought of rejection filled her with fear. Janey Hallahan was never one for showing her emotions, especially not in her line of business. However, she didn't want to give up at the first hurdle.

'Where better than here?' Ciaran said. 'It's a gorgeous day, a relaxed environment. I'm assuming you have her number, if you've already called her before?'

Janey looked at him and exhaled slowly. 'You know me so well,' she said, taking the phone out of her pocket. 'I saved it even though I genuinely thought I'd never use it again.'

She pulled up her daughter's number and hit call. All at once, her stomach started to roll. But before she could change her mind, the phone rang at the other end of the line.

'Orla?' Janey said. A silence hung heavy on the other end of the line. Ciaran looked out across the water and clasped his fingers between hers.

She listened as her daughter began a sudden rant, one that she hadn't expected to come so quickly. Her heart sank in her chest as she listened to Orla, telling her that she didn't need her, or want her. Why was she calling?

'I'm sorry. I only wanted to wish you and your sister a happy birthday. Pass on my wishes to Sinead.'

A few more words were exchanged and the bitterness in Orla's tone made Janey switch off just a little. Once the call was ended, Janey looked out at the water and wished it would roll up from the shore and swallow her.

'She'll come around,' Ciaran said, giving Janey's hand a squeeze.

'I highly doubt that, Ciaran. It's abundantly obvious that she doesn't want to have anything to do with me. It's fine. I can handle it. It's just a sore one, that's all.'

She got to her feet and dusted the sand off the back of her trousers. Her phone rang in her hand and, for a moment, she hoped that it was Orla calling back to apologise and maybe they could chat properly. When she looked down at the screen and saw Kristo's name, she scolded herself for thinking such a stupid thought.

'Hello?' Janey answered, pushing Orla to the back of her mind.

'Boss, we have a problem.'

Janey eyed Ciaran and put Kristo on loudspeaker.

'What's happened?'

'It's Club Envy. It's been the target of an arson attack. The entire building is gone.'

Janey closed her eyes and her jaw tensed. 'For fuck's sake.'

'I'm sorry to have to tell you this over the phone,' Kristo said.

'That's your job, Kristo. We'd rather you told us,' Ciaran replied.

Janey opened her eyes and turned her back on the water before heading back up to the house. As if today wasn't hard enough, some little bastard had to go and burn down one of her properties.

'What would you like me to do, Janey?' Kristo pressed.

'I'll be there in a few hours,' Janey said, slipping off her shoes before stepping into the kitchen. 'I just need to sort a flight. Hang on for me and we can discuss it when I get there.'

'Okay. Let me know when you're due to land and I'll pick you up from the airport.'

Janey thanked Kristo and hung up the phone. Ciaran slid the patio door closed and locked it behind him.

'Do you have any idea who could have done this?' he asked, as Janey sat down at the breakfast bar and opened the laptop.

'It'll be some little fucker thinking that because Danny McInroy is now out of the picture, they can swoop in and claim the territory. They obviously don't know Danny was a cog in a bigger machine. I'll find out who it was and deal with them later.'

Janey tapped away on the keys and smiled. 'There's a flight leaving at four o'clock this afternoon.'

'I take it you're booking a one-way for now?' Ciaran asked.

'It makes no sense to do a return. This could take a while.'

Janey booked and paid for the flight, then closed the laptop. 'At least we get to spend some time in the new house. We've barely been in it since the build was completed. Wouldn't mind living there for a while as we figure out who torched our property.'

Ciaran smiled, and moved out to the hallway and opened the cupboard under the stairs before removing two suitcases. 'Beats living out of these things in hotels. And maybe you should let Kristo take charge of finding the arsonist. You said yourself that you wanted to take more of a backseat and let the lads take on more responsibility. Sounds like a good idea to me. Less work, with the same, if not more, income?'

Janey thought about it. She knew Kristo could do the job with his eyes shut. Along with the lads she'd enlisted as her seconds in Manchester, Birmingham and Liverpool. But did she want to take a step back? Her thoughts would only have more time to torment her; make her question her decision to give up the girls all those years ago. Thirty-eight, to be precise.

'Maybe. I haven't fully decided yet,' she replied. 'This has been my life since… well, forever. I can't make that decision on a whim.'

She stole a glance at Ciaran, who simply nodded. 'Fair enough, Janey. It's your business, your decision. Just don't make yourself ill because of it. You've set us up with a life. We'll never need to worry about money. Ever.'

For Janey, that was not what it was about. It was about her legacy, her father's legacy. Yes, she and Ciaran didn't have children through choice, but if she gave this up, who would carry on the Hallahan name? The Hallahan business?

She wasn't ready to let that come to an end just yet.

Chapter 4

Staring down at the phone in her trembling hand, Orla Hunter felt her blood boil inside her. After all this time. After all these years.

'Just hang up the phone,' Oliver, her husband, mouthed from across the dining table.

Orla shook her head and placed the phone to her ear again. 'I'm sorry. I only wanted to wish you and your sister a happy birthday. The last thing I wanted to do was to upset you.'

'You don't have the capacity to upset me. You're *nothing* to me. Nothing to do with my life. How did you even get this number? I told you the last time you got in touch, I didn't want to hear your voice ever again.'

Her voice was sharper than she'd ever thought possible, but Orla had to say it like it was.

'I hear that, loud and clear.'

'Do you, though? Because you said as much the last time. You better not be here, in Glasgow. I don't want to see you, Janey,' Orla replied.

There was a pause, a heavy silence that, for just a split second, allowed a wave of guilt to wash over Orla. But then she reminded herself why she was being so cold to the woman on the other end of the call. Her so-called mother. Only in DNA and that was bad enough.

'I'm sorry. Happy birthday, Orla. Pass on the message to Sinead, please.' The line went dead, and Orla set the phone down on the table in front of her.

'She has some balls, I'll give her that,' Oliver said, placing his glass of red down and taking a breath. 'Are you okay?'

Orla sighed in annoyance. 'I don't know. First Sinead and all her shit to deal with. Then *she* gets in touch again after I told her to piss off the last time. I don't bloody need her. I've never needed her.'

'Look, we've got a restaurant booked for your birthday meal. That will cheer you up a bit,' Oliver said.

'Cheer me up? Seriously?' Orla said. How could he think that anything would bring her out of this mood now?

Oliver looked at her silently, his eyes unblinking.

'Don't look at me like that, Olly,' Orla said, pushing back her chair and getting to her feet. She picked up the plates from the dining table and glanced up at the clock on the wall above the door. It was just after nine in the morning and Molly Rose wasn't home. She'd left school and didn't have a job, so had nowhere to be. No message to say where she was or when she planned to be home. No phone call. Nothing. Not that she often told her parents much any more. Molly Rose had rebelled against Orla and Oliver. She barely spoke to them these days.

'I just think that you've got some things to unpack with Janey, that's all.'

'No. I don't. She chose to give me up. To give us both up. After thirty-eight years of making it on my own, I certainly don't need anything from her.'

'What about Sinead? Don't you think she might want to talk to her mother? Maybe having a mother figure around is exactly what Sinead needs right now?' Oliver asked. From the way he'd said it, she felt like he was judging her.

'Sinead has her own phone. If Janey wants to contact her, she can. But you know what? Unless the woman has a lifetime supply of heroin and booze, Sinead won't give a shit if our mother turned out to be the fucking Queen.'

Oliver lifted his coffee cup, drank back the last drops and joined Orla at the sink. He slid his arms around her and she felt herself melt into his embrace. She'd never admit it, but he knew her better than she knew herself. As much as she'd got by in life without a mother, it still made her angry that she and her twin were cast aside so easily. Having been adopted wasn't the issue; from what she could remember of them, Orla and Sinead's adoptive parents were loving and caring. But they'd been in an accident when Orla and Sinead were just ten years old and that had left them in foster care. Going from foster family to foster family had been brutal, especially knowing that there was a woman out there who could have taken care of them and chose not to. Growing up in care hadn't been easy and it would have been textbook for Orla to turn to the grittier side of life because of it. But she'd chosen a better path than that. She'd managed to get herself into college, then university to study a degree in business management. Now, she was the owner of an Early Years franchise, with nursery centres up and down the country. She was living the life she could only have dreamed of and her company was being run by area managers. She didn't need to do much, other than request to see the accounts every month. She really was living her best life – or at least from the outside looking in, that was how it would seem.

'It's okay to be angry, you know,' Oliver said, kissing the top of Orla's head. 'I would be too.'

'I'm not angry. That would mean I feel something for this stranger who has randomly started to contact me. And that's all she is, just a random. What does anger me is that she thinks it's okay to do this. Having her interfering like this just makes everything else seem so much worse. With Molly Rose refusing to talk to me because I chased Dean away and my sister off God only knows where shooting up and getting blind drunk every day, Janey can piss right off.'

Oliver was quiet for a moment and Orla knew what he was thinking. That he didn't believe her; that she did care about Janey. In truth, she *was* angry, but she was never going to say it out loud.

'Molly Rose will understand one day why you did what you did, Orla. She was just fifteen and he was eighteen. It was wrong, illegal and just...' Oliver took a breath. 'Enough to send a dad to jail. So I'm glad you dealt with it because I'd be behind bars right now if I had.'

Orla smiled. She knew that wasn't true. Oliver was the kindest, gentlest man she'd ever come across. He just didn't have that kind of thing in him. And as much as Orla had threatened to harm Dean, she wouldn't have been able to, even if she wanted to.

'I know. But right now, she is seething that I ruined her relationship with *the one*. She told me I had no right, that it wasn't up to me who she chose to be with.'

Oliver shook his head. 'That's exactly your job as her mother.'

Orla nodded. 'What if Dean comes back, now that she's sixteen? He's bad news, Oliver. I just know it. I mean, what eighteen-year-old do you know in their right mind would want a relationship with a child? Because in the eyes of the law, that's what she is.'

Silence fell between them. As much as Orla had it mapped out in her head that she wouldn't let that happen, she knew deep down that if Dean did come back to start things up again with Molly Rose, there would be nothing she could do about it. In the eyes of the law, sixteen and nineteen was of legal, consenting age for a relationship.

'Honestly? I don't know. I suppose we just have to hope that she'll have a bit more understanding as to why you warned him off and accept it; that way, she'll stay away from him. But to be honest, he took heed of your warning. He's not been around; Molly Rose's attitude proves that. So, I doubt he'll come sniffing around again.'

Orla wished she could share in Oliver's optimism, but for some reason, something in her gut told her that this Dean situation wasn't over.

Chapter 5

Sinead sighed loudly as she waited in the queue at the chemist for her daily dose of methadone.

The woman stood next to Sinead was staring at her through narrowed eyes, like she was studying her face.

'What?' Sinead challenged, although her tone didn't match how she'd wanted it to come out. Being an addict meant her voice had changed. Everything came out slower, a little more sluggish than intended. She hated that about herself. There was no hiding the fact that she was a full-blown junkie even if her voice didn't sound that way. She just had that appearance and could barely look at herself in the mirror any more.

The woman, who looked like one of those West End mums who was nothing other than perfect in the eyes of society, turned, said nothing and if Sinead had more energy, she'd have asked her what her bloody problem was. It was obvious Sinead's whole image was the complete opposite to this person. She wore what Sinead could only imagine as a designer coat over her jeans and blouse. Her ankle boots looked brand new, or well-looked-after. Sinead looked down at herself and sighed inwardly. Her extremely old and worn Converse trainers, which used to be white but were now a muddy-puddle colour, sported the biggest tear at the front. Her ripped-at-the-knee jeans looked like they'd seen better days and her fingernails were long, with chipped nail polish crying out to be removed. Not to mention the state of her skin, which had been off-colour for years and exhibited plum-coloured patches, alongside some battle scars that came from living on the streets as a junkie.

Jesus, she thought to herself. That woman was probably older than Sinead, and yet she looked at least ten years younger. For thirty-eight years of age, Sinead knew her life should be going down a better path, like Orla's. But for some reason, once Sinead had turned to drugs and alcohol when she was in her twenties, it seemed like there was no reason to get off it. Seeing what her sister had – a hugely successful business, a loving husband and a daughter of her own – didn't even spur her on. Orla gave her money every month. A decent amount. So there was no real incentive to do better.

The designer-coat woman glanced back at Sinead and gave her a smile. 'Are you okay?'

Sinead frowned, confused by the sudden kindness. Usually, people like her did nothing but judge. Sinead gave her a once-over and wondered how much the entire outfit she was wearing was worth and if she'd be able to get some cash for anything she mugged from her.

'I'm fine,' Sinead replied, a little more harsh than necessary.

'You *don't* remember me, do you?' the woman asked.

'Should I?'

'Alyssa? We used to go to high school together.'

Sinead stared into Alyssa's eyes and couldn't believe that it was her former best friend. The one who'd left halfway through school to move to America with her family. If only someone had scooped Sinead up and whisked her away, maybe she'd be in a better situation. Instead, she was taking methadone while still scoring a bag every day. She didn't give a shit what the doctors said, methadone didn't work for anyone and she continued to take both in the hope of a better high.

'Fuck *me*,' Sinead gave a throaty laugh. 'Alyssa? What the hell are *you* doing here?'

Alyssa hesitated, as if she'd just realised what Sinead had become. But there was no way to backtrack without causing offence and Sinead took offence easily because being an addict was something she still couldn't quite believe herself.

'I moved back years ago. But I'm living on the Southside, only over here to pick up something for my gran. How are you?' Alyssa asked.

Sinead glanced down at her appearance and then at Alyssa. She wouldn't get away with the age-old, 'I'm good' but she'd wing it. 'Yeah, I'm great. Life's good. You?'

She could tell by Alyssa's face that she didn't believe Sinead. Not that Sinead blamed her, it was relatively obvious. But what was she going to say? *Oh, actually, life's a bit shit. I'm a junkie and an alchy, and I shag strangers for a tenner just to get a bit extra for said substances. And how are you?*

'I'm great, thanks. Married, have two kids and my own dental surgery in Hyndland.'

That's when it hit Sinead, what an absolute cluster-fuck her life was. But then, that realisation hit her regularly, but never enough to do anything to change it. That would be too much hard work. It was easier to shoot up and push all her troubles to the back of her mind.

The door to Alyssa's left opened and one of the pharmacists appeared in the doorway. Before the woman could call Sinead's name, ready to administer her methadone, Sinead said: 'That's brilliant, Alyssa. Look, sorry to cut you short, but I've got to go. Things on, you know how it is.'

The pharmacist smiled at Sinead and said: 'How are you today, Sinead?'

Sinead pulled her lips into a thin line and then forced a smile. 'Fine.'

Alyssa glanced between the two and then a look crossed her face as if she knew what was going on. Of course she did. She wasn't stupid. 'I'll let you get on. Tell Orla I said hi. Maybe we could all meet up for a coffee?'

Sinead knew it was a passing comment. There was no way someone like Alyssa – someone at her level of success – would want to be seen dead with someone like Sinead. Alyssa was exactly like Orla; as soon as she could get away from the junkie, she would.

Sinead stepped into the private room where she would knock back her daily dose of methadone, before going back on to the street and looking for ways to make some extra cash to score. 'Yeah, yeah no worries,' she called back before disappearing into the room and closing the door.

Sinead quickly knocked back her dose as the pharmacist watched, like they always did. Couldn't be trusted to take it on her own. 'Right,' Sinead said. 'See you tomorrow.'

She left the chemist and walked round the corner before heading along the street towards the hostel in Park Terrace. That was the thing about Glasgow. On one hand, it was a stunning city, with tall, Victorian-style buildings and well-kept streets. Then smack in the middle, there was a hostel, a drug den, and a few streets away, curb crawlers looking to pay a tenner for a quick blowjob before heading home to the wife. What was even the point of taking the methadone? It didn't curb the withdrawal the way heroin did. And she was still shooting up as much as she could. She knew the risks involved in taking both. But it wasn't enough to deter her. Nothing was. Not losing her family, her dignity. Not even the darkest reality that was death.

The thought of what lay ahead of her pressed down heavy on her shoulders again. Another long, cold night on the streets. Another night wearing the skimpiest of outfits to attract the scummiest men just to get enough cash to pay for her heroin and buy a little more food. Just enough to scratch the itch. She'd already spent the money her sister had sent over to her that month and if she asked for more, it would only cause another fight.

She missed Orla. Her twin. The only person in the world she could call her own and she'd deserted her. 'I'll pay you every month to stay alive, Sinead. What you do with that money is up to you, but I don't want anything to do with you unless you get off that shit and sort your life out.'

Those contradictory words had been said ten years ago. And they'd echoed in her thoughts every single day since. *Get off that shit, but here, let me give you money so that your temptations won't last long.* Sinead, however, wasn't complaining. Having money was all that she needed to keep her habit fed.

Chapter 6

Perched on the edge of the wall that surrounded the fountain in Kelvingrove Park, Molly Rose watched as a couple of young children threw coins into the water, before their parents clapped their hands as they all ran towards the play park.

She rolled her eyes and sighed. She thought back to a time where her and her own mother got along fine, before she'd interfered in Molly Rose's relationship with Dean.

'I don't appreciate you spying on me,' Molly Rose had shouted in Orla's face.

'I'm sorry, Molly Rose. But as your mum, it's my job to keep an eye on you while you're still a child.'

'I'm not a child. I'm fifteen.'

'And in the eyes of the law, you're still a child. And Dean should be well aware of that, which I'm sure he is on some level. Which almost makes this worse,' Orla had said.

'You can't stop me from seeing him,' Molly Rose had replied defiantly.

'I won't have to. He's going to end it with you.'

Molly Rose had stared at her mum when the words left her mouth so abruptly and her heart sank. 'What are you talking about?'

'I warned you to stay away from him. He's too old for you. He's an adult and you're not. What he is doing is illegal and I will not have my only daughter involved with a…' Her words trailed off.

'A what?' Molly Rose challenged. 'You think he's a nonce, don't you?'

'For want of a better expression,' Orla replied, shaking her head. 'Like I said, he'll be ending it. And I've warned him that, if he doesn't, I'll be reporting him to the police.'

Molly Rose's jaw almost hit the floor. 'You can't do that. He's not a bad person, Mum.'

'Well, he's not a good one if he's going around, sleeping with fifteen-year-old schoolgirls, is he?'

Molly Rose was speechless. She hadn't slept with Dean; things hadn't gone that far.

'You'll ruin his life.'

'I won't have to if he does what he's told.'

She'd slammed her bedroom door that night and sobbed into her pillow. It had been at that point she thought she couldn't hate anyone more. But that was before Dean had actually been stupid enough to listen to Orla and do what she'd said, because later that night, Dean had dumped her by text message.

We're done. Sorry.

Reading those words, her hands had trembled. She'd tried to phone him, tell him not to listen to her mum and that they could carry on their relationship in secret. But he'd blocked her number. And she hadn't seen him since. That was just over a year ago. She hated her mum more now than ever, because Molly Rose's feeling for Dean hadn't simply disappeared when Dean did. She was left with a gaping hole in her heart and he wasn't there to make her feel better.

'Hey you,' a soft voice interrupted her thoughts. Looking up, she was shocked to see her Aunt Sinead staring down at her.

'Auntie Sinead?' Molly Rose said in disbelief as she looked back at her. She looked ill and that was putting it lightly. Getting to her feet, she hugged Sinead.

'A'right wee yin, how are you?' Sinead said. Molly Rose noted how slowly she spoke, how slurred her words seemed to be.

'How are you?' Molly Rose asked wearily. 'Are you okay?'

Sinead pulled away and smiled. 'I'm doing… okay. And less of the "auntie". Makes me feel pure ancient. But more to the point, how are you?'

'I'm… okay. Happy birthday, by the way,' Molly Rose replied. She saw a look of confusion on Sinead's face.

'Is that today?' Sinead asked. 'Jesus, I didn't realise.'

Molly Rose forced a smile. 'It's Mum's birthday too; obviously. That's how I knew.'

'Ha!' Sinead laughed. 'Glad one of us did. So, you still got that wee boyfriend of yours? What was his name?'

Molly Rose took in Sinead's appearance and was shocked at how bad she looked. Molly Rose had had contact with her auntie on and off over the years. Sometimes she was around, other times she wasn't. This was the first time she'd seen Sinead in well over a year. She'd lost weight from the last time they'd seen each other. Her eyes were heavy and drawn in; her cheekbones were very prominent and not in a good way. Her entire body trembled, but it was especially noticeable in her hands. 'Erm, no. We're not together.'

'Aw hen, that's a shame. What happened?' Sinead said, perching herself on the end of the fountain wall. Molly Rose sat back down next to her and lit a cigarette, knowing that she could be herself around her auntie without judgement.

'My mum happened.'

'What do you mean?'

Molly Rose cleared her throat and took a long draw on the cigarette before saying, 'She wasn't very happy about the age gap.'

'Age gap?' Sinead narrowed her eyes.

'He was… a little older than me,' Molly Rose replied with caution. 'He was eighteen when we were together.'

Sinead's eyes grew wider. 'Eighteen? Jesus, Molly Rose. That's bang out of order. He was in a relationship with a child.'

Molly Rose rolled her eyes. 'Don't you start. I've had enough off Orla.'

'You mean your mum,' she said, and it wasn't a question but a correction.

'He wasn't a bad person,' Molly Rose continued. 'He was the one.' Sinead didn't say anything and Molly Rose continued. 'I loved him and my mum fucked it up. Told him to end things with me or she'd tell the police. Just because there was an age gap didn't make it wrong.'

'You're right, an age gap doesn't make it wrong. But the fact that there was a legal line in the middle did. He was legally an adult and you were legally a child.'

'You sound like my mum,' Molly Rose sighed. 'She ruined something special to me, Sinead, and no one seems to get it.'

Sinead scratched at her arms and looked away in the distance. Molly Rose wasn't blind, she could clearly see her aunt was an addict, but not sure of the substance.

'What does your dad say about it all?'

'Not much, to be honest. He just keeps out of it. But he's on her side.'

'Well, he would be. Orla's his wife and you're his daughter. He'll want what's best and Orla clearly thought that was best for you. If I'm honest, I'd have to agree. And if I was your mum, then I'd have done the same,' Sinead said.

'Dean didn't ever hurt me. He never pressured me into doing anything I didn't want or wasn't ready for. She had no right to do this, Sinead. It's my life. I can make up my own mind. If I'm honest, it's fucking broke me.'

Sinead placed her hand over Molly Rose's and gave it a shaky squeeze. 'I get it, Molly Rose. I do. You loved him, he probably did everything he could to make you think that he loved you too. And in his own way, he may well have. But he was a man in the eyes of the law. He should have known better. I'm sorry, but you'll get over this and when you do, and you see things a little more clearly, you'll realise that what your mum did was the right thing.'

Molly Rose took a draw of her cigarette and thought about that. After the last year, knowing how she felt about Dean and pushing him away anyway, she couldn't see a way back for them.

'Time's a healer,' Sinead said. 'I'm hoping that with time, me and your mum can get back to the way we used to be before…'

'Before what?' Molly Rose pressed.

'Before I became this.' She looked down at herself. 'A scumbag junkie.'

'Is that what she said to you?' Molly Rose asked, shocked that Orla would say that to anyone, even if she did mean it.

'Not in so many words,' Sinead replied slowly. 'But look at me, Molly Rose. Homeless, an addict and probably not far from my deathbed. Sweetheart, things could be worse for you. All you have to do is look at me to see that. Adopted at birth with your mum by a lovely couple who die in a car accident when we were just thirteen. Then we get put into care separately and—'

'Separately?' Molly Rose asked. 'As in, the social workers split you both up?'

Sinead nodded. 'I thought you knew that?'

Molly Rose shook her head. 'No, she never told me.'

'Aye, we got split up. Orla fought for us to be kept together, but they couldn't find a family who could take both of us. Orla had a nice foster family right up until she was self-sufficient and even then the family kept her on. I had a foster family from a shit area who only gave a shit about the money they could make from being fosterers. That's when I met the crowd that got me into the mess I'm in now. Don't get me wrong, my arm wasn't twisted or anything. But I wanted to fit in. So, I did everything they were doing: drinking, taking drugs, sleeping with boys I shouldn't have been near. Now, I'm this. Anyway, what I'm trying to say is, get things back on track with your mum. You only get one shot at this life. Don't do what I did and fuck it up.'

Sinead's speech was becoming slower, far more slurred than it was when they first started talking. Glancing at her aunt, Molly Rose noticed how Sinead's eyes were closing. It was like she'd fallen asleep as they sat on the wall surrounding the fountain. Placing her hand on Sinead's shoulder, Molly Rose gave her a gentle shake and Sinead opened her eyes.

'Sinead, wake up. Come on, over to this bench so you've got some back support at least.'

Sinead tried to stand and walked with Molly Rose slowly over to one of the benches. People were looking, but Molly Rose ignored them. She couldn't just leave Sinead on her own in this state.

'Sinead, what are you on? Heroin? Is that what this is?'

Molly Rose felt, for the first time in her life, that she'd been sheltered from the real world. She was sixteen and sat here in a park with her auntie who her mum had abandoned and tried to keep Molly Rose away from. However, she saw something in her auntie that Orla didn't: she had it in her to get better, to get clean and become a better person. Orla didn't see that and forced Sinead away; in the process keeping Molly Rose from having a close relationship with her. It seemed that Orla wanted to control a lot of her life. And she was surprised by her mother's behaviour, given what they'd both gone through. They'd been separated at a time it was crucial to stay together. Sinead had gone through life being abandoned by everyone, it would seem.

Molly Rose wanted to wrap Sinead in cotton wool and take her home. Give her good food and a bed. But Orla wouldn't allow it.

'I'm fine,' Sinead said. 'I'm just nodding in and out. It happens.'

Molly Rose held her hand. 'Does this happen a lot?'

'Mm hmm,' Sinead replied. 'It's just the high, hen. It'll wear off.'

'Oh my god,' Molly Rose whispered, taking her phone out and glancing down at the time. It was early afternoon.

She could phone Orla, try to get her to take Sinead in and help get her clean. It would be one way to sort the family dynamics out. Something maybe she and her mum could do together to help Sinead get better.

Molly Rose stared distantly at the people walking through the park with friends, families, dogs. She wished she could be them. Live another life and not have to deal with the shit she had been dealt. Then she looked at Sinead. Her situation was far worse than Molly Rose's. She hadn't just lost a boyfriend. She'd lost everything.

Dropping the cigarette onto the ground and stubbing it out with her shoe, Molly Rose hit call on her mum's number and waited as it rang.

'Molly Rose?' she answered, sounding happy if not surprised to hear from her own daughter.

'Mum,' she began. 'Can I ask you something about Auntie Sinead?'

'What about her?'

'Why don't you have a relationship with her any more?'

There was a long pause on the other end of the line. Molly Rose waited, holding Sinead's hand as she dozed against her.

'Why?' Orla asked. 'What's happened to make you ask that question?'

'I'm with her.'

'You're *what*?'

'Don't get angry. She needs help, Mum. Not for us to abandon her.'

A hard sigh and then: 'Molly Rose, you don't know anything about this. I don't want you around her, she's bad news.'

Molly Rose looked down at Sinead and felt so sorry for her. 'She's *not* bad news. She's just in a bad place and needs help. If you could see her, you would agree.'

The silence that followed was deafening. 'Molly Rose, I do things that you don't agree with because you don't understand them. You will in time.'

Molly Rose closed her eyes and shook her head. 'Don't go there. This isn't about Dean and what happened. This is about your sister. Like I said, if you could see the state she was in, you'd want to help.'

'I do help. Every month. I give her money. In fact, why am I explaining myself to you? Just stay out of things you don't know anything about.'

Sinead shifted a little next to Molly Rose. She glanced down at her aunt to see bruising on her arms, just below the elbow joint. Needle marks and scars, both old and new stared back at her.

'Why do you send her money?'

'That's none of your business, Molly Rose. Now, I'm at work and I don't have time for this.'

'You don't have time to save your twin sister's life, but you had time to fuck up mine?'

Orla started to answer when Molly Rose jabbed at the end call icon on the phone screen.

'Waste of time,' Sinead said wearily. 'She's not inter-ested.'

Molly didn't say anything in response. What could she say? Her mum was stubborn and a hard one to crack when it came to making her change her mind.

'Just leave it, hen. Honestly, she's better off without me and I'm better off without her.'

Molly Rose sighed as Sinead sat up straight. 'No, you're not. You guys are twins. You should stick together. She should be helping you.'

'Says the girl who let a boy come between her and her mum. Sorry, my mistake. A *man*.' Sinead looked at Molly Rose with a raised brow and began tapping her temple with her index finger. 'You know I'm right. I might be a junkie, sweetheart, but I still have a brain in there.'

Molly Rose thought about everything. If she could get Sinead to come with her back to the house, if she could just get her mum to take a look at Sinead and see that she needed support and not to be abandoned, then maybe they could start to rebuild their own relationship.

'Come home with me.'

Sinead shook her head. 'Not going to happen, hen. She'll take one look at me and tell me where to go. But you go on home. You and your mum have a lot to deal with. Like I said, she did what she did because she's your mum, not your enemy.'

'Giving you money every month when you're addicted to, what, heroin? You think that's doing best by *you*?'

Sinead stood up, a little unsteady on her feet and smiled. 'This isn't about me, hen. It's about you. Go home. Being here in this place with me isn't good for you.'

Molly Rose stared up at Sinead and tried not to cry. Everything was such a mess and, in the past year, Sinead had been fighting the darkest demons. It made the Dean situation seem so trivial and for that, Molly Rose felt stupid for her reaction to him leaving. Not that it made her feelings about Dean invalid, just in the grander scheme of things, it was nothing in comparison to what Sinead was going through.

Sinead gave her a hug and said: 'We can swap numbers. We can meet up now and again. But the way I live my life isn't good for a lassie your age, Molly Rose. You've got your whole life ahead of you. Don't waste it worrying about me.'

Molly Rose took Sinead's phone and tapped her number into it, called it and then logged Sinead's number in her own phone.

'I'll make her see sense,' Molly Rose said.

Sinead smiled, and Molly Rose noticed the yellowish tinge to her teeth. 'Nah, you won't. But that's okay. I'll see you around, wee yin.'

'Wait,' Molly Rose said. 'Can I take a picture of us for my phone? I don't have a recent one of us. And, well, we don't see each other that often, do we?'

Sinead hesitated. 'You're not going to put it all over that bloody Facebook, are you?'

Molly Rose laughed. 'Facebook? That's for old people. I'm more an Instagram girl.'

'Oi, less of the old. Okay fine, but just don't post it, eh? I don't look the part to be plastered all over that internet.'

Molly Rose laughed. 'I won't. I promise.' She pulled out her phone and took their picture. Sinead did smile, but she didn't look happy. Neither of them did.

'Right then, see you around, Molly Rose. Look after yourself.'

Molly Rose watched as Sinead walked off and thought about the strong possibility that it could be the last time she ever saw her. But Molly Rose was determined to make her mum see that she was the only one who could help her sister.

Chapter 7

The Merchant City was one of those places in the city centre of Glasgow that was beautiful to look at, with its old buildings, incredible architecture and seventeenth century tolbooth. Home to the old fruit, vegetable and cheese markets from the nineteenth century, the place had an interesting history. But when you really broke it down today, the streets were often home to people. Cardboard boxes and sleeping bags were folded up in corners of disused shop doorways, while the owner was out begging for just enough money to get them a hot drink. Or money for booze. Or food. Or, like Sinead, for heroin. Not that it mattered to the rich people using the city for shopping, dining and socialising. The ones at the bottom were often missed by the ones at the top. It made her see her family members in categories like that. Orla, her mum, was one of those at the top; Sinead at the bottom. Molly Rose wasn't even in the middle, just floating around somewhere in between, with troubles of her own yet not quite old enough to lead her own life.

As Molly Rose stood outside the coffee shop with her own coffee in her left hand and a second in her right, she walked across the road to the girl, not far off her own age. She was sat on a step outside one of the disused shops, with a denim jacket on that had seen better days. Her hair was dirty, scraped back from her face, revealing an exhausted expression.

'Hi,' Molly Rose said as she approached the girl. 'Do you like coffee?'

The girl looked up at her and nodded.

'Then this is yours,' she said. 'I have sugar sachets and a milk in my pocket if you need them.'

The girl shook her head and took the coffee from Molly Rose's hand. 'Naw, a take it black, hen. Cheers.'

Molly Rose's heart broke for the girl. It could possibly be what it was like for Sinead in the early stages of her addiction and homelessness state. 'Do you want something to eat?'

The girl glanced down at the money and then up at Molly Rose as she handed her a tenner. 'Here, get yourself some food.'

'Cheers, pal. Yer a good wan.'

The girl took the money and shoved it into her pocket. There was a chance she'd spend it on drugs, Molly Rose accepted that. But then, Molly Rose felt like she had to make up for not being able to help Sinead.

A loud bang made them both jump, and suddenly, a huge cloud of black smoke rose above the buildings towering over them. 'Fuckin' hell, whit the fuck wiz that?' the girl said.

The sound of people screaming and gasping in shock in the surrounding streets filled the air, followed by sirens. She looked up to see several fire engines speeding up Ingram Street along with some police cars. *That was quick*, Molly Rose thought to herself.

When she turned, the homeless girl had disappeared. Looking down the road, she couldn't see her anywhere. Molly Rose didn't want to end up like that. Homeless.

Hoping for passing strangers to give her money to get by. The shit with her mum wasn't worth that.

The smell of smoke began to grow and the air around her was becoming cloudy. She could tell by the way the sirens sounded that the fire engines had stopped not far from where she was.

Molly Rose's curiosity got the better of her and she headed in the direction of the sirens and smoke. As she rounded the corner on to Ingram Street, she could see where the smoke was coming from. A building that housed the old nightclub, Club Envy, which Dean had once tried to get her into back in the day, but they'd been knocked back. Not because Molly Rose was underage or because she didn't have ID, but because it was a members-only club. Molly Rose hadn't known such a nightclub existed but Dean had said he'd heard lots of good things about it.

The place was already being cordoned off and the flames rose out from the top of the building. Police were screaming at the public to move back as they cordoned off the street from where she was standing.

The chaos of it all made her think that leaving home for good, and possibly ending up like that girl she'd given the coffee too, would be the same as life on the street. Chaotic, unsafe, miserable.

Pulling out her phone, she looked at the time. It was three in the afternoon, just a few hours after she'd last spoken to her mum. She had two missed calls from Orla, one from her dad too. No voicemails.

'Right,' she muttered to herself, pushing through the throngs of people who'd gathered to watch the drama of the fire unfold. 'Time to make you see sense, Mum.'

Chapter 8

'I can't believe I'm actually doing this,' Cameron said as Janey opened the door to him.

'Well, if you want to keep seeing me, you don't have much choice. But don't worry,' she said, failing to hide the smile creeping on to her face. 'I checked his gun before you arrived. It definitely isn't loaded, so you're grand.'

Cameron shook his head at her mockery. She couldn't help it. After their brief falling-out, Janey had accepted Cameron's apology after saying he didn't want to meet Finn due to the rumours of what he did for a living. She knew exactly who her dad was and what he did. She'd had time to get used to the idea. Not that she ever confirmed the rumours, or denied them for that matter. What Finn did for a living was no one else's business, and it had annoyed her that rumours had caused her and Cameron to fall out. Although, considering they lived in a small town, the people of Donaghadee would talk, and they'd fill in the gaps if they didn't know the entire story. Dangerous, Janey thought, to be making up your own shit about someone like Finn Hallahan. Times were hard enough for people in Northern Ireland without that kind of crap being added into the mix.

'My da's in the kitchen. Next to all the knives,' Janey joked again, closing the door behind him.

'I'm not kidding, Janey. Stop it or you'll have to explain to your da why there's a Cameron-shaped hole in the door.'

Janey laughed, took Cameron's hand and led him down the long, narrow hallway towards the family room. Not that there was much of a family to warrant having a family room, or a house this size if she really thought about it. Her mum had died a few years earlier, leaving Janey to be brought up by her dad. He never wanted to give the house up after her mum went. Giving up the house would mean giving up the farm and that was one of the things that kept Finn from being consumed by his grief. Not that he ever said it, but Janey could tell just by looking at him that losing her had almost killed him. If Janey didn't exist, he'd have gone off the rails, maybe started drinking heavily.

'Wow, I still can't believe you live in a house like this. It's a castle. Should I call him King Hallahan?'

'Don't take the piss or he really will shoot you,' Janey smiled, rounding the corner at the end of the hallway, which opened into a communal space. It housed a piano, an eight-person dining table and a winding staircase in the corner.

'Where is he?' Cameron asked, staring at the piano.

'He'll be upstairs in his office,' she replied and then, projecting her voice, she called out, 'Daaaa!'

She watched as Cameron looked up the winding set of stairs and she was certain he held his breath. It was quite amusing to see him so terrified of her dad. At least she knew he wouldn't mess her about.

A door above them clicked and footsteps sounded along the hall before Finn came into view at the top of the stairs. He wore a navy woollen jumper with a neat white collar resting over the top, smart trousers and navy-coloured moccasin slippers. Janey kept an eye on Cameron to see what his reaction was like. He didn't seem to blink.

'Hi Da,' Janey smiled as he reached the second step from the bottom before stopping.

'Hello Mr Hallahan,' Cameron said, his voice a little shaky. She hoped her dad wouldn't notice.

Finn reached out a hand and offered it to Cameron. 'You must be Cameron. Good to finally meet ya, boy.'

Cameron shook Finn's hand and Janey held in her laughter. Cameron looked terrified as Finn plastered on his most threatening expression.

'It's good to meet you too, sir.'

Finn raised a brow and started to laugh heartily. Janey followed.

'What's so funny?' Cameron asked, glancing back and forth between them.

'You should have seen your face, son. It was like you were shaking hands with a bear.'

Janey saw Cameron's expression soften a little and she gave him a nudge. 'Relax. He doesn't bite, he's just my old man.'

'Oi, you,' Finn said, stepping down off the last step and smiling at Janey. 'Less of the old.'

'Sorry, Mr Hallahan. I'm just really nervous.'

'You needn't be. I'm a nice man. Really, I am. So long as my daughter is being looked after, and respected, then no one needs to worry about me.'

Cameron let out a breath and Janey smiled before she said, 'So, lunch?'

—

The three of them sat at the table as they finished off a luscious tray of food made by the chef. Finn had arranged it especially. He'd told Janey earlier that he wanted Cameron to feel comfortable and that he was sorry he'd been scared by the rumours. She knew her dad well, he'd ignore the chit-chat because it wasn't important to him in the grand scheme of things. In his line of work, it was important to remain composed; that's what he'd always told her.

'So, you're doing well in school, Cameron?' Finn asked. 'Janey tells me you're very into science?'

'I like the experiments, aye,' Cameron said.

Finn was about to reply when Janey heard the back door open; heavy boots stomped on the tiled floor at the entrance.

'Mind and take those boots off, Charlie. You're not dragging horse muck through this house again,' Finn called.

Janey swallowed the rest of her water and placed the glass down on the table as Charlie came into the kitchen. She saw the look on Cameron's face. Confusion.

'You never said you had a brother,' Cameron said, looking at Janey.

'He's not my brother,' Janey replied. 'Well, not by blood anyway.'

Cameron raised his brow in surprise.

'It would explain why he's the only pain in the arse in my life,' Finn laughed. Getting to his feet, he moved out from the table and met Charlie at the door.

Cameron leaned over to Janey and whispered: 'So, if he's not your brother, then who is he?'

Janey glanced down at the table. Telling Charlie's story was difficult, especially in front of him, even if he couldn't hear what was being said. 'It's complicated. All you have to know is that he's here and part of the family.'

Cameron looked on, shrugged and then leaned back in his seat.

'Do you actually roll around in the muck out there or do you do the work I give you? Look at the state of you, boy,' Finn said with a sigh. 'Get in for a shower and then you can have some lunch.'

Charlie went to speak and Finn raised a hand. 'I won't have any backchat. It's your own fault you're in this state. If ya hadn't gone out and acted like an arse and given me a showing up, then you could be out with your mates. Let this be a lesson to you. Let's not forget what I've done for you, boy.'

Janey shook her head.

'I'm almost eighteen, Finn. I can do what I want,' Charlie said.

'Erm, correction. You're not almost eighteen. You're still seventeen and it's illegal to be going into pubs at your age. But to get into a bloody brawl and punch the local vicar's son, that's another issue.' Finn lowered his voice and continued. 'You're lucky I didn't leather you after what you did, giving me a showing up like that. If you're going to be a Hallahan, you'd better start respecting the name, or so help me God, I won't be responsible.'

Janey caught Cameron's expression and wondered what he was thinking. She rarely spoke about Charlie. He was a bit of a rogue. Always getting himself into situations that would result in her dad having to pay off the local police to get him out of his weekend prison visit. The one thing Finn liked was discretion and Charlie didn't know how to be discreet. In fact, he was so indiscreet that Janey wouldn't be surprised if Cameron already knew who Charlie was before meeting him. His behaviour was disrespectful, considering everything her dad had done for him since his childhood.

'Jesus, it would be nice to be able to go about with my mates and have a laugh. Everything is so fucking serious these days,' Charlie said.

'Serious? You're damn right it's serious. You know, we're quite fortunate to be living far enough away from all the Troubles and my business could be affected by all that's going on. I don't

50

need more shit coming from you, Charlie. Now, upstairs and shower. Get yourself together and do not embarrass me. Janey has company this afternoon and you will behave.'

Charlie huffed in annoyance and looked up at the ceiling.

The phone rang in the hall. Finn excused himself to answer it.

Charlie walked past the table, ignored Cameron and gave Janey one of his menacing smiles. She knew he hadn't taken Finn seriously. He didn't take anyone seriously these days.

He stopped at the edge of the dining table and turned, looked down at Cameron and said: 'You're my wee sister's boyfriend, then?'

Cameron looked up at Charlie and shrugged. 'We're... just friends.'

Charlie nodded. 'Better hope it stays that way. Otherwise, you'll end up like the local vicar's boy when I give you a broken nose.'

Janey pushed back her chair, stood up and jabbed Charlie in the shoulder with a finger. 'Shut it, Charlie. If you're not careful, my dad will throw you out. He's had enough of your games.'

Charlie laughed. 'He's my dad too and he wouldn't do that to me. As much as I drive him nuts, he wouldn't see me on the street with nothing, I think that's obvious, otherwise I wouldn't be here. I'm going to inherit it all one day and, when I do, I'll be the one bailing folk out of jail. Just you wait.'

Janey took a steadying breath. Sometimes, she hated Charlie. Other times they got on fine; just like normal siblings, she supposed. He was just a show-off, using the Hallahan name to exert power over people. In short, he was a bully. But so far, Janey hadn't experienced the wrong end of his behaviour. He wouldn't dare, because Finn wouldn't stand for it.

Chapter 9

NOW

Kristo handed Janey a set of keys and the code for the alarm. 'You can change it to whatever you like,' he said as she unlocked the door and punched the code into the keypad. The entrance hall of the house fell silent as the alarm stopped.

'Thank you, Kristo,' Ciaran said as he placed two suitcases on the wooden floor.

Janey walked through the large, high-ceilinged hallway and into the open kitchen diner. The floor-to-ceiling windows, which led out to a balcony, overlooked the water from Rhu towards Rosneath. The sky was bright blue, the sunlight bouncing off the water, making it reflect off the ceiling.

'Tell me, why don't we come here more often?' Ciaran asked, slipping his arm around Janey's shoulder.

She smiled. 'Because as much as this view is beautiful, there's nothing quite like home.'

'It is just like home, actually,' Ciaran replied. 'Aside from the fact that we don't have our own private beach here. But I can live with it if you can.'

Janey couldn't help but allow Ciaran's mood to affect her. That was something she loved about him, he could always help lift her up when things were heavy.

'So, dinner and then we work out which of these Glaswegian bastards burned down our club?' Janey said.

Kristo was stood at the doorway between the kitchen and hallway. 'I'll get going. If you need me for anything, you know how to get a hold of me. My phone is always on.'

Janey nodded in acknowledgement. 'Thanks, Kristo.'

He left and Janey opened the bifold door and stepped out on to the decked balcony. She took in the spectacular view overlooking the caravan park at Rosneath, and beyond to Greenock. This place did remind her of home – that's why she had bought the land and built a home in Rhu.

'Okay, I could be persuaded to stay here,' Janey said. '*Could*,' she eyed Ciaran as he stood behind her in the kitchen.

Ciaran smiled and lifted a bottle of red from the wine rack. 'Shall we?'

Janey shook her head. 'Not right now. I need a shower first.'

Turning her back on the crystal-clear water, Janey walked back into the house toward the bathroom. Closing the door, she ran the shower and put down the toilet seat before perching herself on it. She pulled out her phone and looked down at the screen. The message on it made her stomach flip, instantly transporting her back to when she was a young teenager. A time when she was vulnerable. There was no number, no way of knowing for a fact who'd sent it. But she knew, deep down, exactly who it was behind that text.

It's been a while, Janey, we need to meet and have a chat. There's a lot to discuss. The past, the present. There's so much burning inside me that I want to talk to you about. Speaking of burning, it's a real shame what happened to Club Envy. I hope that hasn't left your business in dire straits.

Chapter 10

'And I want a list of all the show rounds from each nursery in the last month. I want a breakdown of how many took up places in each centre and I want each manager to contact those who didn't, for feedback,' Orla said before ending the Zoom call with each of the area managers.

The screen went blank; Orla sighed heavily. Pulling up Spotify on the home screen, she selected her favourite Moby playlist and connected to the Bluetooth speakers in the rest of the house. She put the volume up slightly, then pushed the chair back from her desk and got to her feet. She left the office and headed downstairs to the main lounge. She opened the door and almost leapt in the air when she saw Molly Rose sitting on the sofa.

'Jesus Christ Almighty, Molly Rose,' Orla startled, her hand on her chest.

'Nice to see you too,' Molly Rose replied, with that teenage roll of her eyes.

'I just didn't hear you come in, that's all.'

'Still listening to that shit? Moby? It's crap,' Molly Rose said.

No one seemed to like him except Orla. She shook her head and said: 'Music is subjective. I think your taste is shit too.'

She saw the eye-roll intensify but decided not to react. That was what it was like between them now. A constant battle to win the argument. Pettiness. Sometimes, there wasn't even an argument to be won and still they fought, like with the little digs they'd just had over music. Molly Rose would never admit it, but she was exactly like Orla. And Orla often wondered if she herself, was like her own mother.

'Happy birthday, by the way,' Molly Rose said. It sounded forced, but Orla would take it if it was going.

'Thank you,' she said. 'Tea?' Orla got to her feet and moved out of the lounge, through the grand hallway and into the kitchen. She sensed Molly Rose following her. She knew what was coming. Molly Rose was going to bring up Sinead again. Or Dean. Either way, it was going to be one of those conversations that immediately turned into an argument.

Flicking on the already full kettle, Orla turned and leaned against the counter. She could see in her daughter's face that something was bothering her.

'Your dad has booked a table for dinner tonight for my birthday meal. Are you joining us?' Orla asked.

'Mum,' Molly Rose replied. 'Before we get into that, I want to talk to you about something. As you know, I was with Auntie Sinead today.'

Orla felt the anger bubbling away inside her, but she couldn't show it – it would only set Molly Rose off on one of her rants and Orla didn't have the energy to fight with her daughter. The past year had been tough. Having your daughter openly hating you was draining.

Orla nodded but didn't say anything. She wanted to see what else Molly Rose had to say about her aunt and the kind of state she was in. But more importantly, she wanted to see what crap Sinead had fed Molly Rose, about how she could stop immediately. Orla had heard it all before.

'Aren't you going to ask me how she was? What we talked about?' Molly Rose pressed. The frustration on her face annoyed Orla.

'I'm sure you're going to tell me anyway.'

Raising a brow, as if she didn't know how to take Orla's words, she continued. 'We talked about *us*, mostly; me and you. How you only ever want what's best for me and that what you did was for my benefit and that I'd see that for myself one day.'

Orla felt a flicker of emotion then. She'd never imagined Sinead to say anything nice about her; to speak in her favour, given that the last time they had a proper conversation it was to tell Sinead that she was dead to Orla unless she got clean. Every day since, she wished she hadn't been so harsh on Sinead. But at the time, it felt like the right thing to say. And then Orla remembered what Sinead was really like when she was in withdrawal. Aggressive, abusive, full of apologies and promises that she'd change. But when Orla wouldn't shift on her decision to put the boundary in place not to have any contact, the aggression and abuse started again, before begging for more money came into the conversation.

'She probably wants more money.' The words rolled off her tongue before she could stop them. But strangely enough, Molly Rose didn't bite.

'She doesn't look well, Mum. She's too skinny, her skin is a mess and she...' Molly Rose trailed off and Orla thought she could see tears pooling in her daughter's eyes. 'I think she needs our help.'

'She already gets our help. Every month. Five-hundred pounds of our help to be exact.'

'Yeah, and how far do you think that goes these days, Mum? Cost-of-living crisis doesn't just affect those of us who are lucky to have a permanent home. She needs to make that money stretch. Cover hostel costs, food, clothes.'

'Hmm, drugs, alcohol. You do know she works on the streets too? To pay for her habit?' Orla spat.

'And maybe if you actually *fucking* helped her instead of just throwing your money at her then she wouldn't have a habit? Maybe if you gave more of a shit about other people instead of yourself, and your fucking business and reputation, then she'd have enough strength to get clean. But right now, she doesn't have anything or anyone to get clean for.'

Orla felt her jaw drop. Of all they'd gone through in the past year, Molly Rose had never used that kind of language towards Orla. 'Don't you *dare* swear at me.'

'Is that all you've got to say? You're more disgusted with my swearing than your inability to give a fuck about your own twin? That says more about you than it does about me, or even Auntie Sinead for that matter.'

Orla pushed herself off the counter as Molly Rose stomped through to the lounge. She returned just seconds later with a bag and her phone. 'Do you know what? Auntie Sinead made a lot of sense today. I really did think that you and I could work things out. But you've just shown me your true colours. You don't care about anyone but yourself and what having her around might do to your reputation. You're the other side of scum, do you know that? Sinead might have her flaws, but she's got a good heart. You're made of stone. After what you did to me with Dean, now you're refusing to help get your own sister off the streets and get her life together. I can't stay here with someone like you.'

Orla was dumbstruck; she couldn't get the words out. She wanted to put Molly Rose in her place. Remind her she was only sixteen, she knew nothing about anything, didn't understand what addiction had done to Sinead. But that simply wasn't true. She'd hit the nail on the head, as much as Orla would never admit it. She *was* worried about what Sinead being around would do to her reputation. She owned a franchise of nurseries across the country. She couldn't have a junkie living at home with her, could she? Not with access to computers that had login details to bank accounts with thousands upon thousands of pounds in them. That would be like a child finding keys to a sweet factory. Plus, how would that look to inspectors and employees? The childcare business was a small world. It would get out, and if parents at the centres found out, they might start pulling their wee ones out.

'She won't help herself, Molly Rose. I kept this side of her from you for as long as I could, but the truth is, she's an addict and with that comes certain behaviours. She'll draw you in, make you think she will change then *bang*, she's taken money from your purse, or she's—'

'She's what, Mum? She's just human like the rest of us. We all make mistakes. I'm sure your own mum did. I would have thought being given up as babies and then losing your adoptive parents before you were teenagers, then having to go through the care system separately, you'd want to stick by her? Surely you must feel some kind of guilt about abandoning her?'

It was like a knife to the stomach. Sinead must have told her about the foster care separation; another thing Orla wanted to keep from Molly Rose. There was so much she could say in response, but all she could muster was: 'This has *nothing* to do with the woman who gave us up.'

'It has *everything* to do with her. If she'd been around, then you two wouldn't have been adopted, only to lose those parents and be put into care separately. Sinead might not be this way if none of that had happened and you'd have a better relationship with her. Fuck, maybe you'd have a better relationship with me. You might claim to know everything about child development because you own a couple of fucking nurseries, Mum, but you don't know how to be a mother. After everything you two have been through together, after everything you know she's been through and you still won't help her. You've driven me away because of what you did to me with Dean and you're keeping Sinead away from the family when, now more than ever, she needs us. I can't be around you, Mum. You're the most selfish person I've ever met and I just can't understand why.'

Orla watched as Molly Rose strode out of the kitchen towards the front door. Molly Rose had known from a young age that Orla and Sinead had been adopted, that they'd gone into care. She knew as much as Orla did about her birth mother. She'd considered keeping it from her, but when Molly Rose had started asking questions about why she didn't have grandparents like the rest of her friends, she'd sat her down and told her the truth.

So much went through her head then. Orla stood by her decision about Dean, but Molly Rose had been bang-on with everything else she'd said. She had an old head on young shoulders. Sinead was in a terrible state now. She'd fallen in with the wrong crowd years ago and now she just couldn't get out. These days, people say it's fine to remove family members from your life if all they do is bring toxicity. When they were growing up, there was no way Orla could ever have imagined not going through life with Sinead. But Orla couldn't go back to being around her now. She couldn't be trusted around money.

And then the comment about her own mother.

Maybe Molly Rose was right? Maybe Orla had no clue how to be a mother because in reality, she'd had no one to show her. And for that, she could never forgive Janey. She knew how to be a sister to Sinead before all her issues came about. It pained her to think of Sinead out there, on her own. But it was a bed she had to lie in. As much as Orla missed the Sinead she used to know, she couldn't go back there. She couldn't allow her sister to break her heart over and over again.

Chapter 11

'Do you have any idea who it might be?' Ciaran asked after Janey had showed him the anonymous text.

Shaking her head, she glanced across to Rosneath. She wasn't ready to admit to herself that she knew who was behind that text, let alone admit it to Ciaran. She'd tell him in time, once she had cast-iron proof.

'It could be anyone, Ciaran. It could be an old McInroy coming out of the woodwork for all I know,' she lied 'But whoever it is, we need to find out and put an end to this shite. I can't just stand back and wait for this fucker to attack the rest of my businesses.'

Ciaran put the phone down on the dining table and handed Janey a glass of red wine. 'You won't have to. It won't come to that.'

'Won't it?' Janey replied, taking the glass from his hand and taking a large gulp.

Janey walked out on to the balcony. The sun was setting over the hills and the sky was a deep orange colour. She took a breath and drank in the scenery to help calm her.

'Between us and with Kristo's help, we'll find the bastard, Janey. Have you ever known a Hallahan to lose?'

She drank from her glass, placed it down on the table next to her and folded her arms over her body. Maybe that was the problem. Hallahans very rarely lost a fight.

Maybe this was her sign that it was time to step back from it all. She wasn't sure she had the strength or energy to carry on any more. What had happened the last time she was in Glasgow had taken a lot from her.

But who would she hand down to? As much as she trusted Kristo with her life, she wasn't about to hand the Hallahan empire to someone who wasn't blood. Charlie of all people knew that would never be the case.

Now was the only time that she regretted not having children with Ciaran. And it was for a selfish reason. However, she hadn't climbed to the top of her game in a male-dominated criminal underworld by being weak. She'd faced bigger challenges than this, far bigger. Finn hadn't handed down to her for her to give up now. She was his daughter, and she had a fight to win and an empire to protect.

'No,' she replied. 'Never.'

Chapter 12

Stood outside the hostel in Park Terrace, Molly Rose tried Sinead on her mobile a handful of times before giving up and deciding that the best place to find her would be the streets. Not that she knew where to start, or what she was even going to say to her if she did find her. *Hey, my mum has basically told you where to go, so I thought I'd join you out here.*

Where did sex workers go? She'd heard that Blythswood was notorious for them, but that was all the way in the city centre. Surely Sinead wouldn't go far to work, if she had to walk back to the hostel? Or maybe being as far from the only place she could call home was a better option? That way, punters wouldn't know where she was residing?

'Fuck,' Molly Rose muttered as she stepped down from the front entrance to the hostel and made her way down to the street. She didn't know where to start, but anything was better than nothing. So, she made her way along the street towards the stairs that led into the top of Kelvingrove Park.

Dusk was setting in, and it made the park feel that little bit more threatening. She'd heard things about the place at night and she didn't know if it were just rumour: older and younger people being attacked unprovoked; sexual assaults. She'd even heard of a murder. It probably wasn't the best idea for her to be walking through the place by herself unless in broad daylight, but then that would be true of anywhere these days.

Reaching the fountain where she'd met Sinead earlier that day, she looked around and felt like she was searching for a needle in a haystack. If she didn't find Sinead tonight, she'd be just like that homeless girl she'd met earlier; the one she'd given the coffee to just before that building had gone on fire. She couldn't go back home. Not now. She'd be going against her principles if she did. If her mum would just swallow her pride and help her sister, then things could start to mend.

The skatepark sounded busy from where she was standing, so she headed in that direction. Being around crowds of people would be safer for her than being on her own in one of the darkest parts of the park. Although being around people in general made her nervous. Losing her friends because she'd put everything into her relationship with Dean, and then him ditching her, had knocked her confidence to integrate herself into new social circles. Yet being around others was better than being alone. Her friends had ditched her since she'd become involved with Dean, and ever since she'd been away from Dean, the girls hadn't come back. It saddened her that she was so lonely at such a young age. It wasn't normal. But it wasn't fair that she'd been punished by her friends for having a boyfriend. Or maybe it was her own doing? Spending every waking second with Dean when she wasn't at school might have led her friends to distance themselves because Molly Rose wasn't putting in the same effort as she used to. Orla had always said it wasn't a good idea to put all her energy into just one person; that it wasn't healthy. Molly Rose wondered if Orla had been right, although she'd never say that out loud. And it still didn't take away the pain of losing him.

Heading down there, she saw groups of teenagers dotted around various parts of the skate park, a few people out with younger kids on bikes, and a few dog walkers. Relief flooded her veins as she moved in their direction. She found a bench to sit on and pulled her rucksack up onto her knees, before lifting out a bottle of vodka from the side pocket. Staring down at the vodka she nicked from the drinks cabinet at home, she knew it would taste rank, but it would also warm her up a bit and help her to feel numb against the pain of losing Dean because of her so-called mother. She still missed him, felt like she could have had a different life if Orla just hadn't intervened. She'd been secretly drinking a lot throughout the last year. Nothing she couldn't handle but enough to take the edge off.

Unscrewing the cap, she gave the vodka a sniff and pulled away in disgust. How anyone could drink the stuff was beyond her. Maybe vodka was one of those drown-your-sorrows kind of tipples? Taking a deep breath, she placed the bottle to her lips and sipped. Her mouth immediately burned. She couldn't drink that straight. No way. Placing the vodka down on the ground, she pulled the two litre bottle of Coke out of the rucksack and emptied half onto the grass before refilling with vodka. She gave it a swirl and drank straight from the bottle.

'That's a bit better,' she whispered to herself, before she began to guzzle back more and more.

She felt warmer, a little more relaxed. Her head was fuzzy but in a nice way. She sunk back into the bench and continued to drink.

'Here?' a voice called. Molly Rose ignored it. 'You lot better get tae fuck before I knock ye the fuck oot.'

Molly Rose tried to open her eyes, but they felt heavy. Her head began to pound and a strong wave of nausea washed over her.

'And who the fuck are you? Her fucking maw?' a male voice laughed.

'Ye don't wantae know who a um mate, now get tae, otherwise that bottle's gawn in yer face.'

Confusion took over and Molly Rose managed to open her eyes. *Shit*, she thought as she stared up at the sky. It was darker now and stars were appearing above her. How much had she actually drunk? She couldn't remember much after opening the vodka on that bench.

Slowly, she sat up and noticed a girl standing in front of her and a group of boys standing on the opposite side of the path. Molly Rose counted. There were three of them.

'The zombie's up,' one of the boys said. 'Here, look at the state ae her.'

The other two laughed and Molly Rose felt ashamed of herself. Then she retched and quickly leaned over the bench.

The sounds of glass smashing made her jump and she looked up to see the girl holding out the vodka bottle. The end was jagged and the boys took a step back.

'Hink yer aw hardmen, trying tae take advantage ae a young lassie sparkled on a bench?'

'Aye, a'right. Calm doon, ya nutter.'

She moved closer to the boys who quickly scarpered, but not before laughing in that exaggerated way that neds did.

'Aye, keep running, ya bunch ae wee dicks!'

Molly Rose retched a few more times before sitting back and realising that this was what a proper hangover felt like. Hell. Death. Shame.

'Are ye a'right?'

Looking up at the girl, Molly Rose nodded and immediately regretted it as a thundering headache kicked in. 'I've felt better,' she replied.

'If am honest, ye don't look too clever.'

Molly Rose smiled. 'Thanks.'

'Naw, sorry. I just meant ye look a bit rough fae the bevy.'

'I mean thanks for stopping those boys from doing... whatever they were planning to do.'

'A hink they were just gawn tae mug ye. No that that's a'right, but whit a mean is, that's the worst that wis gawnae happen.'

Molly Rose rubbed at her bleary eyes. 'I dread to think what would have happened if you weren't here.'

'Us hameless lassies huv got tae stick taegether, ye know?'

Molly rose nodded and looked up at the girl who'd saved her as she sat down on the bench next to her. She seemed familiar, like she'd seen her before. Then she realised where she knew her from. 'Did I give you coffee earlier today?'

'A didnae hink ye'd remember me. Not most folk remember the face ae a hameless lassie,' the girl said. 'I'm Kassy, by the way.'

Molly Rose smiled. 'Of course I remember you. I'll never forget you now. I'm Molly Rose.'

'Ye got a fag on ye?'

Molly Rose reached into her pocket and pulled the pack out before offering one to Kassy.

'Cheers,' she said, holding out her hand and taking it from her.

'I like your tattoo,' Molly Rose said, pointing to Kassy's wrist.

Kassy placed the cigarette between her teeth and rolled her eyes. 'Urgh, a hate it no I'm on the streets. It's in a place ye kinda cannae hide it. A mean, why a got ma name inked on me in the first place a'll never know. But it's ma grannie's handwritin' so a suppose a cannae complain. Ye got a light anol?'

Molly Rose handed her a lighter and watched as she attempted to spark it a few times before she lit the cigarette. She handed it back to Molly Rose and inhaled loudly. 'Whit ye dain oot here on yer ane getting tanked up, then?'

'I was looking for someone,' Molly Rose replied. 'My auntie. Her name's Sinead. She's kind of homeless too. Well, she's in and out of hostels around here. Do you know her?'

The girl pursed her lips and her eyes narrowed. 'She got a last name?'

'Coyle. Her name is Sinead Coyle,' Molly Rose replied, hoping that the name would ring a bell to this girl and she could point her in the direction of her auntie.

'Nah, don't recognise the name. But a might know her face. Whit age is she?'

'Thirty-eight.' Molly Rose pulled her phone out of her pocket and showed Kassy the picture she'd taken of them earlier that day.

'*Awe*, a do know her. Well, a say know, whit a mean is, I've seen her aboot, maybe hung aboot waw the same folk, had a brief encounter, but a don't know her, know her. She's the auld burd who knocks aboot the streets. She's a crackin lassie mind ye, fae whit I dae know ae her. Always up fur a laugh. But she calls herself something different when she's working.'

Molly Rose raised a brow. 'What name does she go by?'

'Orla.'

Molly Rose burst out laughing and a fresh wave of pain stabbed at the inside of her head. 'Are you joking?'

'Naw. How wid ye hink am jokin?'

Molly Rose couldn't help but find it funny that her auntie was going around as a sex worker using her mum's name. That would put the final nail in the coffin between the two of them.

'Never mind,' Molly Rose replied. 'Do you know where she might be? I need to see her.'

The girl shook her head and took a long draw of the cigarette. 'She's probably no far fae here. Maybe up near Fitzroy, roon the back ae the park. Willnae take ye long tae fun her if ye start lookin noo. Just watch yer back up that end, though,' Kassy pointed towards the other end of the park. 'Pure fannies always hingin aboot, they'll stab ye as quick as look at ye.'

'Right. Thanks,' Molly Rose said as she looked up to the other side of the fountain.

'Dae ye want some company? A've got nothing else tae dae and a kinda owe ye fae earlier. Ye know, better fur someone who knows the area tae tag along so a can tell the fuckwits tae get tae fuck, ye know?'

Molly Rose couldn't help but smile. She liked this girl. She seemed genuine.

'Yeah, why not? Suppose I'll have back up if those boys come back.'

'Ha, those wee bastards willnae come back. Shat it when they saw that bottle coming at their scrawny wee faces.'

Molly Rose sighed in relief that she had someone like Kassy at her side.

They started walking together, a few feet apart from one another.

'So, how come yer sleeping on the streets then?' Kassy asked.

'It's complicated,' Molly Rose replied. 'Family stuff.'

'An you've nae pals ye can sleep on their sofa?'

Molly Rose sighed. 'I don't really have any friends.'

'How come?'

Molly Rose thought back to her relationship with Dean. How she spent every second with him when she wasn't at school. Even when she was at school, she'd spend lunchtimes on the phone to him or he'd come to see her. He'd pick her up from school, drop her off at school. She stopped walking home with her friends and, in the end, they stopped trying with her. Now she was completely alone.

'Again, it's complicated.'

'As complicated as yer step da battering fuck oot ye every day until ye don't huv nae other option but tae live on the streets?'

Molly Rose glanced at her in horror. 'Oh my god.'

'Aye, *he* didnae dae much aboot it either.' Kassy gave a humourless laugh.

'Fuck, my story won't sound half as bad as that. In fact, you'll think I sound like a spoiled brat.'

'Nah,' Kassy shook her head. 'If ye felt like leavin' wiz the only way, then it's reason enough.'

Molly Rose took a breath and decided that she needed one of the cigarettes herself even though the hangover was getting worse.

'So, wit happened?'

'Well, I was seeing this guy, Dean. He was amazing and I loved him. But he was eighteen and I was fifteen.'

'Paedo,' Kassy remarked.

Molly Rose stopped walking and stared at her. 'What?'

'He was a paedo. Probably still is. You said you were seeing him. Yer no noo?'

'No. My mum forced him away.'

'Fucking bang-on, yer maw.'

Molly Rose felt her jaw drop. 'You think she did the right thing? I was miserable after it happened.'

'Nae offence hen, but aye, ye dae sound like a spoiled brat. Think aboot it. The guy was three years older than ye. Doesnae sound much, but when yer only fifteen and he's eighteen, it's just fucking wrong. Whit does a man like that want wae a fifteen-year-old lassie, eh?'

Kassy sounded exactly like Orla, just the ned version.

Molly Rose swallowed hard and tried not to let Kassy see that her comments had bothered her. But in truth, they had. It was the first time someone of her age had said the same thing as her mum. 'Anyway, I kind of let the relationship consume me and when I came out the other side of it, I didn't have any friends left.'

'How long were ye with him?'

Molly Rose blinked and said, 'Best part of a year.'

'Jesus, so you were fourteen and he wis seventeen? That's even fuckin' worse. Ye really were just a wean. So, now whit? Yer just oot here, drowning yer sorrows an' sulking aboot yer maw actually looking efter ye?'

Molly Rose was so stunned that she let out a laugh.

'Well, it's not just that. My auntie, she's in a bit of a state and I asked my mum to help her and she refused. We got into a blazing row about it and I stormed out.'

'So yer oot here oot ae principle?'

'No. I want to find my auntie and take her home. She needs help to get clean.'

'Druggies don't want tae get clean, hen, they want tae get high,' Kassy said, raising her hands. 'But hey, you know yer family better than a dae. So, all a'll say is, you helped me earlier, I helped you. If we stick taegether we'll find yer auntie and then you two can work it oot fae there. Deal?'

Kassy flicked the cigarette into the fountain on their way past and Molly Rose watched the orange embers instantly die out. There was no other alternative, really. And if Molly Rose was honest with herself, she felt safe with Kassy. There was something about her that made Molly Rose want to stay with her.

'Deal,' she replied.

They headed to the east side of the park where An Clachan Cafe sat, and Molly Rose suddenly felt her mind wander to the idea of food. Her stomach rumbled loudly.

'Jeezo, you sound hungrier than me,' Kassy laughed.

'Sorry, I feel like I haven't eaten in years and it's only been a few hours. I don't actually know if I'm hungry or if I'm going to throw up.'

'Ha, the joys ae bevy. Ye got any cash on ye?' Kassy asked.

'Yeah.'

'Well, the cafe's open late the night. Why don't we get something before we start looking fur yer auntie?'

Molly Rose didn't care about the assumption Kassy made about food being bought for her. She'd buy her anything she wanted; she'd stopped those boys from mugging her, or worse. If she was going to help Molly Rose navigate her way through the city to find Sinead, she'd do anything for Kassy.

They went into An Clachan Cafe and chose a table at the back, near the rear exit.

'The muffins in here are fuckin' brilliant. Want tae split wan?' Kassy asked.

'Why don't we get one each?' Molly Rose replied. 'It's the least I can do in exchange for your help and protection tonight.'

'Awe, cheers, Mol. I can call ye that, eh?'

Molly Rose smiled. 'My dad calls me that sometimes.'

Kassy raised a brow. 'Here, whit did yer da say aboot awe the paedo stuff?'

'He wasn't a paedo,' Molly Rose replied sternly.

'Aye, if ye say so.'

Sighing in annoyance, Molly Rose said, 'He let my mum handle it.'

'Seriously? A'd huv thought most dads wid huv murdered the wee cunt.'

Somehow, Kassy was able to turn serious conversations funny. Laughing, Molly Rose replied, 'It's not in his nature to do that.'

'A tell ye, anyone tries that paedo shit on any ae ma weans in the future, a'd fucking murder them,' Kassy said, getting up. 'Right, a'll be back in a minute,' she said before going to the counter. She ordered two blueberry muffins and two coffees, before returning to the table.

'Ye know whit? A've never had a real pal in ma life. A mean, a've had pals that only want ye fur goin hoffers fur fags, or bevy, or coke. But yer no like that, a can tell.'

'Am I that boring?'

Kassy shook her head. 'Naw. Yer sound. Ye huvnae judged me. Ye huvnae looked at me in pure disgust like most folk dae. Yer kinda like a wan aff.'

She wouldn't say it out loud, but that meant more to Molly Rose than Kassy would ever know. She'd clicked with this girl, who she'd only met on the street earlier in the day and who'd stopped her from being mugged. If she'd believed in fate, then this wasn't a chance meeting.

'Thanks,' Molly Rose said.

'Naw, it should be me thanking you. A hink we're gonnae be best pals.'

The smile on Molly Rose's face grew, along with the nausea from the hangover that was fast becoming a big regret, and she nodded. 'Yeah. I think so too.'

Chapter 13

'Are you *actually* fucking kidding me?' Sinead shouted at the woman stood at the front door of the hostel. 'If you throw me out, you do realise I'll be homeless. You're putting a vulnerable woman on the street, you do realise that, don't you?'

Sinead hoped that the bluntness of her words would appeal to the softer side to the woman running the hostel. Not that Sinead believed she had a softer side. She'd witnessed her do this to people before who couldn't pay their way or bent the rules slightly.

'Look, hen, I don't have time for this. You never pay on time, you never follow housekeeping rules, and quite frankly you're a cheeky bastard and I'm sick of your shit.'

The words angered her, because the woman had proven her right. There was no softness, no gentle disposition. She was a grade-A bitch.

'Fuck you then,' Sinead said, picking up her rucksack and heading down the stairs. Turning, Sinead looked up at her sniggering, shitty little face. 'I've just realised I don't know your name.'

The woman frowned, confused by the sudden change in direction of the conversation. 'Karen.'

'Ha,' Sinead laughed. 'Suits you.'

Karen rolled her eyes and folded her arms. 'Piss off, will you. I've got a room that needs cleaning and you're holding me up.'

Sinead took a step up and pushed her face into Karen's. 'I'll do more than fucking hold you up. I'll put an end to you if I ever see you away from this shithole.'

Karen backed away, and for a moment, Sinead considered hawking up and spraying the woman in the face. But that was what she'd expect from a scum junkie; something that Sinead didn't want to be any more.

'Off you go,' Karen shouted, shoving her hands into Sinead's shoulders, which resulted in her falling down the stairs onto the street. 'You've got thirty seconds to get away from here or I'll get you jailed.'

Sinead got to her feet at the bottom of the stairs, her rucksack having broken her fall, and looked up at Karen.

'You're brave, I'll give you that,' Sinead said. She climbed back up the stairs and stood so close to Karen that she could smell her cheap perfume.

Sinead kept her voice low, menacing. 'What's to stop me from rag-dolling you down these stairs and stamping all over you? Eh?'

Karen blinked and Sinead saw regret creep across her face. 'I'll get you lifted.'

'That would be a good thing. At least I'd have a fucking bed for the night. But you know what? I'm not going to touch you, because I'm not the scum junkie you want me to be. You *want* me to do that to you, so you can watch the police cart me off. I'm not going to give you the satisfaction. I'll get clean, I'll get my life in order. But you,' Sinead eyed her up and down, 'you'll always just be Karen, the judgemental hostel receptionist who thinks she's better than everyone else. You might not be a junkie,

Karen, but you're the biggest piece of scum I've ever come across. Enjoy the rest of your shift.'

Karen backed away, moved inside and slammed the hostel door shut. Sinead pulled herself together, half of her wishing she'd skelped her across the face and the other half glad she didn't. 'Bitch,' she muttered as she turned her back to the building.

Shit, she thought. Where was she going to go now? She didn't have any money left, hence why she hadn't paid for her room at the hostel. Working the street tonight really wasn't something that she wanted to do with how she was feeling, but she didn't have much of a choice. Her skin itched, her bones ached, and the overwhelming need for a drink and a few lines was unbearable.

Sinead puffed out her cheeks, zipped up her jacket and headed along Park Terrace towards the city centre. If she was going to be guaranteed money, then she would have to look for it where more men were hanging around and willing to pay.

Park Terrace became Woodside Terrace, and Sinead couldn't help but look in the windows of the ground-level flats. People would have to shit money to be able to afford one of these, she thought. It would be nice to have somewhere to go. A comfy bed. A warm living room; nothing huge, just simple. Somewhere she could curl up in front of the telly with a cuppa at the end of the day. But Sinead's life wasn't that simple. It never had been. Being abandoned by her birth mum when she was a baby; her adoptive parents dying when they were at a vulnerable age. Becoming a young woman and going through a massive change in family circumstances and ending up in care had been where it all started. Her downward spiral of self-sabotage and destruction. Orla was different. She saw their crap start as a challenge and she smashed that challenge in the face every time. But not Sinead. No, she drank or snorted away her problems.

Traffic noise grew louder as Sinead headed on to Sauchiehall Street. The M8 motorway was below her before it disappeared into the tunnel she was stood on top of. As she watched the cars speed through it, she considered jumping off. It wouldn't hurt. It would be quick, she thought. No more pain, no more addiction. She wouldn't have to worry about any of it if she just put an end to it all. The idea of it was quite appealing, when she really considered it. She had nothing more to live for. There was Molly Rose, but she had her own problems and Sinead didn't want to add to them. She might be a mess, but Sinead considered herself a good person at heart. Taking herself out of the equation for her family would be a good thing, the noble thing to do.

'Excuse me?' A voice made her turn. It was like looking in a mirror. A woman, clearly a sex worker and an addict of some kind, was staring back at her.

'Yeah?'

'You got any spare change? I haven't eaten in days.'

Fuck's sake, Sinead thought.

'Look at me, do I look like I have spare change?'

The woman, who looked to be in her early thirties, didn't even respond. She simply moved on. It was likely she was going to ask the next person she came across the same question. Is that how bad the streets of this city had become? Homeless begging the homeless?

Maybe it was time to put her tail between her legs and go to Orla for help. She'd have to get clean. She'd go there, sober; well, as sober as possible. She'd tell her that she was going to get help because maybe now, it *really* was time to make a change. She hadn't seen her sister in a few years. In fact, she couldn't remember exactly how long. And for as long as Sinead could remember, Orla hadn't wanted to be in Sinead's corner. She'd had enough of the lies, the stealing, the manipulation that came with being a heroin addict. But now, Molly Rose seemed to be the only blood relation that wanted to see Sinead do well. Now, there was someone who could fight her corner with her.

She'd fucking beg Orla for support if she had to.

Chapter 14

1985

Janey unclipped the lead from her Alsatian, Hamish's collar, and watched as he bolted off across the unoccupied field after the ball she'd thrown for him. Charlie lit a cigarette and offered one to her. She took it and allowed Charlie to light it for her.

'Why did you punch the vicar's son?' Janey asked, trying not to laugh at the question. She didn't agree with it, but she knew why Charlie would have done it.

'He's a snivelling little fucker who was born with a sense of entitlement because he's the son of a vicar. Thinks he can get away with anything because of who he is.'

Janey blew smoke out of her mouth and raised a brow at Charlie. 'Hmm, I think I know someone else who has a sense of entitlement.'

Charlie shook his head. 'I don't think I'm entitled, Janey. I know I am. Come on, Finn Hallahan is our dad. And everyone in this village, in surrounding towns and cities, even other countries, knows who he is and what he's capable of. Just having the Hallahan name attached is enough to make people scared of you. Look at that little runt, Cameron. He didn't want to meet Finn for fucking weeks. Was terrified of the stories he'd heard.'

Janey sighed and took another draw of her cigarette, while keeping an eye on Hamish as he chased the ball she continually threw for him. She didn't want to say it, but Finn wasn't Charlie's dad at all. Yes, he'd taken Charlie in when Grainne left and Gerry was killed after getting drunk and being hit by a car; best thing that could've happened to him, Janey had always thought. However, other than that, Charlie was just a lad that Finn looked after. He wasn't a Hallahan in any sense of the word; Charlie didn't even call Finn "Dad". She wouldn't, however, say that to Charlie. He'd never admit it, but he'd been hurt enough in the past when his mother left and his dad was killed; even though he'd been beaten by Gerry, it still hurt Charlie when he died.

'Is it any wonder? I would be scared if I was him,' she said. 'But just because the stories are out there doesn't mean you should go around acting like the big man. If it's going to put a bad spin on the Hallahan name, then you know how Dad will react. He doesn't like undue attention, Charlie, and getting into a fight and breaking the boy's nose brought a lot of attention to us.'

Charlie tutted. 'No, it didn't. It brought the attention to me. And anyway, he deserved it. Said I was nothing but a gangster wannabe pretending to be a Hallahan and I'd end up in jail like the rest of them. Then he laughed with his holier-than-thou mates, so I lamped him. He's fucking lucky I didn't shove a Bible doused in petrol down his throat and a match up his arse.'

Janey rolled her eyes at the scenario. She knew Charlie's ego was dented by the comment about pretending to be a Hallahan. He'd lost who he was back when they were just kids. Janey couldn't really remember a time where Charlie wasn't around. He'd come to live with them when she was just five. Finn had brought him up as a Hallahan and he really was part of the family.

Hamish dropped the ball at her feet again. She picked it up and launched it across the field.

'You should be careful with Dad. You know what he's like. He takes no prisoners. You make enough wrong moves with him, Charlie, and—'

'And what?' Charlie snapped. He bowed his head, sighed and said, 'Sorry. I'm not annoyed with you. But you've got to understand how hard it is to be the lad who had to be taken in because his mum fucked off and his dad was an abusive drunk who got himself killed after a skinful. You know the story about me and so does every other fucker in this town. My old man was abusive. My ma couldn't handle it so pissed off and left me with him.'

She saw a flicker of sadness cross his face.

'You're the only one who doesn't look at me like I'm some kind of parasite.'

'That's because you're not. I know your backstory is a bit shit, Charlie, but that doesn't give you the right to go around acting the way you do. People don't deserve to have you take out your problems on them.'

Charlie glanced at her in annoyance. 'Easy for you to say. You've had the perfect life. You know where you come from. Your mum died, she didn't just up and leave you. And Finn has never laid a hand on you.'

Sighing inwardly, Janey said, 'You think I have the perfect life? You said it yourself; my mum died. I'd say that's far from perfect, Charlie. And yes, I do know where I come from. And now, you come from Hallahan stock too. Try to focus on that, Charlie. It'll do you the world of good. And just try to behave. Because he won't hesitate to throw you out if you don't buck up your ideas. And he won't fall for the sympathy stories. Bring the police to the door again and he'll do it. He will. I don't want to see that happen to you. You deserve a place at our table and you'll lose it if you don't stop all this self-destruction shit.'

Hamish returned the ball to Janey's feet and Charlie bent down to pick it up before lobbing it so far that Hamish was difficult to spot as he dove into the long grass to retrieve it.

'It won't happen. He won't throw me out.'

Janey watched his expression contort and then relax. Was he considering the possibility that Janey was right? He looked worried.

'You're right. He won't, so long as you do what I suggested and stop all this. Our reputations are his. Trust me on this, Charlie.'

Chapter 15

NOW

Janey got out of the car and looked up at what remained of Club Envy just outside the cordoned area. She'd never liked the club, but then, she didn't have to. All she needed was the revenue from the person who ran the business from her property. It just so happened that the fucker who'd had it before it closed had caused a lot of bother. She'd thought about renting the place out to someone else, but stipulating that it would be her business plan and the person would literally manage the place. Then she'd considered selling the property altogether. Now, she was looking at its ruins.

Water still dripped from the rafters and the building was smouldering in places.

'Janey,' Kristo said. 'I have spoken with a few contacts, and no one in the city seems to know who could have been responsible for this. It looks like it might have been a lone wolf.'

Janey breathed slowly, smelling the smoke on intake.

Glancing up at the surrounding buildings, at the cafes, the shops, the other bars and restaurants, Janey wondered if everyone had been warned to keep their mouths shut. Someone must have seen something; *heard* something at least.

'Yeah, it sounds more plausible. I think I'll do some digging. See what I can come up with,' Janey said, thinking back to the text she'd received. She knew who'd sent it. She just had to get proof.

'Do you want me to come with you?' Kristo said, a shadow of concern crossing his face.

Janey smiled at his concern. 'No, I'll be fine. Ciaran will join me. Why don't you head down to Carbeth. There's a shipment due soon and you need to be there for it.'

Kristo nodded and said: 'Of course. I have my phone on me. You call if you need anything at all. And if you find out something that doesn't quite sit well, get in touch and I can be back with you.'

Janey placed a hand on Kristo's lower arm and squeezed gently. 'Thanks, Kristo. Now, get going. With weather like this, everyone will be heading for the Devil's Pulpit. You know what those roads can be like when the sun is shining.'

Kristo headed along Ingram Street and out of sight, and Janey watched as Ciaran immerged from one of the shops on the corner next to the entrance to the Candleriggs.

'One pack of Club cigarettes, at your request,' Ciaran said, handing Janey the packet.

'Thanks, love,' she replied, pulling one out and lighting it.

'What you thinking?' Ciaran asked, watching her as she took in the surrounding streets of the Merchant City.

'This place, it's a small part of the wider city. A more expensive place to come, have a drink, socialise. Not a lot of people do these days, given the state of the country's finances.'

'Hmm,' Ciaran replied.

'I know some of the business owners around here. They weren't all too happy with how McInroy was running things, from what I can gather. So, if it was one of the opposing businesses, why now? Why burn the place after McInroy is out of the picture?'

Ciaran shrugged. 'Revenge? A warning not to allow it to happen again?'

Janey narrowed her eyes. 'No. That's not it. These people, these business owners... they wouldn't go up against me like that. Not when half of them know what I'm about: that the Hallahans aren't a threat so long as you don't cause a problem.'

'That does make a lot of sense.'

'Someone around here must know something, surely? I mean, it happened during the day, so it's not as though the partygoers and the staff had all gone home for the night and the only people left on the street were sex workers and curb crawlers.'

'Police? CCTV?' Ciaran suggested.

'Yeah, we should get on to our contacts at the local station,' Janey said, although she wanted to deal with this by herself. 'But I do want to talk to people face to face.'

Ciaran sighed and then shoved his hands in his pocket. Janey eyed her husband. 'What is it?'

'I don't know. It's just...' he hesitated. 'Janey, we're getting on a bit.'

'Ha, speak for yourself, you cheeky bastard.'

'No, what I mean is, shouldn't we just let the heavies do this for us. Bring the person to us when they find out who it is? I mean, after what happened a few months ago, don't you think we should be relaxing?'

Janey's thoughts went back to the summer of last year. Lucie. Christina; all the terrible things that happened

87

under Danny's watch. She shook her head. 'This has nothing to do with last year, Ciaran. And just because I'm approaching my mid-fifties doesn't mean I can't deal with this.'

'No,' Ciaran said. 'That's not what I meant at all. All I meant was, we employ people like Kristo for a reason.'

'Ciaran, the person who sent that message, teasing about how they hope the fire hasn't left the business in dire straits, wants to meet *me*. They aren't going to reveal themselves to Kristo. Or you. Or anyone else close to me for that matter. They want me to figure it out. And I will.' *I already have*, she thought.

Janey headed down Candleriggs and on to Merchant Square. Approaching a bar named Cocktails and Cake, she pushed the door open and went inside. The place was empty, not open to punters yet. She glanced up at the poster on the wall, stating that high tea could be booked for a starting price of forty pounds. Janey rolled her eyes. Forty quid for cake and some shit prosecco? Did people pay for that?

'Can I help?' A male voice filtered through from the bar towards where Janey was standing.

'I'm looking for Max, the owner?'

Cocktails and Cake had a similar layout and décor to that of Club Envy, or at least what Club Envy used to look like before it became a pile of charcoal.

'You're Janey Hallahan, right?' a man stood up from behind the bar. 'I could tell by the accent.'

'We've met once before,' Janey replied. 'When Danny McInroy took over Club Envy?'

Max nodded and dried his hands on a tea towel. 'Aye, I remember. I wasn't too happy about that arrangement.'

'Well, he's gone now.'

'Aye and so is your club from what I've been hearing.'

Janey didn't like his tone. It was almost as though he sounded happy about what had happened. Surely not? Surely this man wasn't that stupid to be so open to Janey about that?

'Yes. I just wondered if you'd heard or seen anything?'

Max pursed his lips, rolled his eyes up to the ceiling in mock thought. 'Nope. Sorry.'

Janey's brow furrowed before she crossed the floor. Max busied himself behind the bar as if he didn't know she was there, approaching him with rage inside her.

'Max, this is serious. If my property was attacked, then yours could be at risk too.'

A slight smile raised the corner of Max's mouth.

'Nah, I don't think so. You see, I don't have enemies. And I don't bring in fuckwits like Danny McInroy to run things for me. You'd have to be brain dead to do something like that.'

'No, you just have Daddy's money, don't you?' Janey replied. Max shot her a look of disgust, but when he saw the expression on her face, it changed to regret.

'Aye, you see, I know all about you. I know all about every business owner in this city that could potentially rival me. Who could cause me problems. And I know that little Maxwell George Clark is a snivelling little shit who wouldn't be standing here now if it wasn't for dear, dead, Daddy's money. So, I'll ask you again, did you hear, see or know anything about my property being burned to the ground?'

Max had stopped what he was doing and was staring at Janey, wide-eyed and open-mouthed. 'No. I didn't. And no, I don't.'

Janey nodded, took a step closer to Max. The only thing between them was the marble-topped bar, still wet from having been cleaned. The smell of disinfectant was overwhelming. Quickly, Janey shot a hand out, grabbed Max by the collar of his white, Ben Sherman polo shirt and pulled him down onto the wet marble surface, forcing his face down with her other hand.

Max cried out in pain, or shock, Janey wasn't sure which, as she dug her long, manicured nails into the back of his neck.

'Listen to me, you little shit, I don't have time for your attitude. If you know anything, fucking tell me now otherwise I won't be responsible.'

Max's skeletal frame struggled under Janey's grip, and all she wanted to do was pull him right over the bar and onto the floor. He was that tiny, she would manage it without issue. But instead, she held him there, awaiting his response.

'I don't know anything.'

'Are you sure?' She dug her nails in a little harder.

She felt him tense under the pressure and then suddenly, his attitude changed. 'Okay. Okay, just let go, for fuck's sake.'

Janey kept him in place. 'Okay, what?'

'A guy was here.'

Janey let go, allowing Max to stand up and try to regain at least some of his dignity. She eyed him as he tried to gather himself. Was he trying to come up with a lie? Something that would get him out of this situation? No, Janey thought. This little runt wasn't clever enough for that.

'What guy?' Janey pushed.

'I don't know. Just a guy. He was drunk, or on drugs. I couldn't tell which.'

'When was this?'

'A few weeks ago.'

Max went silent and looked beyond Janey to the door of the bar. She clicked her fingers and said: 'Oi, eyes on me. We're not finished yet.'

Max sighed and threw his dishtowel down onto the bar, but he didn't say anything.

'Max, if you don't tell me, I'll fucking squeeze it out of you.'

He sighed loudly and his shoulders slumped in defeat. 'He came in, asking if I knew what had happened to Club Envy and why it had shut down. I told him I didn't really know details, only that the guy who ran it was no longer around. Then he started muttering something about you.'

Janey felt her stomach lurch. 'What did he say?'

'I couldn't make him out. Like I said, he was off his face one way or another. Anyway, I asked him if there was anything else I could do for him and he replied saying, no, he would do it himself.'

'Do what himself?' Janey pressed.

'He didn't say. But I'm assuming it's not just a coincidence that a few weeks later, your club goes up in smoke.'

Janey looked Max up and down and raised a brow. 'Anything else?'

Max shook his head. 'Yes. There is one thing.'

'What?'

'He had the same accent as you.'

Janey closed her eyes and her stomach lurched. She knew who this was; the mention of an accent all but confirmed it.

'Do you have CCTV?' Janey asked, already making her way around to let herself in behind the bar. Max stopped her, letting himself out.

'Yeah, it's in my office.'

She followed behind him, watching as he attempted to smooth out his polo shirt after she'd held him down. Max took a set of keys out of his pocket and unlocked a door, before letting himself into an office. Again, the place looked like the office at Club Envy and Janey felt like she was back there.

'Let me just pull up the date and you can have a look,' Max said, sitting down at the computer and tapping away on the keyboard. 'It was the day before Merchant City Festival started, so I know the exact date. When he came in, I thought he was a delivery guy; I was expecting a delivery so didn't bother to look up until he was right in front of me.'

'You've changed your tune all of a sudden.'

'Yeah,' Max replied. 'I don't fancy having to explain to the missus why I've got nail marks on my neck. You weren't going to let go until I told you.'

'Correct.'

Max was quiet for a moment and then he turned the screen towards Janey. She leaned down, resting her hands on the desk as she watched the scene play out in front of her.

The man staggered into the club and approached the bar. Max was in shot behind the bar, doing some paperwork but had his back to the camera. The man came into full view of the camera, on the other side of the bar. And that was when she saw his face. She couldn't be a hundred per cent certain. But in her gut, she knew that it couldn't be anyone else. It all made sense; it was all connected now. The text, his face.

Janey frowned. 'He didn't give you a name?'

'No. Do you know who it is?'

Janey turned and headed out the office door and across the floor towards the exit. 'You need to clean your bar top again. Your face prints will be all over it and that'll shine up on that expensive marble.'

She pushed the door open and once outside, she took a deep breath. And another, until she could feel herself calming.

Ciaran was walking towards her, concern on his face.

'What's happened?'

'I know who burned down the club.'

Ciaran looked on expectantly and when she didn't answer, he said, 'Janey, who?'

'An old face I haven't seen for years and, quite frankly, I hoped I'd never see again.'

She opened the car door and climbed inside, trying to breathe through the nausea that had crept up on her. Ciaran got into the car and looked at her, waiting for her to give him a name.

'Janey, tell me who it was.'

She pulled a cigarette out of her pack, lit it and put the window down. 'Just drive, eh? I'll tell you on the way back to the house.'

Chapter 16

'And she said she couldn't be around you?' Oliver asked after Orla had told him what had happened.

'Correct,' she replied. 'Actually, she said she couldn't be around someone like me. I mean, all I've ever done is care for and protect her and this is how she thanks me, by storming out of the house and refusing to answer her phone.'

Oliver sighed. 'She'll come back. She's not the type to stay away.'

Orla tapped her fingernails against the crystal wine glass in her hand. 'It's not like she's got anywhere to stay. She lost all her friends after Dean isolated her from them all. It was one of the reasons I wanted her away from him. And I know Molly Rose won't see that the reason her friends are gone is because of him, but it makes me feel sad for her. She's only sixteen and has no friends, no life. Oh God, what a mess, Oliver.'

Oliver held his breath for a moment and Orla knew that meant he was going to say something she didn't like.

'Go on, say it.'

'I mean, couldn't you just agree to what she's asking? We could pay for Sinead's rehab or something?'

Orla stared at her husband in disbelief. 'Did you seriously just say that to me? Are you actually telling me that you want me to allow Sinead back in the house after last time? She was shooting up in the guest bathroom and had an actual dealer come to the house, Oliver. What the hell is wrong with you?'

Frustration crossed Oliver's face and he closed his eyes momentarily. 'I know. I remember. But it was five years ago, Orla. Maybe now, we could give her a chance to show us that she really does want to change. She doesn't have to stay here. I don't want to take the risk again either, you know, of her proving your distrust again. We could pay for her rehab, in a facility somewhere.'

Orla sighed. 'Maybe that's what I should have been paying for in the first place, instead of giving her money every month just to keep her away. Jesus, what kind of person am I, Oliver? I've buried my head in the sand about this and now our daughter has taken the dramatic action of leaving home because of it. I'm an arsehole.'

A smile raised the corners of Oliver's mouth. 'You're not an arsehole. You've only been doing what you thought was right all this time. But like you said, now it's time to change things. If Molly Rose feels so strongly about getting Sinead help, then maybe we should too?'

Orla hated to admit it, but Oliver was right. It seemed Molly Rose had a mature head on her shoulders, for this at least. And perhaps doing what she asked would mend their relationship after all the drama revolving around Dean.

'So, when did you last speak with her?'

'Yesterday when she stormed out. I haven't been able to get a hold of her since. In fact, her phone just keeps going to answering machine. So, she's either blocked me or she's run out of battery.'

'She could be staying with friends?' Oliver asked, looking concerned.

Orla shook her head. 'No, she doesn't have any friends left. The ones she did have ended up so distant because of Dean and now they don't bother with her. So, if I'm brutally honest, I don't have a clue where she could be.'

Oliver pulled out his phone and Orla watched as he made a call, presumably to Molly Rose. 'Hi, sweetheart, it's Dad. We just want to know that you're okay. Please, come home. We can discuss Sinead and a possible solution to getting her some help. We love you.'

He hung up and Orla knew it was a message he'd left.

'What if she's lost her phone? What if something has happened to her?'

'I think we should report her missing,' Orla said, fighting back tears.

When everything was going on with Dean, she thought that was the worst thing she could go through with her daughter. But now, knowing that Molly Rose was potentially missing, that something horrible could have happened to her – because she wasn't the most street-wise girl out there given her privileged upbringing – made her feel sick.

'Yeah, I agree,' Oliver said. 'I can do it, if you want?'

Orla felt tears pool in her eyes as she watched Oliver make the call to Police Scotland. Before she knew it, there would be officers in her house, taking details and a description. They would ask questions about the circumstances surrounding her disappearance. Disappearance? Was that what it would be classed as? She was uncontactable. Orla didn't have a clue where she could be or who she could be with.

'They're sending someone round now to take details,' Oliver said as he hung up the phone.

'Oliver, what if she's with Dean?'

He sighed. 'The police will handle it. But we have to remember that she's sixteen now. If she wants to go there and they get back together, the law can't do anything about it. And neither can we, really.'

She'd tell the police about Molly Rose's connection with Dean. Surely that would be something they'd look into.

'It's my fault she left, Oliver.'

'No, it's not.'

'It is. If I'd just… I don't know. I just can't help but think that if I'd handled everything with a little more respect for her feelings, we wouldn't be in this situation right now.'

Silence fell between them.

The doorbell rang and Orla went to the door with Oliver. As he pulled the door open, Orla had expected to find two officers at the door. When she saw who was actually standing there, she froze.

'Hi,' Sinead said timidly.

Orla peered over Sinead's shoulder. 'Is Molly Rose with you?'

Sinead frowned. 'No. She's not here?'

Orla shot her twin a dirty look. She appeared weathered. Her skin was dull, with a deathly film of sweat over her face. She trembled. *Withdrawal*, Orla thought.

'No. She's not here. She's been gone for twenty-four hours. We've reported her missing.'

Sinead's eyes narrowed as she folded her arms across her body. 'But I told her to come home and sort things out with you.'

'Well, she did come home. But we got into an argument and she left again. And neither of us can get hold of her. So, the police are on their way to take statements before they start looking for her. If you've got any heroin on you, you might want to do one.'

Orla felt Oliver's eyes on her. She turned and the look of horror on his face surprised her.

'I'm trying to get clean,' Sinead said, her voice barely a whisper.

Orla tutted. 'Ha, aye right. I've heard that one before.'

'I am. Seeing Molly Rose yesterday made me realise how much life I've missed out on since falling into the wrong crowd. But mostly, I've lost you. And I need to get myself sorted. But I can't do it without your help, Orla. And I don't mean money. I mean actual support. Please, I'm desperate. I'm begging you. Do you want me to get down on my knees?'

Orla stared at her in disbelief, confusion, anger.

'How long have you been clean? I'm guessing by the shaking, longer than a few hours?'

Sinead nodded and scratched at her arm. 'I've not had any since last night. Less than twenty-four hours. But that's the longest I've ever gone.' Oliver gestured for Sinead to step into the house. She took a cautious step, keeping her eyes on the floor and Oliver closed the door behind her.

'We need to focus on finding Molly Rose right now,' Orla said. 'I don't need your shit alongside that, Sinead.'

'I promise not to cause you any problems, Orla. I just need somewhere safe to try to get my head together and figure out how I'm going to get off this shit.'

As she stared at her twin, she wondered how things had got so bad for her. She'd fallen into the wrong crowd and been swept away by that lifestyle until it wasn't fun any more. Orla often thought about how things would have turned out if she'd been the one placed with that awful foster family instead of Sinead. Would she have become what Sinead was now?

'And you really think that now, after all these years, you can get clean?' Orla asked.

Sinead shrugged. 'I don't know. I've never really tried. But I was someone else before this, Orla. We were close once before I fucked it all up. The difference now is, I want to stop. Hopefully that'll be half the battle.'

Oliver grazed Orla's hand with his and she looked up at him. 'I think we owe it to Molly Rose to help Sinead.'

Orla sighed. 'Fine. As soon as the police have been, we start looking into how to get you clean. But I'm warning you, Sinead. One foot out of line, if even a penny goes missing from this house, you're out and I will never speak to you again. Do you understand?'

Sinead exhaled slowly and unfolded her arms. 'Yeah. Loud and clear.'

As she took in Sinead's appearance, Orla felt sorry for her for the first time in years. Sinead's lack of self-respect and her inability to say no to all the wrong things had turned her into a shell, and Orla couldn't see her sister behind those eyes at all. The one she'd grown up with, gone through so much with.

'Good. Because believe it or not, Sinead, I do want you to get better. I'd like my sister back.'

But before that, she wanted Molly Rose home.

Chapter 17

Sinead sat on the edge of the bed in the guest room of her twin sister's house and dropped her bag onto the floor. The ensuite bathroom door was open. This wasn't any old ensuite with a basic toilet and shower. It was like a five-star hotel bathroom, with a free-standing bath, the kind with the huge, fancy gold legs. It had a shower head attached to the gold taps and an assortment of toiletries for Sinead to choose from. In the corner was a larger-than-most shower cubicle with a rain shower head at the top.

'Jesus Christ, who the hell is she expecting to stay here? The fucking King?' she whispered as she moved into the bathroom and turned on the hot water tap to fill the bath.

She'd only been off the heroin for less than a day and already the withdrawal was brutal. It would be so easy to just get a hit to ease the symptoms. Sinead shook her head. No. She wasn't going to fall at the first hurdle. If she wanted to do this, she had to be serious because the alternative was to go back to the streets. Sell her body. Live in fear that she wouldn't wake up the next day. She had to focus on a future that didn't involve drugs. One where she had a relationship with her family that didn't include rejection or being accused of theft.

A gentle tap at the door made Sinead turn. Orla was standing in the doorway of the guest bedroom with a pile of fluffy white towels in her hands.

'Thought you might need these,' she said. Sinead could tell she'd been crying.

'The police have been?' Sinead asked.

Orla set the towels down on the king-sized bed and then perched herself on the edge of the mattress.

'Yeah. They took our statements and said they'll start an investigation.'

'Fuck,' Sinead whispered. 'I'm sorry, Orla.'

'Yeah, me too.'

Sinead sighed and sat down beside Orla on the bed. 'I just want to thank you for taking another chance on me, Orla. I know you've got a lot going on right now and the last thing you need is me hanging around.'

Orla was silent. She wasn't looking at Sinead, but staring down at the floor.

'Our lives are very different, Orla. I don't know what it's like to live in your world and you don't know what it's like to live in mine. But I want to do this. I want to get clean. I want us to be sisters again. And *when* Molly Rose comes home, we can start to rebuild things.'

A teardrop fell to the plush, cream carpet and Sinead watched as her sister tried to compose herself.

'What if something's happened to Molly Rose? Out there on her own, because I pushed her away.'

'She's your daughter, Orla. She'll be fine. And it won't be long before she's home. Trust me. A day out there is tough. She won't last much longer.'

Orla glanced up at Sinead. 'Do you think?'

Sinead nodded before getting up and turning off the tap in the bath. She caught a glimpse of herself in the mirror and sighed.

'I really do look like shit,' she said, turning back to Orla, who was still sitting on the bed. 'I wonder if we get our looks from her.'

'Who? Our mother?' Orla replied. 'I hope we don't get anything from her. Selfish bitch.'

Sinead sighed. Orla had always been bitter about what had happened to them. But they never knew the backstory of their birth mum, or what caused her to give them up.

'You can't say that if you don't know her. She could have had multiple reasons for giving us up.'

'Then she should have told me.'

Sinead frowned. 'What do you mean?'

Orla shook her head and got to her feet. 'Nothing. Never mind. You don't need it on top of trying to get clean.'

Orla moved to the door, but something in Sinead's gut told her that there was something she should know. She shot out a hand and grabbed Orla by the wrist.

'No. You clearly have something to say. So say it.'

'No.'

Sinead let go and crossed her arms over her chest. 'This is about our birth mum, isn't it? Have you spoken to her?'

Orla didn't respond.

'Orla, if you've had contact with her, I deserve to know.'

'Fine,' Orla shouted. 'Yes. She contacted me.'

Sinead felt a wave of nausea pass over her. 'Oh my god. And you didn't think to tell me? You didn't think I'd want to know?'

'You were off doing other things, Sinead, you know, like heroin? Sharing needles with God knows who. And no, in all honestly, I didn't think you'd be that interested purely for that reason.'

She felt her jaw drop. 'What the hell is *wrong* with you?'

Orla sighed loudly and ran her hands through her hair.

'What did she say? When did this happen?'

Orla's shoulders slumped and she fell back onto the bed, the thick, fluffy duvet crumpling around her.

'Okay,' Orla said. 'About ten years ago, our mother turned up in Glasgow. I was out having lunch with some friends and she approached me when I was in the bathrooms. She told me who she was and I… I don't know. I flipped. Freaked out. Walked out of the restaurant and got in a taxi. But she followed me back to the house and when I got home, she was there. She said that she didn't mean any harm or upset. She only wanted to talk.'

'Ten *years*? Are you fucking kidding?' Sinead couldn't believe what she was hearing. Was she off her face and this was all some kind of lucid dream?

'I told her that I didn't believe who she was claiming to be. That she could have been anyone who saw an opportunity to make money. She pulled out her ID and a copy of some adoption paperwork, which by the way, I have no idea how she even got a hold of. I saw our adoptive parents' names on there. I slammed the door in her face. But not before I told her to piss off and never to come anywhere near me again.'

Orla sat up and rubbed at her eyes.

'So then what? She just left and you haven't seen her in ten years? I can't believe you never told me this. You're a selfish cow.'

'She phoned me yesterday, on our birthday,' Orla said, ignoring Sinead's remark.

'What did she say?'

'Wanted to know how we were doing.'

'So, she turned up ten years ago, then disappeared again. Now, she's calling to see how we're doing as though she's been around all these years? What did you say?'

'I told her where to go. That we weren't interested.'

Sinead felt sick. Also, curious. This woman obviously wanted to make amends and Orla had pushed her away.

'You spoke on my behalf? You had no right, Orla. Where is she now?' Sinead asked.

Orla shrugged. 'I have no idea. But I have a feeling that won't be the last time I'll hear from her. Especially now that Molly Rose is missing. If this makes it on to the news, she could see it and try to make contact again.'

'I'd like to speak to her myself, if she contacts you again,' Sinead said.

Orla shot her a look. 'What? No. Why would you want to speak to the woman who abandoned us?'

'And why would you *not*? Don't you have questions that you want answered? I have tons. Give me her number.'

Orla laughed. 'No way.'

'It's not up to you whether or not I have a relationship with this woman, Orla. You don't have to, but it's my choice whether I do. Now, give me the number she rang you from.'

'Do you think it's a good idea, given that you're about to make a dramatic lifestyle change? This could send you over the edge, Sinead. It could tip you the wrong way and you could fuck it up. Is she really worth it?' Orla asked. And then she thought about what Molly Rose had said to her just the day before. If the woman had been around, then maybe things would have been entirely different for both Orla and Sinead. Sinead might not have gone down a bad path at all.

Orla stood up abruptly, pulled her phone from her pocket and began tapping away on the screen. Then, shoving the phone at Sinead, she said: 'Here.'

'You'll have to write it down for me. I've lost my phone.'

Orla left the room and reappeared a few moments later, dropping a piece of paper onto the bed.

'Don't say I didn't warn you. She'll hurt you, Sinead. You'll feel the abandonment all over again and you'll end up back on that shit. You're better off without her.'

Sinead ignored her sister, picked up the piece of paper with a trembling hand and stared down at the number. 'What's her name? Our mum.'

Orla almost spat the name out of her mouth. 'Janey Hallahan.'

Chapter 18

1985

Janey watched as her dad refilled the water trough for the horses and brushed the tail of his favourite mare, Freya. He adored the horses on their farm. He'd spend hours out on the horse field every day and she often wondered how they ever had so much money if that's all he did all day. In reality, she understood the secret moneymaker behind the business. She'd grown up around it and, if she was honest, as much as there wasn't much she could do or say about it, she did worry for the future. For Finn and herself, and now her unborn child. Her dad being a crime boss could mean danger for her, although Finn didn't seem to think that danger would befall the family. She'd only found out about what he did for a living when Charlie started to work for Finn when he was just fifteen. She didn't know much about what they did when they went out, but she knew that it affected Charlie in a way that changed his behaviour. He was cocky and arrogant, even more so than he'd been before. Janey had started asking questions and Finn gave in when she didn't relent. He gave her the basics, but she understood that their family business wasn't legit.

She missed her mum and often wondered how things would have turned out if she hadn't died when Janey was nine. She liked Charlie, treated him like her own and his manners were softer when she was around. But when she died, Charlie resorted back to having that mean streak in him that Janey truly disliked and it had escalated from there.

She loved her dad with everything she had. But as she glanced down at the ever-growing bump that she'd been doing well to hide up until now, she wondered again, how he'd react to his fifteen-year-old daughter telling him that he was going to be a grandfather. She wanted him to be thrilled. To take Janey in his arms, tell her that everything would be okay and that he would look after her and the baby. But she knew that was never going to be the case. Finn Hallahan was a traditional man. The marriage-before-babies kind. Not that Janey had anyone to marry. She needed her mum now more than ever. The feeling of fear at the prospect of living without her had never gone away and it was fully present now.

Finn turned and waved to her across the field. She shielded her eyes from the burning sun and waved back, hoping that the raised arm wouldn't reveal her belly. It didn't. How had he not noticed yet? She was huge and surely ready to go any day now. Not that she knew her due date. She hadn't even told the doctor.

It was now or never. She couldn't stay hidden forever. It would be worse to have the baby before telling her dad she was pregnant. He'd die of a heart attack from the shock.

She forced one foot in front of the other and made her way across the field towards her dad. She would tell him today. And he would be okay. He wouldn't abandon her. He was her dad and always said it was them against the world.

'Hi Dad,' Janey said as she reached him.

'Hi Janey,' he said, continuing to brush Freya's long, chestnut-coloured tail.

'Dad, I have something to tell you.'

Chapter 19

NOW

Janey got out of the Defender and walked up to the front entrance of the house. Pulling her keys from her pocket, she saw that her hand was shaking with rage.

'Here,' Ciaran said, 'let me.' He reached around her and attempted to open the door, but Janey snapped round and gave him a warning stare.

'I've got it,' she said, unlocking the door and pushing her way inside. She walked quickly to the kitchen and slammed her bag down on the counter. She heard Ciaran close the door behind her and approach the kitchen with caution.

'Are you going to tell me who the *hell* you think started the fire?'

Janey took a breath and closed her eyes. She'd been quiet on the journey back from the Merchant City to Rhu. It was a long bout of silence, but she just couldn't bring herself to say it out loud or even believe it. She always suspected that he'd come back one day. But for it to actually be true made her feel angry that she hadn't dealt with him long ago. 'It's Charlie *fucking* Hallahan.'

Ciaran frowned. 'You're *related* to the guy who burned down Club Envy?'

She shook her head and took a steadying breath. 'Unfortunately, yes. Well, no. It's complicated.'

'How have I never heard of him before?'

'Because I've never let his name cross my lips. He doesn't deserve to be alive, never mind have his name mentioned.'

'Why? What happened? Did you two have a falling-out or something? And who is he? Like, how are you related?'

Janey lit another cigarette and gritted her teeth. 'Jesus, Ciaran, one question at a time.' Janey took a deep breath and filled her lungs with smoke and her bloodstream with nicotine. 'Because he's a fucking bastard, that's *why*.'

'And *how* are you related?'

'He's my stepbrother… *was* my stepbrother. A very, *very* long time ago,' Janey said. Saying the words out loud made the anger come rushing back.

'You have a stepbrother?' Ciaran said again, shocked.

Janey blew out a cloud of smoke and took another draw. 'Had. But like I said, he was an utter bastard. A troublemaker. Thrived on making people miserable.'

Ciaran was quiet, like he was trying to make sense of it all. And then he asked: 'Why have you never told me about him?'

'He left the family a long time ago. I haven't seen him in decades.' Janey took another long draw on the cigarette, hoping that when she exhaled, the memory of those times would float away on the cloud of smoke as it left her lungs.

'I mean, if it's been that long, maybe you were mistaken?'

'It was him. I saw his face,' she said with the cigarette between her teeth. 'I never forget the face of a bastard. Certainly not his.'

The security monitor in the kitchen alerted Janey to Kristo's car pulling into the driveway. Ciaran had called him to meet them at the house.

'Why did he leave the family?'

Janey tapped her perfectly manicured nails on the counter and turned to look at Ciaran. Could she tell him the truth about what went on back then? She'd never spoken a word of it to anyone, not even Finn. She'd made a promise to herself not to let any of it cross her lips.

'He's another one of those fuckers who hates women. Another Danny McInroy. Hated the fact I was being handed my old man's business. Said it wasn't a place for women and certainly not *me*.' She shook her head at the memory. 'And he's not one to stand back and do nothing when he thinks he's owed something, or he thinks he's been crossed.'

'You think he's still pissed about that after all these years? Could that be why he did it?'

Janey shrugged. 'It sounds a lot like the Charlie I knew back then. I can't imagine he's changed for the better after all these years.'

She knew she'd come face to face with him in the coming weeks or even days. But Janey really didn't want to face Charlie. She worried that she'd lose all control and murder him the second she laid eyes on him; even though it was something she should have done a long time ago.

The front doorbell sounded and Ciaran got up to let Kristo inside. Janey sat on a stool at the breakfast bar and contemplated sinking back the remains of the red-wine bottle Ciaran had opened the previous night. But that wouldn't help her.

'Janey,' Kristo said. 'Ciaran told me to come to the house. He said you know who set the club alight?'

'Hmm,' Janey replied, taking another long draw on her cigarette. 'The man who razed Club Envy to the ground? It's my stepbrother from long ago.'

Kristo frowned, his eyes going between Janey and Ciaran. 'You have a stepbrother?'

'Did. His name is Charlie Hallahan. And I haven't seen him for close to forty years.'

Kristo nodded, taking it all in.

'Janey thinks he could have done this because he'd lost out on a stake in the family business back when Janey took over from Finn.'

'So, this could be revenge, perhaps?' Kristo suggested.

'Yes. But why now? Why not back then, when it all went down?' Janey glanced out of the window and across the water, wondering why on earth Charlie would do this now. Unless there was another reason?

'So, we go and find him,' Kristo said, making it sound so easy.

'He won't come to me. I'll have to find him.' Janey knew that as much as Charlie was a nasty, evil bastard with the bit between his teeth, he was also a coward and would never admit to his wrongdoings, no matter how big or small.

'That won't be a problem,' Kristo said.

'It might be,' Janey said as her thoughts took her back to that night. 'He might not go by the name Charlie Hallahan any more. My dad demanded he change it. Said he wasn't fit to be a Hallahan.'

'What did he do to make your old man say something like that?' Ciaran asked.

Janey shrugged and pulled open the door to the decked balcony.

'Janey, do you know what he might have changed his name to?' Kristo asked. Janey turned back to look at him.

'I don't know. Like I said, I haven't seen him for a lifetime. His name could be Jiminy Cricket for all I know.'

It would be hard to find Charlie, but not impossible. It would just take a while. But Janey hoped that in the time it did take, that he wouldn't do anything else as reckless as setting the club on fire. He'd done enough damage to her family.

'But I do know one thing. If he deliberately set the club on fire, then he certainly knows where I am and what I've been doing. Question is, how long has he been watching me?'

That very thought terrified her. Janey wasn't usually scared of anyone or anything, but Charlie was different. He had no morals, no empathy. He cared only about himself and what he wanted. And that was what made him reckless. He'd stop at nothing to get what he wanted.

Her thoughts of Charlie were interrupted when her phone rang in her pocket. She took it out and when she glanced down at the screen to see the number was withheld, she said: 'Maybe this is the little shit now.' Her stomach lurched at the thought of hearing his voice.

She jabbed at the green answer icon with her index finger and said: 'Charlie?'

Silence on the other end of the call made her roll her eyes. He wanted to build the tension, but Janey wasn't going to allow it. She pressed the speaker icon and allowed Ciaran and Kristo to listen. They gathered around the phone in silence.

'Charlie, I know what you did. So, save us all some wasted time and tell me what it is you want, or what the hell you plan to do next?'

An eerie silence came from the other end of the line and Janey reluctantly pictured Charlie with a phone to his ear, listening to Janey's voice. She remembered the last time she was with him, the last time she heard his voice.

Ciaran mouthed. 'What's he saying?' but Janey stared back at him blankly and listened some more.

'The entire point of making a phone call is to *talk*, Charlie. Are you incapable of that?'

Another bout of silence, then the line went dead. Janey stared down at the phone in annoyance.

'What did he say?' Ciaran asked.

'Nothing. He said absolutely nothing, the cowardly fucking bastard.'

Janey wondered where he was and what he'd be thinking his next move would be. Taking a deep breath, Janey prepared herself for the fact that with Charlie, it could be anywhere and he would do anything to get what he wanted, whatever *that* might be.

Chapter 20

Two weeks had passed since Molly Rose had left home. Inside that time, she'd created a friendship with a girl who, just a year previously, she wouldn't have dreamed of even speaking to let alone becoming friends with. She'd been surprised with herself that she'd enjoyed not only the time away from home and the freedom to discover a little of who she was, but not having her mum on her case twenty-four seven. Drinking with Kassy, smoking weed and meeting some of the people Kassy hung around with had been an experience. Sometimes it was scary, especially finding somewhere to sleep for the night if it wasn't the odd hostel here and there. But overall, she'd discovered that she wasn't the girl she thought she was. She could survive on her own. She hadn't lifted a penny from the bank account that her parents put money into for her. If she did that, then there was a chance they'd find her. And she knew her parents, they'd have reported her missing. Molly Rose felt a little guilty about that and had considered sending a message to say she was okay. But then, what if the police tracked her phone?

Two whole weeks of dossing about in the springtime with her new best friend, someone who she had more in common with than she could ever imagine. They were both free spirits, really. People who didn't want to be controlled by the system, or anyone else for that matter.

But now, things were starting to go downhill. They'd run out of money and Kassy's ideas on how to make more were turning dark.

'It's no that bad, especially if you've had a couple bevies beforehaun,' Kassy said, standing next to Molly Rose as they watched some of the women on the street up in Blythswood Square. 'Some ae them warned me of certain men who wid come roon, chancing their arm at a freebie. They showed me how tae deal wae them if they got a bit aggressive. It's no happened tae me yet, but a know others who've had tae defend themselves. It's a dangerous job, but we all need tae get paid. Especially now, Mol. We've literally got nothin' left an a dunno aboot you, but am gettin tae the point where if a don't eat something soon, am gonnae chew ma ane arm aff.'

Molly Rose felt sick; she was so hungry too. But she was more averse to the thought of having sex for money. She'd never had sex in her life, not even with Dean – despite what her mother thought. She didn't want to be doing it for the first time for cash.

'Nah, it's not for me, Kassy,' Molly Rose said.

Kassy shrugged. 'Fine. But how're ye gonnae pay fur a hostel room fur the night if you've no got any money? Or are ye gonnae skulk aff hame tae that bitch ae a maw ae yours – your words, no mine – and ask fur money? How d'ye hink that'll go doon since you've been away two weeks?'

'I don't know,' Molly Rose replied. She hoped that Orla would welcome her back, even if she was furious with her. Molly Rose was her daughter after all, surely, she wouldn't do to her what she did to Sinead? 'She'd be raging, that's for sure. Enough to keep me away from home a bit longer, I suppose.'

Molly Rose felt like she was stuck. The thought of turning to prostitution for money was a step too far. She wanted to go home more than ever now. She hadn't heard from her auntie since and going home would only result in Orla wanting to keep Molly Rose imprisoned in the house so she didn't disappear again. The fun of living free was slowly becoming less and less appealing. Going from street to street, doorway to doorway and the odd hostel room hideout wasn't exactly paradise in the cold light of day.

'It probably won't go in my favour, but I can't do... *this.*'

'Whit? Shag a random for a couple quid? You can choose who ye dae it wae, ye know? Ye don't huv tae shag em all,' Kassy said, unwrapping one of the blueberry muffins she'd stolen from a shop earlier. She picked off a piece and popped it in her mouth as though she wasn't starving. As though they *both* weren't starving. It was getting to the point where they'd have to nick their next meal. But that was something else that Molly Rose couldn't bring herself to do either.

'If I'm honest, I'm a bit shit at this whole life. At first it was a laugh. I mean, I got to do my own thing, make my own choices. But now...'

'Here,' Kassy said, handing the second muffin to Molly Rose. 'An ye don't huv tae actually huv sex. Ye could dae something else. Ye know, offer other services.'

Kassy wasn't listening to her. But she wasn't being particularly forceful either. It was almost like she was making a sales pitch.

'Like what?' Molly Rose asked as she pulled back the wrapper and took a bite. It tasted better than anything she'd ever eaten in her life.

'Blowjob. Hawn job. That kind ae thing.'

Molly Rose almost choked on the mouthful she'd just bitten off. She felt properly sick now.

'Or, ye could take the hard way oot. Sleep on the street. Or worse. Go hame.'

Going home wasn't worse than what Kassy had just described. Molly Rose shook her head. 'I'm not cut out for this. I'm not. I'm sorry, Kassy, but I think I need to call it a day. I don't care what my mum says. I can't do this.'

Just then, a car pulled up beside them and Kassy's face lit up. 'Right, just watch me. Ye'll see how easy it is tae make a bit ae cash.'

The window rolled down and Kassy bent her head low, peered into the car and said, 'Hiya. Whit ye efter?'

The man leaned across to the passenger seat and looked at them both: Kassy and then Molly Rose, a little longer than was comfortable.

'What you offering?' he asked, finally glancing back at Kassy.

'Blow or hawn job fur a tenner. Full lot fur forty quid,' Kassy replied.

The man smiled creepily. 'And a price for both of you?'

Shit, Molly Rose thought. She felt Kassy's eyes on her.

'Naw, she's waitin on a regular. She's aff limits the night. It's me or naebody,' Kassy replied, as if sensing the fear in Molly Rose.

He reached over and opened the door for Kassy to get in. Molly Rose felt herself going into a blind panic. She needed to get away from here and she wanted to take Kassy with her.

'I'll get ye back at that place where yer auntie wiz staying,' Kassy said. The look in her eyes told her not to mention the name of the place in front of the guy.

'Wait,' Molly Rose whispered, grabbing Kassy by the arm. 'Come with me. Back to my mum's.'

Kassy's face contorted. 'Aye, that wid go doon well. You turn up after two weeks ae ghostin' yer family and you've got me at yer back? I don't hink so. Nice eh ye tae hink ae me though. Like I said, I'll get ye later, where I said.'

Molly Rose hesitated. She really didn't want to see Kassy get into a car with a strange man. A creepy man. But there wasn't anything she could do about it.

'Okay.' Molly Rose succumbed to the idea that she could talk her friend out of what was about to happen. She watched helplessly as Kassy climbed into the car and shut the door.

The car drove off and rounded the corner before heading down Douglas Street. And then, she was on her own. In the darkened streets of Glasgow's red-light district.

At that point, it was as though reality had kicked her in the stomach. She wanted to cry. And she wanted to go home. But she couldn't leave Kassy on her own back at the hostel to fight for a room on her own. She'd convince her to come back to the house with her. Surely Orla would allow it if it meant Molly Rose returning home. If she knew that Kassy had looked after her, protected her from being mugged on that first night, then she'd hopefully welcome Kassy with open arms. Perhaps it could be the start of a new life for Kassy. She was getting ahead of herself. She needed to get back to the hostel and wait for her, then she could present the idea to Kassy.

It was only a twenty-minute walk back to Park Terrace. She'd be fine walking back on her own. But then a series of questions began to rush through her head. As much as

Kassy thought she knew what she was doing, was she safe with strange men who were paying her for sex? What if she turned up dead?

She pushed the thoughts out of her head. She didn't want to go down that dark path of thoughts while going it alone in the city at night. She'd never felt as vulnerable as she had in that moment. If it hadn't been for Kassy, Molly Rose wouldn't have coped with living on the streets. In fact, she might not have stayed away from home as long. She was thankful to have found Kassy. She was a good soul, with her own issues. But the connection they had together was something Molly Rose had never experienced. Somehow, she felt like she owed a lot to Kassy.

Turning on her heel, she pulled the straps of her rucksack a little tighter before she made the journey back to Park Terrace, nibbling on the muffin Kassy had stolen for her.

Chapter 21

Hands in pockets and head down, Molly Rose walked as quickly as she could to get back to the hostel to wait for Kassy, who'd said she wouldn't be that long. Molly Rose was still hungry, even after having finished the muffin.

She reached the Bank of Scotland building on Sauchiehall Street and glanced up at the park entrance. Molly Rose had chosen to stick to the main roads since she was by herself. There was much more traffic on this route compared to the side streets. She felt safer that way. She knew it would take longer, but longer was better than the idea of potentially being mugged, or worse, because she'd chosen the quickest route.

The entrance to the park was busy. A crowd of teenagers about her age were gathered at the gate. They were drinking and their rowdiness made her feel uneasy. Instead of using that gate to get into the park and up to the hostel, she walked further along towards the Sandyford Hotel on the main road and into the park that way.

She crossed at the lights and continued her longer-than-planned walk. Passing through Fitzroy Place, Molly Rose kept her head down but her eyes on every car and person who passed. She was good at that, making herself look like she'd logged out, when really she was aware of everything.

She listened to snippets of conversations as people walked past her. Little moments between people, friends, couples. One person mentioned something about a family funeral, another talked about getting a bit of weed from their neighbour but it was utter shit. Someone else passed while on a phone call, and they said that the money had definitely been transferred and there were no two ways about it, they weren't going to be scammed out of more money.

Molly Rose sighed. As much as she didn't know these people or their life circumstances, she would have given anything in that moment to be them. To not be herself right now would be a relief.

Molly Rose felt tears prick at the corners of her eyes. Her dad wouldn't want this for her, and neither would her mum, as much as she interfered and was a pain in the arse.

Reaching the Big Slope bar, Molly Rose noticed a few men stood outside in the narrow beer garden, which wrapped around the corner of the building. They were arguing about something, but Molly Rose didn't stop to listen. She turned onto Kelvingrove Street and crossed over to the side where the hotel was situated. Glancing up the street, the park was just ahead of her. Thankfully, its entrance was free from drunk teenagers.

As she approached, she noticed the gates were locked.

'Oh, for fuck's sake,' she moaned. Glancing along the street that ran parallel to the park, Molly Rose knew that she would have to walk along there to access the park via another entrance.

She headed along Parkgrove Terrace, passing the two nurseries and thinking about her mum. Her nursery franchise had taken over her life and she rarely had time for anything else these days.

Parkgrove Terrace became Gray Street and Molly Rose noticed an entrance to the park she hadn't known was there. Crossing the street, she reached the open gate and sighed with relief. But something made her stop and turn.

A figure was stood outside a guest house in the next building along. It was dark, so she couldn't see the person's face. But she had this terrible feeling in the pit of her stomach. And then, he called her name.

'Molly Rose. Come here for a second, eh?'

She froze. Who the *hell* was this guy? She didn't recognise his voice.

Choosing to ignore him, she gripped the straps of her rucksack and entered the park, checking behind to see if the guy had followed. All the while, her inner voice was screaming at her not to be like those idiots in horror films who head in a direction where there was more danger. Entering the park certainly didn't seem safe. But she could see and hear people darting around – not too many, but enough to give her some sense of safety.

She half-walked, half-jogged down the sloped path into the park and found herself at a crossroads. She could exit the park and walk along Kelvin Way, and head up to the hostel that way but that would take even longer. Or, she could go through the park, past the fountain and up the stairs, which would cut her journey in half.

Molly Rose remembered the words Kassy had last spoken to her. *I'll get you back at that place your auntie is staying at.* Taking a deep breath, her mind threw all sorts of thoughts at her. What if Kassy didn't come back? What if something had happened to her? What if she…?

'Fuck this,' she whispered, pushing her fears about Kassy doing a bunk to one side before continuing. She thought about how long it had been since Kassy got in that guy's car. Twenty minutes? Half an hour? It felt a lot longer, as this was the longest Molly Rose had been out on the streets by herself.

Heading up to the left towards Kelvin Way, Molly Rose looked over her shoulder. Whoever the man was, he wasn't there now. Then, another thought entered her mind. One that scared her more than the imaginary images about Kassy. The man *knew* her name. But how? Maybe he was one of Kassy's friends who she'd met over the past two weeks? She used the term "friends" loosely. Acquaintances who got together to take drugs and get smashed on vodka, or cider, or whatever else they could get their hands on. Yeah, that would be it, she tried to convince herself. Not that it worked. The idea that she was alone in the city with a stranger calling out her name freaked her out and forced her legs to move quicker.

She reached the exit and turned left. The side entrance to the Kelvingrove Art Gallery and Museum was directly across from her. All lit up at night, it was beautiful but also, eerie. Especially in the situation she was faced with.

Molly Rose had no money. Her phone battery was almost dead – she'd reserved as much of it as she could before it switched off. There was nowhere near enough to make a call to her dad. She could send him a text, ask him to pick her up.

She took the phone out of her zipper pocket and tapped out a text message.

> Dad its me. Can you pick me up please?
> Outside the art gallery on Argyle Street? I
> want to come home. Don't phone, my
> battery is about to die. Text me back
> please. M x

She hit send and sighed with relief, before making her way down the street towards where her dad would pick her up. He'd be about half an hour, so long as he saw the message right away.

Her phone pinged and she looked down.

> Of course I can sweetheart. On my way.
> Don't move

'Thank fuck for that,' she said out loud. She'd get her dad to drive up to the hostel and wait for Kassy – there was no way she was leaving her behind without asking her to come home with her. Kassy deserved so much more than a life on the street.

The sound of a car pulling up beside her made her chest constrict. The sound of the engine changed. The car was next to her.

'Are you Molly Rose Hunter?'

Molly Rose smiled and shook her head. 'Nope. Sorry.'

In that moment, she knew she was going to have to run.

Chapter 22

'I can't believe that after all this time, she actually got in touch. I was starting to think the worst,' Orla said as Oliver stopped the car at the traffic lights on Dumbarton Road at the bottom of Byres Road.

Oliver nodded silently and when Orla looked at his face, she could see that he was fighting back his emotions.

'It's such a relief,' Orla said, placing her hand over his as it rested on the gear stick. 'She's safe. Our girl is okay.'

A lump grew in her throat then and the relief that flooded through her was overwhelming. The idea that something horrific had happened to her daughter had been crippling her for weeks. And she'd been blaming herself – rightly so, she was the reason Molly Rose had left, even though she had the best intentions.

Oliver cleared his throat as the lights changed from red to green. 'Yeah, relief is one way of putting it. I never want this to happen again, Orla. We can't have this kind of stress in the family. She's our only daughter. She needs to be our priority and she needs to feel that.'

Orla nodded. Her husband was right. Molly Rose needed to know she was their reason for everything. The long hours to keep the businesses going; the harsh advice; the difficult decisions. But Orla vowed to herself that she would be a better mum, explain herself better, work out solutions to problems *with* her daughter.

Oliver pulled the car up outside the art galleries and Orla got out of the car.

'I'll park. You go and find her and meet me out the back entrance at the charging ports,' Oliver said.

Orla nodded, closed the door and watched him drive along the road before turning on to Kelvin Way and out of her sight. She looked up the wide pathway to the concrete staircase, which led to three large archways under which the glass entrance doors stood. The archways were illuminated in a red light. Molly Rose wasn't there.

Orla pulled out her phone and called her daughter's number. It went straight to answer phone.

'What the hell is she playing at?' Orla muttered. The phone still in her hand, Orla looked up at the archways again, scanning each one slowly.

No, she thought. *Don't be like that with her.* Maybe her phone died? She hasn't been home for two weeks and she didn't take her charger.

Orla approached the stairs and as she stood at the bottom, she glanced to her left, along towards the Partick bridge and then to her right where the bowling green was situated. There was no one else around. Only Orla.

'Molly Rose?' she called out as loud as she could. Maybe she'd found somewhere to sit, so that she couldn't be seen by the scum that often walked the streets at night here. Her voice echoed off the towering walls of the galleries.

'Molly Rose?' she called again, louder this time.

'She's not here?' Oliver asked, appearing from the side of the building.

Orla shook her head. 'I can't seem to find her. But she asked you to come. She wouldn't just leave, would she?'

'Try her phone,' Oliver said.

'I already did. It's switched off.'

Oliver glanced over Orla's shoulder towards the arches and shrugged. 'Maybe she's gone to the pub across the road?'

Orla nodded. 'Maybe. We could check.'

'I'll check. You stay here in case she appears.'

Orla watched as Oliver walked down the wide path and crossed over to the Brewdog pub directly opposite them. He went inside and became lost in the crowd of people. Turning back, Orla looked up at the building and decided to actively look for Molly Rose.

She moved along the right side of the building, heading for the car park at the back. Rounding the corner, Orla pulled out her phone and tried Molly Rose's number again. Still switched off. Something in the pit of Orla's stomach told her this wasn't right. It would have taken a lot for Molly Rose to phone and ask to come home. She wouldn't just change her mind after she'd asked her dad to collect her.

She reached the end of the building and was now facing the car park at the back. There was no one else around. The only thing in front of her was the Ovo bicycle stands and an empty car park. The University of Glasgow peeked above the trees ahead and the bowling green to her right was empty. The darkness enveloped her and she began to panic.

'Molly Rose?' she called, a little more forceful this time as she turned left and headed for the back entrance to the galleries. Maybe she was sitting there, away from the eyes of the road.

She reached the bottom of the stairs and looked up. Molly Rose wasn't there either.

'Oh, for fuck's sake, Molly Rose. Where the hell are you?'

Orla carried on past the stairs and around the building. She scanned the trees to her left and saw the two memorial headstones on the grass. She shivered again and made her way back along the path to the front entrance, just as Oliver was coming back up the path.

'Well?' Orla asked, her arms stretched out to the side.

'No one's seen her. I've tried her phone too, but it's switched off,' Oliver replied. 'Something isn't right.'

Orla felt the rising panic in her throat.

'Olly, something's happened to our girl.'

Chapter 23

She sobbed as her body was thrown from one side of the boot to the other. Every few seconds, she crashed into her best friend.

Kassy was dead. And Molly Rose was lying next to her, kidnapped by some nut job who seemed to know who she was. That's when it hit her. The guy who'd picked Kassy up over at Blythswood. It was the *same* guy. He'd obviously planned this all along.

'Let me out!' Her muffled screams behind the gag were lost on the sound of the roaring engine. Where was he taking her? *Why* had he taken her? And how did he know who she was?

She'd watched a true crime episode once, where the victim in the boot had kicked out the back light to alert the driver behind them that they were in the boot. But the motion of the car was so erratic, and the boot so dark and small that Molly Rose knew she wouldn't be able to do that.

'Help!' she attempted to scream again, desperately trying to unravel her wrists from whatever he tied them together with at the back. She needed to get her phone from her pocket and text her dad.

Kassy's body slammed into Molly Rose, pinning her to the side of the boot. And then the car stopped.

She couldn't hear anything aside from her own, laboured breaths. But the car rocked slightly and then there was a bang, like a car door being slammed shut. Footsteps on gravel. Fingers pulling at the handle of the boot.

Suddenly, he was tying something around her face so that she couldn't see and Molly Rose was being pulled from the car by large, rough hands. He threw her to the ground as he slammed the boot shut, leaving Kassy inside.

She wanted to take in her surroundings, but everything was so dark under the blindfold that she couldn't work out where she was.

As he tried to lift her off the ground, her mobile fell from her pocket. He muttered something she couldn't make out and pulled her roughly to her feet before dragging her along what sounded like gravel.

'You're my bait,' he said.

What the hell did that mean?

Molly Rose started to scream from behind the rag in her mouth, hoping that someone would hear her. She stopped when the sharp sting of his hand made her cheek feel like it was going to explode.

'Shut the *fuck* up, or you'll end up like your pal back there,' he grunted into her ear. 'Now, I don't have to hurt you, if you just do what you're fucking told. Okay?'

Molly Rose nodded, hoping that her co-operation would get her away from this nightmare and home. Her dad would get to Kelvingrove Art Gallery, see she wasn't there and panic when he wouldn't be able to get a hold of her. She'd been gone for two weeks and knew the police would be looking for her. This would spark a wider search, surely? Now that she'd been in contact after fourteen days? *Jesus Christ*, she thought as she began to go over the thoughts in her head. Why the hell had she run away from home again? Because her mum wouldn't give her auntie a second chance? Because her mum had made Dean break up with her? It all seemed so ridiculous now that she was faced with being kidnapped and potentially murdered.

Suddenly, there was a loud, overwhelming thud, thud, thud. Then music; deep house music. People singing. Loud, chants of 'here we, here we, here we fucking go', and the thuds got louder. As she was being kidnapped, a party was going on somewhere nearby. Though it was far enough away, yet still *loud* enough that if she screamed for help, no one would hear her.

Wherever he'd taken her, the place smelled clean, like it had just been disinfected. All sorts of thoughts were going through her head now. Had he killed someone in here before bringing Molly Rose to this place? Was this where he killed Kassy? The car journey hadn't been too long. But then, if that was the case, why was she in the boot of his car?

'Sit down and keep fucking quiet,' he said, forcing Molly Rose down onto a chair. She held her breath, trying to listen to what he was doing or if anyone else was there. Then the rag was pulled from her mouth.

'Scream and I'll kill you,' he said quietly into her ear.

Molly Rose had never felt so terrified in her entire life. All she *wanted* to do was scream but she believed this guy was telling the truth – he'd kill her if she did.

The blindfold was yanked from her face, and she expected a sudden rush of light. But there was nothing, only a darkness that was less black than when her eyes were covered. She still couldn't see anything properly but could make out the outlines of things in her peripheral vision.

Again, nothing that would help her identify where she was or what she was surrounded by.

'So, *Molly Rose...*' Her name slithered from his lips as his voice trailed off. His accent was changing. He'd sounded Irish when he'd called on her from outside the guest house, but there was a Glaswegian twang to it now. And then she remembered the guy who'd picked Kassy up had the same accent. It was definitely him.

She wanted to respond. Ask him what he wanted with her. Why had he killed Kassy?

'Do you want some water?' His voice softened.

Molly Rose pushed the questions from her head. If she wanted to survive this, then she needed to stay calm; deal with the here and now and do exactly what he said. She nodded in answer to his question, and she saw a shadow get up and move away from her. She tried to track him, but the further away he got, the harder it became.

She sensed him sit down again in front of her, sensed his hand near her face. He pulled the rag from her mouth and placed the open bottle of water to her lips. She sipped slowly, so as not to take in too much too quickly. If she did that, she'd vomit and that was the last thing she wanted to do.

'Thank you,' she spoke, although her voice was quietly raspy.

'Where's Janey?' he asked, his tone so calm it made her feel more scared than before.

Molly Rose though for a moment. *Janey?* She had no idea who he was even talking about.

'Molly Rose, I asked you a question,' he said, becoming frustrated.

Swallowing hard, Molly Rose replied, 'I don't know anyone called Janey.'

132

'Your *grandmother*, where is she?'

Molly Rose wanted to cry. If this guy thought she was lying, she worried what he might do to her. 'I *swear* to you, I don't have a grandmother called Janey. I don't know *anyone* by that name. Please, let me go. I won't tell anyone about this.'

He sighed loudly, clearly annoyed by the answer she'd given him. The calmness in his voice was gone now, replaced with the rage that was there when he'd first taken her. 'Don't fucking lie to me, Molly Rose. She's in Glasgow, you live here. Your mother and auntie too. I *know* Janey wouldn't be here if she didn't know about you. So, I'll ask again. *Where* is she?'

Molly Rose began to panic. If he thought she was no use to him, he could kill her right there and then. Her young, all-but-lived life snuffed out because of one person she'd never even heard of.

'I… I,' she stumbled. She didn't want to lie in case that got her into more trouble. But if she continued to tell the truth – that she didn't know who he was talking about – the same outcome was inevitable.

'You really don't know who I'm on about, do you?' the man asked.

'No. I'm sorry. If I did, I'd tell you,' she sobbed.

'That means they haven't told you.'

'Told me what?'

She heard the man snigger and begin to pace the floor. She waited for his response. The words that followed chilled her to the deepest parts of her soul.

'Told you who you are and where you're really from. You'll just have to stay here. If she finds out I have you, she'll eventually come out of the woodwork. Sorry, Molly Rose, but you won't be going home for a while.'

Chapter 24

Back at the house, Orla paced the floor with a glass of wine in her hand. Not that she'd taken a sip yet; just having it there as an option to help was enough for now.

The police had arrived at the house just fifteen minutes after Orla and Oliver had called them to give them the news that Molly Rose had been in touch, but then disappeared again.

'And you're absolutely sure that was where she said she would meet you at the art gallery?' Officer McGhee asked Oliver.

'For the millionth *fucking* time,' Orla exploded.

'Orla, for God's sake. You can't speak to them like that,' Oliver replied, turning to the officer. 'I'm sorry, she's just very upset.'

'It's okay, Mr Hunter. We understand. We just want to be clear, that's all,' Officer McGhee replied.

Sinead placed a hand on Orla's shoulder but she shrugged her off.

'Orla, the police will do their job and bring her home,' Sinead said. Orla turned and stared at her sister. The twin she'd allowed back into her life just two weeks earlier. So many contrasting things had happened in that space of time. Sinead was two weeks clean, from what Orla could tell. She was *really* trying her best and with Molly Rose missing, she was acting like a proper family member and being as supportive as she could. It was like being in the presence of a new person. And even though the withdrawal was a struggle most days, Sinead said she'd do whatever she could to help the family. Orla never – ever – thought her sister would achieve this amount of time clean, but this was overshadowed by the cloud hanging over them: that Molly Rose was missing. They'd been so close to bringing her home and then... nothing. She disappeared again, after asking to be collected. In those two weeks, Orla and Oliver had been frantic with worry that something awful had happened to their daughter and Sinead had been there to support them both. She'd even offered to go out and look for her niece, which would have meant going back on to the streets that could tempt her back to the thing she was trying to stay away from. Orla had refused to let Sinead put herself at risk like that but had been so grateful for the offer.

'What if it wasn't her who sent the text?' Sinead said, interrupting Orla's thoughts. 'I mean, it's possible. I've lived on those streets, there are all sorts of idiots out there. Scum who would do anything for money; trust me, I was one of them,' she paused, looked disgusted with herself and then continued. 'Maybe someone did this for a ransom or something?'

Orla looked at her, horrified by the thought. 'If that's the case, then why haven't they asked for a sum of money? There's no amount I wouldn't give to have her home.'

She looked at the wine glass in her hand and, as the red liquid sloshed around inside, she raised it to her lips and took a large mouthful. Then another and another, until the glass was empty.

Everyone was silent, even Officer McGhee, and Orla couldn't help but wonder if they all thought Molly Rose was already dead.

Chapter 25

Charlie paced the floor, back and forth, back and forth. He ran his hands through his hair, thinking about what he was going to do next. He just needed to put his thoughts in order.

The thump from the music in the SWG3 club just along from where he was keeping Molly Rose masked that they were even in the abandoned lockup. A train thundered above them and Charlie looked up. In a world this huge, no one would even think to look for him here. Or Molly Rose.

'Please, let me go. I won't tell anyone about this,' the teenager said. His great-niece.

'Shut the fuck up,' Charlie said quietly. She was scared. He couldn't blame her. He'd killed the girl she'd been with earlier. He didn't even know her name. But the girl wouldn't tell him anything. She was useless to him; well, not completely useless. Prostitutes did have their uses. But if he'd let her go, he wouldn't have been able to get to Molly Rose without that other bitch trying to stop him. She might even have gone to the police. She'd seemed the type.

'Why did you do that to Kassy?'

Charlie spun around and glared at Molly Rose. 'I said shut the fuck up.'

She started to sob again and a sliver of guilt crept in. But then he reminded himself why he was doing this. He needed Molly Rose to survive. It was *all* about survival.

'Who are you? What is it you want with me?'

Charlie closed his eyes. 'It's not you I'm after. It's your gran.'

'I told you, I don't have a gran.'

'Aye,' Charlie sneered. 'You said. But you'll get to meet her soon. I'm going to make sure of it. Because she's the only reason you'll get out of here alive, Molly Rose.'

He watched as her mouth grew wider. Just as she was about to start screaming, Charlie shoved the gag in her mouth and used electrical tape to secure it in place.

Charlie thought about all the women in his life, all past tense, including Janey. He'd taken control of them the only way he knew how. All except Janey. He should have killed her back then. That way, Finn would have had no choice but to pass down to him. He'd regretted that decision every day since he left Northern Ireland.

'If you want to stay alive,' Charlie said, 'then you'd better fucking pray that Janey responds appropriately to my message, otherwise you'll just join a long list of women to die by my hand. The only difference between you and them is that you're useful to me and that's the only reason you're still alive. If Janey doesn't do what I say…'

He let the sentence hang in the air. Some things were better left unsaid.

Chapter 26

POLICE SCOTLAND MEDIA POST

Police Scotland – MISSING PERSON –
Fresh appeal for information

Molly Rose Hunter (16)

- Last contact with Molly Rose was Tuesday, May 27, via text message to her dad; two weeks after she initially went missing. Had arranged to be collected from the front entrance of Kelvingrove Art Gallery and Museum at 10pm. Molly Rose was not there when her dad arrived.

- Molly Rose is white, 5ft 4, slim build with shoulder length, dirty blonde hair. Last time she was physically seen, two weeks prior to the above date; she was wearing a dark-coloured zipper, jeans, Adidas trainers and a rucksack.

  Do you know anything that might assist the police?

  Get in contact with Police Scotland on the non-emergency number or Crimestoppers.

Chapter 27

It had been a long night since the police left the house. Orla sobbed on and off, Oliver paced the floor in the hallway downstairs and repeatedly boiled the kettle but never actually made any tea.

The past two weeks had been hell on earth for Sinead. Trying to stay clean and sober while living in a house with the twin who'd essentially abandoned her for years was hard enough, doing it while Molly Rose had dropped off the face of the planet made it worse.

Sinead had a bad feeling about it all. She knew what it was like to live on the streets in the city centre and surrounding areas. She was a hardened rough sleeper but Molly Rose was just a young girl, with no clue what she was up against. Sinead feared the worst and that when they did find her, she'd be dead.

Staring down at the laptop screen, she read the missing person appeal on the media pages via Facebook. So many people had replied with generic, yet kind, comments. *Hope she makes it home. Poor family, hope she's found.* And the posts had been shared multiple times too. It was all well and good, but two weeks was a long time.

Closing the laptop, she stared down at the phone by her side and wondered if Janey Hallahan had ever worked out that it was Sinead who'd left her the silent call.

Janey Hallahan. The name of the woman who'd birthed her and Orla all those years ago. Sinead had always wondered about their birth mum and now, she actually had a name. Not calling her back after the initial call two weeks earlier had been difficult. But she couldn't bring more issues to the family to deal with. She'd decided, with difficulty, to wait until they knew what was happening with Molly Rose, one way or another.

Glancing at the clock on the wall, Sinead noted that it was just after six in the morning. The house was silent. Orla and Oliver must have fallen asleep at some point. All through the night, Sinead had fought against the heroin-addicted devil on her shoulder not to go out and find a hit. Two weeks might not sound much, but it was the longest she'd gone in a decade. She wasn't going to fuck that up, not now.

Heading downstairs, Sinead glanced into Orla and Oliver's bedroom. The pair slept soundly, although Sinead noticed how contorted Orla's expression was. She couldn't imagine what it must feel like not to know where your daughter was after all this time.

Padding downstairs, Sinead felt the thick, luxurious stair carpet between her toes and reminded herself how lucky she was to be in the house after everything that had happened over the years.

Sitting down at the kitchen table, Sinead sighed sadly. It should be her out there, she thought to herself. Molly Rose didn't deserve to be out there, on her own; if she was still alive, she'd be suffering.

If Sinead hadn't fucked up her life so much, none of this would be happening, she thought.

'Please, come home,' she whispered.

Chapter 28

Janey Hallahan opened her eyes to the sound of birdsong. She sat up and glanced out of the window that overlooked the Gare Loch and out to Rosneath. A robin was perched on the decking rail that wrapped around the front of the house. It chirped happily as the early spring sun rose.

'Good morning,' Ciaran said, entering the room with a mug of coffee in his hand. 'Did you sleep okay?'

Janey sat up and rested her head against the plush, navy-coloured velvet headboard. 'I think I saw every hour. And when I did drift off, I was having some crazy dreams. More nightmares.'

She took the mug from Ciaran's hand and sipped gently. The robin took flight and Janey tracked it until she could no longer see it.

Turning, she caught Ciaran's eye. There was something about his expression that made her question him. 'What is it?'

'You might want to take a look at this,' he said, handing her his phone. She looked down at the screen and read the description. It was a Police Scotland social media post. A teenager had gone missing. Molly Rose Hunter. Her granddaughter.

'This says it's a fresh appeal. How did I manage to miss the first one?'

'You've had a lot on with all the crap with Charlie,' Ciaran replied. 'Don't beat yourself up about it, Janey.'

'Shit,' Janey said, sitting forward and placing the coffee mug on the bedside table. She read on and saw that the post had been shared a few times on various platforms. Then she saw her daughter's name. Orla Hunter. Her face was on Google searches, alongside Molly Rose. She'd appealed to her own social media followers and friends, and shared on Molly Rose's page too.

If anyone knows where our beautiful girl might be, please get in touch. We just want her home and safe.

'Oh my god,' Janey said, getting out of bed and crossing the room.

'What are you doing?' Ciaran said.

'I need to go to them. I need to help.'

Janey felt frantic, searching for clothes in her wardrobe. Ciaran gripped her by the shoulders and spun her around.

'I'm not sure that's such a good idea, Janey. The last time you spoke to Orla, she pretty much told you to fuck off.'

'Don't you think I know that?' Janey shouted, pulling herself from his grip before taking a dark-blue trouser suit out from the wardrobe. 'My granddaughter is missing. I want to help.'

'Or is it the perfect excuse to try to make contact again?'

Janey closed her eyes and took a breath. 'Ciaran, no offence but they're not your girls. This is not your family. So back the fuck off and let me get on with it.'

She listened as Ciaran did exactly that. He backed out of the room and left her on her own. And then she had a thought. What if this was Charlie?

143

Picking up her mobile, she searched Orla and Molly Rose online. The story was growing. If Orla didn't want her help, that was fine. But she was going to get it regardless.

–

Pulling up to the house she'd visited once before, she took in its grandeur once again. Her daughter had done well for herself. Well, one of them. She didn't know anything about Sinead, purely because Orla had said in no uncertain terms was Janey allowed to get in contact with either of them.

Getting out of the Defender, Janey fixed her jacket and pushed back her shoulders before heading down the rest of the drive towards the front door of the house. There were a few different cars parked in the drive, one of which was an unmarked police car. She'd recognise one anywhere.

The house would be busy with people and police. She was surprised the press wasn't lurking.

Reaching the door, she raised her hand and pressed the bell. Ciaran was right, Orla would only repeat her sentiments. Before she could turn around and head back up the drive, the sound of a key turning in the lock made her freeze. The door was pulled open from inside and a woman was stood in front of her.

'Can I help you?' the woman said, her voice a little rougher than Janey had expected.

'I'm… I'm looking for…' Janey's voice trailed off.

'Who are you looking for?' the woman asked. Janey knew exactly who she was. It was her daughter, Sinead. She looked a lot like Orla, although they weren't identical twins. 'Are you here about Molly Rose?'

Janey felt her heart begin to bang against the wall of her chest. *Turn around. Turn around. Speak to her. That's why you came here.*

'What's your name?' Sinead asked, stepping out of the house. 'Orla and Oliver aren't here at the moment. They're out looking for Molly Rose. But I could pass on a message?'

Janey turned around and smiled at Sinead. She looked a lot like Janey did when she was that age. But something sad about her appearance caught in Janey's throat. She could tell an addict a mile away. 'So, your name?' Sinead asked, folding her arms. A look of suspicion crossed her face. 'You're not press, are you?'

Janey shook her head. 'No. I'm not press. But to you, I might be worse.'

Sinead frowned and uncrossed her arms. 'Who are you?'

Janey sighed. This was it, the moment she met her other daughter. 'I think I'm your mother.'

Sinead's eyes widened and her mouth fell open slightly. '*You're* Janey Hallahan? You're our mum?'

Janey nodded and suddenly felt pathetic.

'I heard about Molly Rose. I wanted to see if I could help.'

Sinead stepped forward and studied Janey's face. 'Is it really you?'

Janey nodded. 'Yeah. It's really me.'

Sinead puffed out her bony cheeks and spun a full three-sixty before running her fingers through her hair. 'Holy fuck. It's actually you?'

Janey laughed nervously. 'And holy fuck, it's *you*.'

They stood in silence for a few moments, simply taking each other in. And then the sound of a car pulling into the drive made Janey turn.

'Oh shit,' Sinead said. 'That's Orla.'

Janey nodded. Orla wasn't going to be happy to see her. And by the look on her face as Orla stepped out of the car, Janey was right.

'What the *fuck* are you doing here?' Orla spat the words out.

'Orla!' Sinead shouted. 'That's bang out of order.'

Janey tensed as her daughter, Orla, the one who was born second that night in the back bedroom of her father's house with a midwife and a priest present, drew her a filthy look as she passed by to go into the house. Her husband, Oliver, got out of the car and closed its door.

'So, you're Janey then?' Oliver said. 'I didn't have the pleasure of meeting you the last time you were here.'

Janey held out her hand to Oliver and to her surprise, he accepted.

'I'm Oliver, Orla's husband.'

Janey already knew who he was, but she wasn't going to admit that to him. 'I'm Janey Hallahan. I wish we were meeting under better circumstances.'

Oliver frowned. 'Yeah. I know who you are. I googled you after your first visit. You're...' his voice trailed off. 'You're an interesting woman. According to Google, you're a successful businesswoman. Orla is too. Seems it runs in the blood.'

Janey was so taken aback she didn't know what to say.

'Sorry, I know that's a bit forward. But once I'd learned that about you, I did some digging. Curiosity got the better of me.'

146

Janey smiled. 'I suppose it would with anyone in this situation.' She was happy that he hadn't seemed to have read between the lines on whatever Google searches came up. Everything looked legit because her money had been cleaned.

'Can I ask why you're here?' Oliver pressed.

'My granddaughter is missing. I thought I could help.'

Orla came barging back out of the house and grabbed Janey by the crook of her elbow. 'You don't have a fucking granddaughter. And you don't have daughters either. You're not fucking welcome here.'

Oliver tried to pull Orla away, but there was a strength in her he couldn't match. Something she could have got from Janey.

Janey allowed Orla to stand there, with her arm in her grip and shout like her life depended on it. It was a form of stress release. It was something Janey had done a few times after she'd given her girls up. She'd stood in the horse field and screamed bloody murder as the pain grew with each second her girls were being raised by someone else.

'Orla, *stop*!' Sinead shouted, pulling at her sister's arm.

'It's okay,' Janey said, holding up her other hand. 'It's fine.'

'No, it's not fucking okay. Don't you hear me when I tell you to go away? I don't want you in my life. None of us do.'

Sinead scoffed. 'Erm, since when did you make decisions for me?'

Orla let go of Janey's arm and glared at Sinead. 'Since you started putting drugs into your body and fucked your life up.'

'Fuck you, Orla,' Sinead retaliated.

147

Jesus, Janey thought as she stood there in silence, stunned by the display in front of her. Was this what had happened to her daughters? They hated each other?

'Look, let's all calm down,' Janey suggested. 'I'm here to help you find Molly Rose.'

Orla tutted loudly and shook her head. 'And what the hell do you think you can do that the police haven't already? Do yourself a favour and piss off, eh? I've got a police officer in there and if they suspect something is wrong out here then they'll come and remove you.'

'No, actually. The liaison officer won't be here until the afternoon,' Sinead said.

Janey glanced at Sinead. And then back to Orla.

'I think I know who has your daughter.'

Orla stepped back and glared at Janey. Oliver came into her peripheral vision and said: 'How would you know that?'

'Can we go inside?' Janey said, lowering her voice.

Orla hesitated. 'Is this your way of getting in with us? You thought you'd exploit what's going on with my daughter? How do I know *you're* not the one who took Molly Rose and this is all just a ploy to get onside?'

Sinead threw her hands up in the air. 'That's fucking ridiculous!'

'Is it? I mean, you take her—' she glared at Janey '—then you claim to know who has her and, bang, you're in with us like you wanted.'

Janey felt the anger beginning to build. She didn't want to get angry at her daughter. But Sinead was right, the thought was ridiculous even though she could see why Orla would come to that conclusion.

'Okay, fine. I'll leave. Good luck with the police finding her.'

Janey headed for the Defender when Orla said: 'That sounded like a threat.'

'It's not a threat. I'm telling you, if the person I think has her is the one responsible then you're going to need me to get her home.'

'And why is that?' Orla pushed. 'What kind of super-power do you have that can bring her back safely?'

'Because the man who has her wants me to find him. And he's targeting the things he thinks are important to me. And Molly Rose, although you might not believe it because I've never met her, is of high importance to me. You all are. Whether you like it or not.'

Sinead stepped closer to Orla and gently took her by the hand. 'Orla, this is the first lead we've had since Molly Rose went missing. I lived on the streets and even I don't know what could have happened. She's literally disappeared. You have to give this at least some of your time.'

Oliver nodded and Orla looked at each of them before stomping back into the house. Janey watched her go as Sinead stood by her.

'Did you really only come back to help find Molly Rose?'

Janey felt her palms begin to sweat. This wasn't how she'd imagined starting up a relationship with her twin daughters. In fact, when she'd found out she was pregnant, she'd never imagined having to give them up, so thinking about meeting them after all this time was something she hadn't pictured.

'Not only Molly Rose, but she certainly is now the main factor.'

Sinead swallowed hard and nodded. 'Okay, you'd better come in.'

Chapter 29

1985

Janey sat back on her bed and rubbed at her swollen, pregnant belly. Tears streamed down her face as she thought about what was going to happen in a few months once the girls were born. She didn't want to give them up. She was being forced to. And yes, she knew that the girls might be better off with a couple who could really give them the best start in life, but surely with her father's help, Janey could do the same? It wasn't as though Finn didn't have money or space for two babies? And they could always hire a nanny for extra help.

Wiping away the tears with the back of her hand, Janey sniffed loudly and stared down at the scan picture of her babies. They were hers. Growing inside her right now. She was building arms, legs, toes, fingernails, eyelashes. All times two. How the hell was she going to be able to give them up?

'Are you going to tell me who the dad is?' Finn had asked her for the millionth time. But how could she tell him? It was an impossible ask. It would break him. It would break her all over again. And she just couldn't do that to him, even though he was making her give up her children. She had a strong, unbreakable sense of loyalty to her dad. How could he think it was okay to make her give up her babies when he lost his own mother at the start of the troubles in 1969? That was a tragedy in his family that could have been prevented. This was being forced upon her

and she felt helpless against it. There was a very strong possibility that they'd question her choice for the rest of their lives.

'I don't know who he is,' she said, again.

'It's that little boyfriend of yours from down the road, isn't it? Little shit had me fooled, playing the nice, fourteen-year-old boy, calling me Mr Hallahan and Sir. I'll fucking kill him.'

Janey felt sick at the thought of Cameron being attacked by her dad. He was just a kid like her. 'It's not Cameron, Dad. He's not the dad.'

'I don't fucking believe you,' he shouted back, slamming her bedroom door. She'd heard him stomp down the stairs in a fit of rage. She'd never seen him so angry. And then, the sound of him coming back filled her with dread.

The door flew open and a finger pointed in her face. 'And get it out of your head that I'll change my mind. Those babies are not staying here. If you want them, you can go too. I'm not allowing you to flush your fucking life down the pan because you were stupid enough to get pregnant.'

Another slam. This time the room shook.

Not only was she losing her daughters. She was slowly, day by day, losing her dad too. But maybe Finn was right. Maybe giving the babies away would be a good thing for them. With their country still in conflict and Janey only a young girl herself, it might be best they go somewhere safe, with people who could give them a better start in life.

Janey sobbed silently into her pillow.

Chapter 30

NOW

He walked across the bridge, taking each step slowly. Counting how many steps it would take to get to the other side. Not that it mattered, it was just something he always did. Counted stairs when he climbed. Counted the seconds it took to get from one floor to another in a lift. He liked to be in control of things. And so far, with what had happened with losing his money, his house, his entire life, he felt utterly out of control.

Taking a deep breath, Charlie glanced up the path to his right where the Kelvingrove bandstand sat and started to walk towards it. Then he stopped, shook his head. No, that was too public. Too open. Even at night. He needed to put her somewhere that was accessible by car, somewhere he could quickly toss her over a wall into long ferns. Someone would find her and that was okay. But she was just a prostitute. No one would miss her. but he certainly couldn't keep her in the car for much longer. He'd already wrapped her in a few binbags, but the smell and the decomposition would attract attention to the car.

'Right,' he said aloud. 'Where can I leave you?'

He looked back at the bridge and headed back across it towards the kids' playpark at the pond.

The pond. It was overgrown at the front. And there were trees in the centre. But it wasn't accessible by car.

'Fuck's sake,' he said. An old woman who was walking her dog glanced at him warily but continued.

He headed to the east side of the park, towards the Park Terrace area. But he wasn't planning on going up to where the hostel was. No. He was headed for the large staircase which led to Park Gardens. He passed by the football pitches and a football flew towards him.

'Oi, auld man, kick that back, eh?' a teenaged boy shouted. Charlie ignored him and kept on walking.

'Ya auld bastard. Probably reeks ae pish!' he shouted and all his little mates started to laugh. If there weren't so many of them, Charlie would knock the little bastard out, but he knew what kids that age were like. He was one of them back in the day; causing havoc and getting into bother. Things hadn't changed in that respect, he was just cleverer than he was back then – understood the need to keep quiet and stay under the radar a little more.

Annoyed that he'd been distracted, he told himself to concentrate. He had a job to do and he couldn't allow himself to be swayed by kids. He followed the path round and found himself at the pedestrian gate that led him straight from the park to the bottom of the Park Garden stairs. He glanced up to the top and then back down. The street mainly consisted of offices. They'd be unoccupied at night, which would be beneficial given his plan.

Large, industrial-sized Glasgow City Council bins sat just next to the gate. *They would hold enough space to contain a body*, he thought.

'This is the place,' he whispered. 'Yeah, this is the place.'

He'd do it at dark, at the point in the night where everyone was inside. He'd cover the registration plates.

He'd wear a face mask, just like they did during that fucking pandemic. That was the only good thing about it, being able to cover your face. No one would know who you were. What you were thinking.

He'd got away with this kind of thing before he'd lost all his money, multiple times. The audacity of those prostitutes asking to be paid had annoyed him. Getting rid and keeping his cash was like all his Christmases coming at once.

And he'd get away with it again. And if Janey didn't pay up, then the next body he'd be getting rid of would be her annoying, snivelling granddaughter.

A thought crossed his mind then. *Maybe* he could use this girl's body for his own gain? As his thoughts grew, he came up with a plan. He smiled at the idea of Janey's face when she realised that Charlie was in control.

Chapter 31

Molly Rose shivered as the draught swirled around the room she'd been locked in. It was so dark, she had no idea how long she'd been there. He'd left the disgusting, dried-up rag in her mouth before leaving her alone. She couldn't scream even if the rag wasn't in her mouth, her throat was so dry and scratchy.

Think, she told herself. *Think about this calmly. You need to untie yourself.*

But how would she do that? She didn't know where she was and had no way of moving so that she could untie herself. This guy had it all worked out.

The sound of an engine outside stopped her thoughts. She held her breath, listening as the engine died out and the sound of footsteps approached. Panic set in again and her breathing became laboured at the sound of a key turning in a lock; the door opening.

'Ah, you're still here,' the voice chuckled. He was mocking her as she sat there in the dark, a blindfold around her eyes and tied tightly at the back of her head.

'I might need you to do something for me,' he said, his tones hushed as he moved around her from one side of the room to another. 'I need you to get in touch with your mother. Or your aunt, I couldn't give a shit which one. I need you to tell them about their mother, Janey. That you need her to come and get you.'

He was going to let her talk to her parents? Surely he was teasing her? If he did that, the police could trace where the call came from, wouldn't they? They'd find him and she'd be set free. Why would he do that? He'd implicate himself and end up in prison.

Her skin prickled as she felt his hands on her; in her hair. Unexpectedly, he was untying the blindfold. She expected light to hurt her eyes, but when she opened them, the place was still dark. Not dark where she couldn't see anything, but dark where her eyes didn't need to be shielded.

She looked up at the man, who was wearing a balaclava. He held a phone in his hand. It was a pay as you go, with lots of buttons and a small screen. She'd never seen a phone like it before in real life; only on a TikTok page where old mobiles were compared to modern makes. It was meant to have a comedy factor to it, but it was lost on Molly Rose.

'Use this to phone them. I'll give you a script of what to say. If they ask questions, you don't answer. Stick to the script and you'll survive. Got it?'

She looked at him and quickly scanned the room. There was a door in the corner, next to some industrial-looking shelves, which housed cans of paint. On the other side of the door was a window. It had shutters down in front of it and Molly Rose wondered if on the other side of those shutters was the outside world. Maybe she could get out.

'There's no point planning the best escape route,' he said. He bent in front of her, leaned in – the smell of his breath almost made her gag. 'Just so you know, you're not getting out of here until your grandmother is standing in front of me and she gives me what I want.'

Molly Rose shook her head and tried to speak, despite the rag still stuffed inside her mouth. He frowned and then, as if curiosity got the better of him, he pulled the tape off and removed the rag.

'Say that again?'

Scream, she thought. *Scream as loud as you can. But what if there's no one around outside?* What if she were to scream and it angered him? He could hurt her and it would have been for nothing.

'I said, I still have no idea who you're talking about. I don't have a grandmother called Janey. And even if I did, how am I supposed to get her here if you won't tell me where I am. And I doubt you're going to tell them when I call, because they'd just bring the police with them and you'd get caught.'

The man stood up and put his hands on his hips. 'Ah, you're a smart little bitch, aren't you?'

'I'm sorry, I don't mean to sound cheeky. I just don't get any of this.'

'You don't *have* to get it. You just have to do what I say.'

Molly Rose watched as he pulled a piece of paper out from his jacket pocket and unfolded it in front of her before holding it up so she could see. He'd written a script, like he'd said. His writing was surprisingly neat and easy to read.

'Your house number?' he said, saying the words so firmly she couldn't refuse to answer the question. She'd do anything if it meant she had a chance of getting away from this psycho.

She said the number aloud and he pushed each button with precision before holding the phone to her ear.

The sound of the ring in the earpiece made her stomach flip. She was going to hear her mum's voice and she knew it could break her. The last time she'd spoken to Orla, she told her she couldn't be around someone like her after how she'd treated Sinead. Now, all Molly Rose wanted was to be with her mum.

'Hello?'

Molly Rose took a long, silent breath and swallowed back all the emotions she was feeling in that moment. Fear, sadness, anger.

'Hello?' the voice said again. It was her mum.

'Hi Mum. It's Molly Rose,' she said as she began to read the script.

She listened as Orla's emotions took over. She choked back tears as she repeated her name. It was a sound that almost broke Molly Rose.

Chapter 32

Janey felt awkward, standing in a house she wasn't welcome in. But she was in and that was all that mattered. Seeing her daughter, Orla, so broken by her own daughter's disappearance, hurt her in a way she hadn't expected. How could she feel this way for Orla when she hadn't been in her life? And more to the point, how could she be so worried for a granddaughter that she'd never met?

Then she thought about Charlie. She could barely think his name without the rage becoming so over-whelming she wanted to scream. If it really was Charlie who had Molly Rose, then she was in a lot of danger. Janey of all people knew that.

'So,' Orla started. 'Go on then. Who do you think has my daughter?'

Janey felt Orla's icy stare pierce right through her. In all her years in charge of her firm – taking on thugs, lowlife scum and big-time bosses – Janey had never felt more vulnerable than she did now, with her rage-filled daughter standing in front of her.

'You blame me, I know that,' Janey said.

'Well, what do you expect? You aren't around our whole lives, then you show up, looking to waltz into our homes, be part of the family, and suddenly my daughter goes missing and you tell me you think you know who has her? Of course it's your fault!'

Orla's husband, Oliver, looked down at the floor and shuffled uncomfortably.

'Orla, would you calm down,' Sinead said. 'We don't know it's Mum's fault.'

Janey shot Sinead a glance. *Mum?*

'Are you *fucking* joking? *Mum?*' Orla scoffed. 'The woman doesn't know the meaning of the word.'

'Janey will do fine,' Janey said softly, looking at Sinead. For a woman in her late thirties, she looked like she'd had a rough few years. Taking in the appearances of both her daughters, it was clear they led very different lives. Orla was successful, with a beautiful, exceptionally large family home. Sinead had a drug addiction.

'No, if I want to call her Mum, I will. You don't get to dictate to me what I call her, Orla.'

'You sound like a child. Oh, but that's right, you're not a child, are you? Because kids aren't addicted to drugs and booze, are they?'

'Right, that's enough. Let's not do this again,' Oliver said, stepping between his wife and sister-in-law. 'It really doesn't matter what Sinead calls her, Orla. You're losing sight of what's happening here. The more people to help with finding Molly Rose, the better.'

Janey felt the weight of the silence as though it was pushing her down by the shoulders.

'Excuse me?' a police officer said, stepping closer to Janey. 'Can I have a word?'

Janey excused herself from the kitchen and followed the officer out to the hallway. The officer crossed the hall and into a lounge. She had to be honest with herself, her daughter seemed to have done well in life if this was where she was living.

'What can I do for you?' Janey asked, folding her arms. She noted that this officer seemed to be the only one in the house. Not that it would matter to her; standing in a house wasn't deemed as illegal activity, no matter who she was.

'You're Janey Hallahan?'

Janey raised a brow. 'I'm Janey, yes,' she said.

'I've been instructed by my boss to let you handle this,' the officer said.

Narrowing her eyes, Janey exhaled softly and said, 'What's your name?'

'It's McGhee,' the young officer replied. She stood tall and pushed back her shoulders, as if standing to attention.

'And your boss is?'

'DS Richards.'

Janey nodded. He was one of hers. 'Okay. I assume you've been briefed on keeping your mouth shut?'

McGhee nodded. 'Yes. We're to carry on the investigation as normal, but let you take lead. If you know who is involved, then it's likely you'll...'

Janey knew what she was going to say. That Janey would likely take her own justice. And she would. When she found Charlie, she would make him pay for what he'd done.

She should have dealt with him a very long time ago.

The police would do their bit to make Charlie's death look like it was an accident. The Hallahan firm paid them enough to do anything she needed.

'I'll let you get back to your family,' McGhee said, opening the lounge room door and crossing the hallway to the kitchen. Janey looked out and saw Orla, Sinead and Oliver watching her.

She wasn't ready to tell the girls about her life yet. Orla was right, it was bad enough that Molly Rose had disappeared because of her, she didn't want to fuel that fire any more than necessary.

'So, what was that all about?' Orla said, her tone venomous.

'Just some routine questions,' McGhee replied before Janey could. 'Still piecing together our information to help find Molly Rose. I've got some paperwork to file regarding Molly Rose's case. I'm just a phone call away if you need me and the liaison officer will be here shortly.'

Janey straightened her jacket, pushed back her shoulders and walked towards her daughters as McGhee left the house. There was a long bout of silence and then the landline phone began to ring.

Everyone turned towards it as Orla rushed across the lounge to pick it up.

'Hello?' Orla said. She waited and it seemed as though everyone else in the house held their breath. 'Hello?' she said again, more forcefully this time.

And then, Orla dropped to her knees and let out a sound that Janey didn't think was possible from a human being. 'It's Molly Rose.'

Oliver was by her side, Sinead too. Oliver took the phone from her and hit the speaker button. 'Sinead,' he whispered, 'run out and get that officer to come back right now.'

Janey closed her eyes and hoped McGhee had already left.

'Molly Rose, sweetheart, it's Dad. Where are you?' Oliver said. Janey was impressed by how calm he sounded.

'Listen carefully,' Molly Rose said. 'It's important. Janey Hallahan is the reason I'm not at home right now.'

Orla turned sharply and glared at Janey. She didn't have to say anything, the look in her eye reiterated the "I told you so" when it came to blaming Janey for Molly Rose's disappearance.

'Where are you?' Oliver pressed again.

'I have instructions for Janey Hallahan. You need to get this message to her,' Molly Rose said.

Janey took a step closer to Orla and knelt on the floor beside her. 'I'm here,' she said. 'I'm Janey.'

Silence followed and Orla started to panic. 'Molly Rose, are you being held against your will?'

Janey looked deep into Orla's eyes and shook her head. She knew the criminal world and the scum who operated out there. This was a set-up and Orla needed to be careful with what she said. Janey placed a finger to her lips and gestured for Orla to be quiet.

'Molly Rose, I'm listening,' Janey said.

'I'm going to send a location to my mum's mobile. When you get there, you need to leave a bag with...' Molly Rose faltered. Janey heard her swallow and then continue, 'With a million pounds inside. I don't care how you get it, just do it. It needs to be done in twenty-four hours from the moment you receive the text.'

Janey knew what was going on on the other end of the line. Molly Rose was being made to say these things. She was either reading from a script or had been forced to memorise these words.

'And is that money for Charlie Hallahan, by any chance?' Janey pressed.

'Once the money is left in the specified location, there will be a second text with information about where you can come and collect me. No police. If I think you've gone against my words…' Another lengthy silence followed and the sound of Molly Rose's voice cracking with fear sent a shiver up Janey's spine. 'I won't ever come back. Is that clear?'

Janey felt sick. This poor, young girl was being used as bait and she fully believed that Charlie would kill her if Janey didn't do something quickly.

Orla stared at Janey, her eyes wide with fear. She looked desperate and confused.

'Loud and clear,' Janey said quietly. 'Send the text and I'll get right to it.'

Orla opened her mouth to speak but Molly Rose wasn't finished yet.

'Come alone. No one else. Just you. I'll be watching. You won't see me. Once I see that you've followed instructions clearly, the next phase will commence.'

Janey felt her heart thump hard inside her chest as the line cut off.

'No!' Orla shouted as she got to her feet. 'No. Get her back, call her back right now!'

Sinead appeared back in the lounge, out of breath and red in the face. 'I tried to chase her down the street but by the time I got to the end of the drive she was gone.'

Janey looked sympathetically at her. 'Thanks,' she said. 'It's okay.'

Orla shoved Janey hard in the shoulders and Janey stumbled back. 'How is it okay? And how the fuck are you going to get a million quid together? What are you, some kind of money-laundering drug dealer or something?'

In that moment, Janey felt more exposed than she ever had in her life. But she wasn't going to let this situation get the better of her. Charlie Hallahan wasn't going to win this one.

'It would be a lot easier if I was,' Janey replied. 'But I said I was here to help and I am. I'll get Molly Rose back for you. You just have to trust me.'

'But that's the problem. I don't trust you. You've come into this all guns blazing, telling me you'll deal with it. The police... I mean,' Orla threw her hands up in the air. 'Something isn't right about you. Or the police for that matter. This isn't right. I don't want you dealing with this. If this person is demanding a ransom of a million from you, then he clearly thinks you have it. Or knows you have it.'

Janey knew she had to tell all for Orla to understand. But just as she was just about to, Orla's phone pinged loudly. Janey watched as Orla scrambled to open the message. She read it aloud.

'Leave the bag of cash at the bottom of the Park Gardens steps in Kelvingrove Park in exactly twenty-four hours. I'll be watching. You won't see me. I won't collect the money until I see you leave the park. Do not follow me. Wait for instruction on where to pick me up. If you deviate from these instructions, I'll be killed. M.'

Orla sobbed and Oliver enveloped her. 'It's okay,' he said. 'We'll get her back. I promise.'

'Can you really do this?' Sinead asked, looking into Janey's eyes. The poor girl was shaking.

All eyes were on Janey. She *couldn't* fuck this up. 'Yes. Yes, I can. And I will explain everything. But let me just do this. Let me get Molly Rose back and then we can talk. About everything.'

Chapter 33

The staff in the local Tesco had just finished putting the crates of food out the back of the shop that they could no longer sell when he crossed the courtyard and filled his rucksack with as much as he could. He hadn't eaten properly in a few days and he needed to keep his strength up so he could carry out his plan. Collect the money from Janey and dump that girl, Kassy, who was still in the boot of his car.

He shoved packaged sandwiches into the top of the bag and some loose fruit into the side pockets, but what he really wanted was a good old bottle of whisky. Any brand would do, but his particular favourite was Glenfiddich Grande Couronne twenty-six-year-old single malt. That was his drink. Well, it was when he had the money. At almost five-hundred quid a bottle, Charlie would now have to settle for a half-bottle of Bells. But he didn't even have the money for that these days. His car had the last of the petrol in it, so he didn't have cash to fill it up. He'd have to keep what was left so he could get rid of the prostitute. The only thing that was keeping him going was the idea that Janey was getting him his money. Although, he knew if Janey was anything like her father was, this could go south for him. It was a risk he was willing to take.

Zipping up his backpack, he slung it over his right shoulder and headed out on to the main road, pulling his hood up over his head. He didn't want to be seen on CCTV.

'Excuse me pal, any spare change?' A voice interrupted his thoughts. He looked down to see a homeless guy sitting on the ground, his back leaning against a council bin, looking up through bloodshot eyes at Charlie in the hope of some money.

Charlie crouched down next to him and said: 'I'm the same as you, mate. Nowhere to go, no money of my own. I did have, once. I had it all. Fast cars, fast women. But I pissed it up against the wall and now I'm raiding the crates of out-of-date food at the back of the shops just to get something to eat But I have a plan, a plan to get it all back. And I will, you know. I will get it all back.'

The homeless guy stared back at him, his eyes bleary and heavy. He probably hadn't taken in a word Charlie had said. Not that he blamed the guy for being off his face. It was easier to be wired to the moon when dealing with being homeless and on the street.

Charlie pulled his bag off his shoulder, dug his hand into the side pocket and took out one of the apples. He handed it to the guy and said, 'Sorry, it's all I've got.'

'Cheers,' the guy said, uninterested in the apple. He wanted money for another hit. The effects of whatever drug he was on would wear off soon and the harsh reality of sleeping rough would creep in again.

Charlie got to his feet and kept walking along Argyle Street, back to the lockup. He often wondered if things would have been easier like this if he hadn't lost his fortune. Because now, he knew what he was missing. And it was all down to that bitch, Janey. She'd taken it all away from him. The money. The entitlement. It was all supposed to be his. He wouldn't be satisfied until the money was in his possession.

'Bitch,' he spat. A woman glared at him, horrified by the sudden outburst. He could tell her it wasn't aimed at her, but why should he?

He glanced up at the doctor's surgery on the corner of the street and saw all sorts going in and coming out – people in designer clothes and others with holes in their shoes. This part of the city was a mix of rich and poor. People slept on the streets with luxurious flats and historic buildings towering over them. The wealthy drove past them in expensive cars, choosing not to see the man sitting in the shop doorway or on the pavement with the bin supporting his back.

Charlie used to be the one ignoring the homeless littering the streets. Now, he *was* the homeless. But not for long. He'd be back in his luxurious home, living his high life soon enough. He just had to be careful not to fuck it up again.

Turning onto Haugh Road, Charlie walked towards the old Yorkhill hospital and kept his head down. Thoughts began to creep into his head as he put one foot in front of the other. Thoughts of his time as a Hallahan. As Finn's stepson. The one who was supposed to inherit it all and instead the old man thought it would be a good idea to put his daughter in charge of the family firm. Finn had no right to think that he could just push Charlie out like he did; pay him off and make him walk away from his right to take over. He might not have been blood, but he'd been part of that family for years before he'd been cast aside. He still couldn't understand why Finn could, on one hand, take him in after his mother abandoned him and his abusive drunk of a father had himself killed.

Best thing that could have happened to Gerry, if Charlie was honest. What a wonderful start to life: one parent abandoning him and the other battering him as often as he liked, just because he could. It was like he'd been angry that he'd been left to deal with the son he'd never wanted in the first place. It was Gerry's fault he'd been born – if he hadn't repeatedly raped his wife, his life would have been a lot different. Charlie thought that things would pick up when Finn took him in – and they had for a few years until, of course, he was disowned. *Story of my life*, he thought.

Charlie gritted his teeth so hard that he thought they might shatter in his mouth. Knowing that he'd wiped out one of Janey's businesses with that fire wasn't enough. Knowing he had Janey's granddaughter and the only way she'd survive was by giving him a million, wasn't enough. He needed to destroy every last shred of her. And he would. He just needed to do it in a way that ended with her looking into his eyes and knowing he was going to do to her what she had done to him. She'd robbed him of it all. And he was going to return the favour. It didn't matter to him if she followed his every instruction. That entire family would be dead by the end of the week.

Chapter 34

Janey climbed into the Defender and placed both hands on the steering wheel before closing her eyes. The phone call had happened just moments before and Janey had to act fast. This wasn't going to be an easy feat but she had to try to save her granddaughter.

Hitting Ciaran's number on the screen on the dash, he answered after one ring and it took all Janey had not to break down.

'Janey, how are things going? Have they found her yet?'

'Organise a meeting with Kristo and some of the counterfeit team. We need a million and we need it now. I want this meeting to take place in one hour out at Carbeth. No questions asked. If they have other work commitments, I want them cancelled and this put ahead of everything, and I mean everything. Deliveries, collections, the lot.'

Ciaran didn't hesitate. 'I'll get in touch with Kristo now. I'll drive out too and I'll meet you there in about forty-five minutes.'

Janey reversed out of the drive. Getting together one-million pounds in counterfeit cash would be just as difficult as getting the real thing.

Janey drove through Milngavie and noted how pretty the town was. Orla had done well to end up here but she couldn't help but wonder about Sinead. What had she done with her life?

Stopping at the red light, Janey stared up at Episcopal Church building. She'd never believed in God, or any religion for that matter. If a god did exist, then why did bad things happen to good people? Like her, when she was just a child herself? Or Molly Rose?

Drawing her eyes away from the building as the light turned from red to green, Janey crossed the junction onto Clober Road and then on to Craigton Road where the residential area became less dense with large homes and the farmlands increased. This area made her think back to the farm she grew up on with Finn and... she couldn't bring herself to even think his name.

With Clober Golf Club on her right, Janey kept her eyes on the road ahead until she came to the junction that took her on to the A809, locally known as the Stockie. On any normal business day as she headed out to Carbeth, Janey enjoyed the drive. This area of the city reminded her so much of home. But now she was here, in Glasgow again, and her girls were in crisis, she wondered if Scotland would become more of a permanent residence for her and Ciaran? Even if things didn't go to plan, Janey wasn't sure she could just walk away from her family, even if they didn't let her in.

About ten minutes later, Janey arrived at Carbeth Holiday Park and drove to the main office. The park seemed quiet. The business had been affected by the discovery of the young girl's body just the previous year, but things were picking up again.

Janey parked the Defender outside the main office – merely a small wooden hut – and went inside. Locking the car door behind her, she pulled back the rug on the floor to reveal a basement door. Unlocking it, she pulled it up and switched on the light from under the desk next to her, illuminating the office door underneath, which even Danny McInroy hadn't known about in the time he'd worked for her.

Descending the staircase carefully, Janey's heels clicked against the metal staircase leading to the underground meeting room. She took a seat at the head of the long, rectangular table in the middle of the room. It wouldn't be long before her employees would start arriving.

Tapping her fingers on the metal, fold-out table, she closed her eyes and thought about Molly Rose and how terrified she must have felt during that scripted call. Being in Charlie's presence was hard enough, but being forced to do what she did and make that call would have been terrifying. She'd have expected him to kill her had she uttered one wrong word he hadn't instructed her to say.

She couldn't sit any longer so she got to her feet and started to pace the floor slowly, her arms folded across her chest. Then, just a few minutes later, she heard a car above stop outside the cabin and a door slam shut. Footsteps entered the cabin and she watched as Kristo appeared on the staircase.

'Janey,' he said. His voice echoing slightly.

'Hi, Kristo. Take a seat.'

'The others are on their way. Shouldn't be too much longer.'

Janey noted how nervous he sounded. It was no wonder given the precise instruction she'd given Ciaran to pass on.

'Thank you,' she replied.

'Is this about Charlie?' Kristo asked.

'Let's just wait for everyone to get here. I don't want to have to keep repeating myself when I could explain everything in one go to everyone. But yes, in short, this is about Charlie. And it's not good, Kristo. Not good at all.'

Kristo's nodded, sat down on the seat at the opposite end of the table to where Janey was stood and waited quietly. Then, moments later, more of Janey's employees poured down the stairs. All quiet, all dressed inconspicuously and, by the looks on their faces, ready to listen to Janey's instructions.

'Take a seat, boys. Ciaran won't be much longer and then we can get this meeting started.'

Everyone sat in silence around the table and waited. And then Ciaran appeared, stood at the bottom of the stairs staring into the room.

'Right,' Janey said. 'Now that we're all here, I'll get right into it.'

Ciaran walked past the lads around the table, and stood next to Janey as she placed both hands flat on the table and looked each and every one of them in the eye. The men who worked for her kept the secrets of the business quiet. Their unwavering loyalty meant everything to her and they were paid extremely well for it. As much as the Hallahan empire belonged to Janey, these men – some in their twenties, some in their forties and some in their fifties – helped her to build that empire. They were involved in drug running, illegal exportation, and counterfeit goods and cash. And they kept it all under wraps from the Serious Organised Crime Taskforce, or at least the ones who weren't on Janey's payroll.

'I'm sure you're all aware of my request,' she said. 'Let me give you more of an insight as to *why* I've requested a million in counterfeit notes.'

They all stared at her, unblinking; waiting for her to continue. She saw the respect they had for her on each of their faces and it gave her an enormous sense of relief to know she had a team she could rely on.

'I know it's a big ask and it's a huge risk. But I know we've got the technology to get this done in a short space of time. The reason for this is because, a lot of you won't know, I have a granddaughter. Her name is Molly Rose Hunter and she's been taken by someone, a man who shares my name but unfortunately not my morals. He's threatened to kill her if I don't give him a million pounds in cash.'

She locked eyes with Kristo at the opposite end of the table, the second man she trusted with her life, and took a steadying breath.

'It's not a problem,' Kristo said.

A look of disbelief crossed the faces of some of the others around the table, but not one of them opened their mouth.

'I think we both know it could be,' Janey said. 'But I would appreciate all of your co-operation on the matter. And as soon as physically possible.'

'I'll organise this with the printers at the press offices we have connections with, Janey. This will be organised and sorted before this fucker has a chance to blink.'

Janey felt guilty for putting her team in such a difficult position because it was a personal matter. But she had no other choice. If she was going to stop Charlie in all his madness, this was the only way.

Kristo stood and glanced down at the rest of the boys around the table. 'You'll break into teams,' he said. 'Four teams of four. I'll get instructions to you all by the end of the working day with which press office you'll be working from.' He turned to Janey. 'You'll have the cash by the end of the working day tomorrow at the absolute latest.

The boys will work through the night. They know how important this is.'

The team nodded and rose from their seats.

'Thank you,' she said to them. 'I understand this is impacting on other works being dealt with. You'll all be rewarded.'

Kristo stood to the side and gestured for the boys to make their way up the stairs. Janey watched them go. Ciaran placed a hand on her shoulder and gave that reassuring squeeze he did when she was stressed. She placed her hand over his and felt a lump grow in her throat.

'We'll get her back, Janey. Charlie Hallahan's feet won't touch the ground after this,' he said.

She nodded. 'I know they won't. Because I'm going to kill him, like I should have done a long fucking time ago.'

Chapter 35

'It's ready,' Kristo said on the other end of the line. 'The teams are on their way back to Carbeth to drop the money to you.'

Janey closed her eyes and breathed a sigh of relief. It hadn't been that long since she'd given her instructions to her team and they'd already completed their work. Janey glanced down at her watch and noted that twelve hours had gone by. 'I don't know what I'd do without you lot, you know that?'

'Could I make a small suggestion?' Kristo continued as Janey opened her eyes and looked out the lounge window in Orla's house.

'Go on,' Janey replied.

'Might I suggest we add some real cash to the bundles? Charlie might check the contents when he picks up the bag. If he does, we need to know what he finds in there is real.'

Janey pulled her top lip under her teeth and pressed down hard. 'The printed counterfeits aren't good enough to fool him?'

'No, that's not what I mean. All I'm saying is it might be worth making the top few layers real, you know, bundles of fifties and hundreds. If he looks at the top layer at least then, even if he did have his suspicions and did a proper check on pick-up, he'd be satisfied that he hadn't been scammed.'

Janey relaxed her mouth and nodded. This was why Kristo was her top man, not just in Glasgow, but of all the cities she ran. Janey had promoted him to top dog not long after the Danny McInroy fiasco. And he'd proven himself worthy, yet again.

'Yes, that makes a lot of sense. Thank you, Kristo. I'll get Ciaran to head to Carbeth now. He can collect the bags and I'll stay here with Orla and Sinead.'

'Okay, I'll talk to you soon, boss.'

Kristo hung up and Janey placed the phone down on the sofa next to her. She was alone in the lounge. Sinead and Orla were in the house, but had barely spoken to each other, let alone Janey. Things had been tense since the text message had come through from Molly Rose twelve hours earlier. Kristo had made his teams work tirelessly to get the money printed and bagged. Now, Janey had to work out a way of explaining to Orla and Sinead how she'd managed to get a million pounds together. How could she explain to them what she did for a living? That she was a crime boss. The biggest crime boss in the country, to say the least.

The lounge door opened and Sinead stepped inside, holding a mug in each hand.

'Hi,' Janey said, wondering if she had been standing outside, listening to the call she'd been on with Kristo.

'I didn't know what you took in your coffee, so I guessed. Milk and two?' Sinead asked.

'Bang-on,' Janey said, getting to her feet. 'Thank you.'

Sinead passed over the mug from a shaky right hand and smiled. 'That's how I take it, too.'

Janey felt her stomach drop. It hit her then, that she'd missed so much of her own daughters' lives, even down to the smallest detail, such as how they took their coffee.

'This isn't how I wanted things to be, you know, with meeting you and Orla for the first time,' Janey said.

'I don't think anyone could have imagined this was how it was going to go,' Sinead said, taking a sip from the mug. 'I heard you on the phone.'

Janey raised a brow. 'You did?'

'Yeah. Something about Ciaran collecting the bags. So the money, it's ready?'

Janey didn't know how to play this. Should she tell the truth, now? Just to Sinead?

'Molly Rose will be coming home today?' Sinead pressed.

'I hope so. But I won't lie,' Janey said in hushed tones so that Orla wouldn't hear her. 'Charlie, he's unhinged. I wouldn't be surprised if he puts another demand up.'

'Will he hurt her?' Sinead asked. 'I mean, I've lived on the streets for a long time. I know what it's like out there. But I can't say I've ever come across someone who would do something like this… use a child the way he has.'

Janey felt sick. 'I won't let him hurt her,' she said, although that wasn't something she could promise because she didn't know how things would pan out. Like she'd said, Charlie was unhinged. She knew that better than anyone.

Sinead's hands trembled a little and she sat down on the sofa. 'You're probably wondering why I ended up on the streets.'

'It's not really my place to ask. I mean, I haven't been around. In a sense, it's none of my business,' Janey replied, staring down at her daughter.

'I'm just going to come right out and say it, Janey. Mum. Sorry, I don't know what to call you.'

Janey took a seat next to Sinead and parted her lips to speak before realising that she didn't know what to say in response. She simply took a sip of coffee and waited.

'I'm a junkie. Well, a recovering junkie. You know, heroin?'

Janey stared at Sinead. It was obvious she was an addict. But heroin? That was a side of the business that she'd refused to go into. Amphetamines, fine. Cocaine, of course. Guns, yes. Counterfeit money and money laundering, not a problem. But heroin? That was a step too far. She refused to have her cities littered with people injecting themselves, overdosing and mugging grannies as they did their bread and milk run to the shop.

'How did you end up down that path?' Janey asked.

'Fell in with the wrong crowd after my parents died.'

Janey stared at her in disbelief. They died? When? How?

'Then we got split up, me and Orla, you know. Sent to different foster carers. Orla got a family she still keeps in touch with now, as far as I know. Me, I got the family who gave zero fucks about anyone but themselves. They did it for the money. I stayed out of the house more and more often, and got pally with a group of kids from the scheme. Got into a bit of trouble, liked the thrill of the chase, started smoking, drinking, taking the odd line here and there. Then, bang, I got that high everyone talks about after trying heroin with a guy I was seeing. I've been chasing it ever since. Orla told me she didn't want anything to do with me and got on with her life.'

Janey hadn't blinked as Sinead told her story. 'I'm so, *so* sorry.'

Sinead narrowed her eyes and asked, 'Why? You didn't put the needle in my arm. I chose to do it. I am who I am because of me, not anyone else.'

Janey looked down at the floor and tried to compose herself. 'If I hadn't given you up, you wouldn't be this version of yourself.'

Sinead sighed. 'Everything happens for a reason, or so they say.'

'I thought you were going to be better off after I gave you and your sister up.'

'We were fine, for a few years at least. In fact, Orla's always been fine. It's me who's the let-down.'

Silence fell between them and Janey couldn't get the image of her daughter on the street as an addict out of her head. How could she have got it so wrong? She'd truly believed that giving the girls to a couple who were friends with Finn and desperate for a family was the best decision.

'I'm still sorry.'

'No one could have predicted what would happen, never mind you. I mean, you must have been young when you had us?'

Staring down at the floor, Janey looked up at Sinead and noticed how her entire body still trembled from time to time. She'd said she was a recovering addict. She was going through withdrawal right now.

'I was fifteen. And I lived in Northern Ireland. Being a fifteen-year-old, pregnant and out of wedlock was hard enough. But bringing you up in the midst of the troubles... I just couldn't do it.'

The sound of footsteps creeping along the hall towards the lounge made them both look up at the door. Orla was stood there, staring at both of them. Her eyes were puffy and looked sore.

'I didn't know that was why you gave us up,' Orla said.

Janey nodded. She didn't want to admit that she was forced to do it, that if she'd been given a choice and had control over what happened to her own children, she'd have kept them. Raised them as best she could. But Finn hadn't allowed it. He had a business to hand down and Janey was the only one that he was going to give it all to. His stipulation was give them up and she could have it all. Keep them and she was on her own with no way to support herself or the girls. Now, when she truly thought about it, she knew she'd made the wrong choice. If she could go back thirty-eight years, and tell herself to take control and keep her girls, she would. Yes, it would have been difficult, impossible at times. But she'd still do it.

'Yeah. I thought you two deserved better,' Janey replied. Lying to them felt wrong. If nothing else, she was lying to herself. 'How are you?' Janey asked Orla.

'Awful,' she replied bluntly. 'It's like the police are off the bloody radar. You'd think they'd be all over this with a million-pound ransom on the cards.'

Janey felt Sinead's eyes on her and she knew she was going to have to explain herself. Orla had already fired so many questions at her about the fact that she could get that kind of money together and she'd dodged them up until now.

'Yeah, about that,' Janey started. 'So, my husband is on his way to collect the money now and is bringing it here.'

Orla stared at her silently.

'And again, how are you able to get together a million quid in what?' Sinead glanced at her watch. 'Twelve hours?'

Breathing through the stress of what was about to come out of her mouth, Janey rubbed her clammy hands on her knees and said, 'Okay. I'm not going to go into detail. But all you need to know is that I'm in the type of business that can conjure up pretty much whatever I need in a short space of time.'

Orla frowned. 'What do you do?'

'Yeah,' Sinead said. 'I mean, do you own a bank or something?'

'I wish it was that simple. Like I said, I'm not going to go into detail for your own good. But just know, that even if Charlie asked for ten million, I could sort it.'

Orla let out a sudden burst of laughter. 'Ha, okay then, Walter White.'

'Pardon?' Janey said.

'What are you doing, cooking crystal fucking meth? There's no way you'd be able to get that kind of cash together if you were doing something legit.'

Janey didn't have an answer for her. All she could do was sit there in silence and hope Orla wasn't able to peel back her mask as far as she thought she could.

'So, are you?' Sinead pressed. 'Are you a high-flying businesswoman with a legit business, or a high-end drug boss?'

Janey felt like her heart was going to burst out of her chest. For the first time in her life, she felt ashamed of herself.

Janey's phone rang and she lifted it from the couch where it sat next to her. It was Ciaran calling her. *Saved by the fucking bell*, she thought.

'Hello?' she answered, holding a finger up to the girls to signal that she'd be a moment on the call. 'Ciaran?'

'I'm on my way to Orla's with the cash, do you want to meet me outside? I'll be about half an hour.'

Janey turned her back to the girls and looked out of the window into the back garden. 'Oh really? And it can't wait?'

There was a pause on Ciaran's end of the line, like he was trying to work out what she was talking about. 'Is there a problem?' he asked.

'Right, if it's urgent I'll come and deal with it now. I don't want our employees missing out on wages because our accountant decided to piss off on holiday and not tell anyone,' Janey said. 'Just you stay there and I'll come to you. I'll be there in about thirty minutes.'

'Janey, are you in danger?' Ciaran pressed, sounding concerned.

'Oh no, not at all. Just want to get this sorted. I'll be with you soon.'

She ended the call and turned to face Orla and Sinead. 'A problem with payroll. I'm sorry but I have to get to the office. It won't take more than an hour.'

Orla threw her hands up in the air. 'What about the money? You can't just walk away from this, Janey.'

'I'm not. I won't miss it. I said I'd sort this and I will.'

'Sounds to me like you're just dodging our question,' Sinead said with a slight smile raising the corner of her mouth.

Janey shook her head. 'Yes, I'm Walter White. My husband is Jesse Pinkman and we cook crystal meth out the back of a shitty campervan. Is that what you wanted to hear?'

Orla raised a brow and crossed her arms over her chest. 'My daughter is missing and being held ransom for a million pounds that has been demanded *you* pay. That money is coming from somewhere.'

Sinead turned and looked at her sister. 'As much as I want to know, does it actually matter, Orla? The main thing is, Janey can help.'

'Yeah, we'll see about that. You don't have the money yet and Molly Rose is still missing. And the police seem to be leaving us to it. Something's not right here, Janey.'

Janey slid her phone into her pocket, picked up her handbag from the floor and smiled. 'I'll be back before heading to the drop-off point.'

She left the house, climbed into the Defender and drove to Carbeth.

-

'It's all here,' Kristo said. 'The team printed in record time.'

Janey stared down at the large, black duffle bag and nodded. 'It's hard to tell which of the piles are real and which are counterfeit. If I'm struggling with that, then Charlie won't see it.'

'Exactly. They all look the same, but there are some slight differences that you would only notice if you knew where to look,' Kristo said, picking up two bundles of one-hundred-pound notes. 'This bundle here is the counterfeit. This bundle is real.' He slid a note out from each pile and handed them to Janey. 'Run your finger over the print at the top where it says "Bank of Scotland". You feel that?'

'The text is raised,' Janey confirmed.

'Yes. And the hologram does what it's supposed to,' Kristo said. 'On this one here,' he gestured to the other note, 'the text isn't raised and the hologram still works but is slightly smaller. It's by far one of the hardest counterfeits to spot. But still possible. Hence why we've put some real notes in there. Which we will get back, once Molly Rose is returned to her family safely.'

Janey was impressed by the work Kristo and the team had put in. 'Thank you,' Janey said. 'All of you have worked hard under pressurised conditions, not to mention through the night. Like I said, a bonus is coming your way.'

They all nodded and thanked Janey.

'I have everyone on standby if you need them with you at the park,' Kristo said.

Janey had considered this. It would be helpful but too risky. 'If we ambush him, he might never give up where Molly Rose is. In doing that, we could put her in further danger. We stick to the plan, Kristo. But thank you for the concern.'

Kristo nodded. 'Okay, boss.'

–

Janey parked the Defender in a bay on Woodlands Terrace, directly across from the Clifton Street stairs. This was a deliberate act, so that she could walk along the street and scan the area. Janey hadn't seen Charlie since before the girls were born. She might not even recognise him. Yes, she'd seen him on the security footage from Cakes and Cocktails, but that was just a snippet and it had been slightly grainy.

Getting out of the car, Janey moved around to the back and pulled the bag out of the boot. Walking through the streets of Glasgow with a million in cash, real or not, was a huge risk to her and her business. Something Charlie would be laughing about as he watched her – if he was watching her.

Slamming the boot closed, she gripped the handle of the duffle bag tightly and moved on to the pavement that ran alongside the buildings. She walked slowly, taking in her surroundings, her entire body feeling tense and on edge.

She reached the top of the stairs at Park Gardens and stood still, looking down to the concrete below. The trees ahead of her were in line with her eyes; to her left, she could see directly into the windows on the top floor of the building that sat on the road at the bottom of the stairs.

'Where are you, you bastard?' Janey whispered as she perched herself on the wall to the right of the stairs. Should she wait for him? Would he appear if she didn't leave? Would that put Molly Rose in more danger?

Just drop the bag and go, Janey, she told herself. *Just go back to the car, keep an eye on the bag and…* and what? She couldn't follow him because he'd be watching for her to leave.

'Shit,' she said, placing the bag on the grass behind the wall she was sat on. Getting to her feet, she scanned the area one more time, looking into the window of each building and car. She looked into the faces of the people who walked past, seemingly not noticing her.

She walked quickly back to the Defender and pulled her phone out. She hit Kristo's number and he answered immediately.

'Boss?'

'Get the team here now. He needs to be followed. He's not going to give Molly Rose up after this, even if he doesn't discover the money is fake.'

'Done,' Kristo said.

She climbed into the car, closed her eyes and took some steadying breaths. She'd promised to find Molly Rose. But what if she couldn't? What if she'd just played Charlie's game and she ended up dead anyway? Janey scolded herself for thinking it was a good idea to do this without eyes on the bag other than her own. She should have taken Kristo up on his offer to have the team station in and around the park, watching the area. But that was her all over; thinking she could do things by herself; cope on her own. That was what she'd done her entire life. After giving the girls up, she'd told herself that she wouldn't rely on anyone for anything; if she needed something done, she'd do it herself. Yes, she'd married Ciaran; yes, she had a team of male employees, but she had never truly relied on anyone other than herself. In this instance, Janey knew she had made the wrong call. But now Kristo and the team were on their way.

Janey's phone rang and Orla's number flashed up on the screen. *Shit*, she thought. She startled and glanced up at the wall where she'd left the bag. She could see it through the decorative concrete.

'Hello?'

Orla's voice was frantic. 'Is it done? I've not had further instruction from Molly Rose. Have you left the bag where you were told to?'

Janey massaged her temples and stared down into the footwell. 'It's done. You'll hear from her as soon as Charlie has the money.'

'You'd better hope this works, otherwise I'm going to make sure you never see the light of day when you go to prison for helping this utter psycho evade justice.'

Orla hung up and Janey focused on the wall again. Charlie would be here soon; especially since he knew that a million pounds was waiting on him. But as her eyes scanned the gaps in the wall, the decorative spacings and the grass beyond it. The bag was gone.

'Fuck!' she shouted, scrambling out of the car before running along the street to the top of the stairs. She looked down to the entrance to the park and saw a man in a long coat with an identical duffle bag walking into the park.

'Jesus, *fuck*,' she said, taking the stairs, two at a time. She almost snapped her ankle as she ran down them in her heels, but she was moving faster than she'd ever thought she could.

Taking a sharp right into the park, she saw the man moving past the benches that overlooked the park below. He glanced behind him, his eyes connecting with hers.

'Stop!' she shouted. 'Charlie, *stop*!'

He moved, quicker and quicker away from her. He was getting away. Then, out of nowhere, Kristo and Ciaran tackled him. The bag flew along the path as Kristo pinned him to the ground and Ciaran fetched the bag.

Her breath caught in her throat as she ran as fast as she could towards them and, when she reached them, Kristo was staring down into the man's face. Ciaran towered over them with the duffle bag in his right hand. Standing by the man's head, she looked down into his face.

'*Fuck*,' her words rasped. 'It's not him.'

A look of confusion washed over Ciaran's face. 'Are you sure?'

'Fucking positive,' she replied, desperately trying to catch her breath.

'Please, take whatever you want, just don't hurt me,' the man pleaded.

'Janey?' Kristo said, looking up at her. 'He had the bag.'

Janey placed her hands on her waist and spun around, looking up and down the park. 'Are you two deaf? I said he's not Charlie. Fucking hell, it's an identical bag. Jesus, I had my eyes closed for a *second*. When I opened them, the bag was gone.'

Kristo stood up and pulled the man to his feet.

'I could have you arrested you know,' the man said, suddenly changing his tune from terrified to blatant cheek.

Kristo rubbed the man's coat down with his hands in a calm manner, then grabbed him by the scruff of the neck. 'Not if you want to keep your fucking legs you won't. What's in the bag?'

The man frowned, struggling under Kristo's strength. 'My gym gear.'

'Janey, are you sure this isn't the bag?' Ciaran asked.

Janey shot her arm out and pulled from Ciaran's grip. 'Do you think if it was, it would be so fucking light that I could grab it from you so quickly? Fucking hell, it weighs nothing,' she said, being careful not to mention the money in front of the man Kristo and Ciaran had tackled to the ground. 'The bastard must have seen me in the car and took his opportunity.'

Kristo shoved the man away and reached out to retrieve the bag from Janey before launching it towards him. 'Get going,' he said.

The man turned and moved away from them, breaking into a run and disappearing from sight.

Janey hunched over, placed her hands on her knees and breathed deeply – not because she was out of breath but because of the sudden nausea that was taking over.

'*He's* gone. He has the money and I don't think we'll find her. He's not going to give her up. It's just not in his nature.'

Ciaran placed a hand on Janey's shoulder and she looked up at him. 'We'll find him, Janey. We will. Our men are all over the city. He's not going to get far.'

'And how do you work that one out? No one knows what he fucking looks like, Ciaran. I've fucked this all up. I should have taken a still from the CCTV in that cocktail bar and passed it around all of you. I should have taken Kristo up on his suggestion to man the park. I didn't use proper logic, only my stupid, arrogant need to prove I can get through these things on my own. Now Molly Rose is going to die and it's all my fault.'

Chapter 36

Charlie stepped into the lockup and dropped the bag onto the table next to the door. He locked the door behind him and caught his breath. He'd surprised himself that he could run for such a length of time. Disappearing into The Park Bar on Argyle Street, Charlie had gone into the bathroom and changed his clothes – he'd hid a bag in the men's toilets. His plan had been to change so that if he was being followed, it would possibly throw whoever it was off the trail. Janey would have people on him, he knew that given the line of business she was in.

He opened the bag and glared inside. The duffle bag was full to the brim with cash. She'd done it. She'd actually got him his money. He picked up two or three bundles and held them in his hands before sniffing them. 'Yas!' he shouted, causing Molly Rose to jolt awake.

'Oi!' Charlie shouted. 'Oi.' He tapped her firmly on the face. 'Looks like your grandmother came through for you.'

Molly Rose startled and sat up straight, and Charlie pulled her blindfold off. He stared into her eyes; she looked terrified.

'You alert? Awake?' He tapped her on the side of the face a little harder this time as she blinked against the light.

'Yes,' she said, her eyes wide with fear.

'Good,' he said, bending down and picking up a bag of clothes before dangling them in front of her. 'You need to get changed into these.'

Molly Rose looked at the bag and frowned. 'Why?'

'Just do it. Don't make this any harder for yourself,' he replied, dropping them at her feet.

'You'll have to untie me.'

'I will, but I won't be letting you out of my sight.'

'I'm not getting undressed in front of you,' she said, sounding horrified.

'I'm not going to touch you,' he said, disgusted at the sound of her voice. 'What do you think I am, a fucking pervert?'

Molly Rose didn't say anything in response. He could tell by the look on her face that she was too scared to speak.

He walked around to the back of her and started to untie her. She was so tense, her shoulders up by her ears; she was trembling.

'And don't think for a second I've left any doors unlocked. You'll get changed and be straight back into the chair. Understood?'

She nodded once and allowed Charlie to pull her up from the chair. 'Right. You've got thirty seconds to change into the clothes in that bag.'

Molly Rose did exactly what she was told in less than the timeframe given to her and sat back down.

'Good girl,' Charlie said as he tied her back up, but leaving her hands free.

Molly Rose shuddered and it annoyed Charlie. He made her skin crawl. 'I really bother you, don't I? I mean, I get it. I've taken you. I've held you against your will because of a member of your family you didn't even know existed. And I can tell by the look on your face that I make you uncomfortable; like I'm going to...' He left the words hanging.

Molly Rose didn't say anything, she just stared at him. He saw traces of a younger Janey in there. The freckles on her face, the way her hair curled at the ends. The way she stared at him, in disbelief or fear... He couldn't tell at this point. In some ways, her eyes were neutral, almost looked like there was no emotion behind them. In others, she looked horrified. It was odd to him.

Charlie pulled a small table from the other side of the lockup over and placed a fresh pad of paper on it in front of her, along with a pen.

'What's that for?'

'You're going to write a letter for your family.'

'A letter?'

'That's what I said.'

'Are you going to kill me and make it look like suicide? Because they won't believe it.'

'Just shut up, listen to me and do what you're fucking told, girl. Otherwise, I'll do worse than make it look like you killed yourself.'

Molly Rose cried harder as he shoved the pen into her hand. 'I hope you're a quick writer, because I'm only going to say this once.'

Chapter 37

Molly Rose listened carefully and wrote the words down as fast as she could, hoping that she didn't miss a word in fear of what he might do to her.

> Janey
>> *You thought I didn't know, didn't you? You thought that when Finn sent me away...*

Molly Rose kept writing and tried not to show the horror she felt at the words she was being forced to scribble down.

When he had finished speaking, Molly Rose put the pen down gently and kept her eyes on the full stop after the last word. He was an animal; the spawn of the devil.

'Right then,' he said, interrupting her thoughts as he took the piece of paper from the table and folded it in half. 'I'll get this to Janey.'

Molly Rose looked up at him and frowned. There was so much she wanted to say to him. But if she did, it would only anger him. So instead, she kept her thoughts to herself and simply asked, 'What about me?'

'What about you?' he asked, seemingly confused.

'I've done everything you asked.'

He stared at her, as if waiting for her to go on.

'You need to let me go now.'

He smiled and raised a brow. 'Molly Rose, I don't have to do anything. Do you really think that after all this, I'm going to just let you walk out of here? You know too much. You know what I look like. I can't risk you taking this to the police. No, sorry. But I don't have a use for you now. So, like I said, I'll get this to Janey and when I'm done—'

'No! You said I could go.' Molly Rose got to her feet but he was too quick for her. Before she could say or do anything else, he was tying her to the chair again and shoved the disgusting rag back into her mouth.

'Shut up! Like I said, when I'm done, I'll deal with you. But I will promise you one thing. I'll make it quick. You won't feel a thing.'

Molly Rose watched as he strode out of the lockup and slammed the door behind him, locking it before he left.

Panic took over and, as she began to hyperventilate, black spots skewed her vision.

He was never going to let her go. It was his plan to kill her all along.

Chapter 38

Walking along Sauchiehall Street towards the city centre, Sinead felt like she was betraying herself even being in the area. It was like sending a child into a toy shop and telling them they couldn't have a toy. There were so many corners of the city she could go and she'd be able to get hold of a bag. It would only take one hit to get rid of the shakes, the aches and pains, and the constant headache. Her withdrawal was lasting a lot longer than she'd ever expected it to, even with the methadone every day. But then, that was just like swapping a cigarette for a nicotine patch. You were getting the desired drug without the satisfaction. Or a non-alcoholic beer instead of the real deal. *What was the point?* she thought.

Sinead wrung her hands together and tried to ignore the headache that paracetamol and ibuprofen combined hadn't touched.

Just once, that's all it'll take, then you'll feel better.

'Fuck off,' she whispered to her inner junkie and kept walking. She couldn't give in to temptation now, not when she was supposed to be helping find Molly Rose. Not that she expected to find her. From what she could gather from the contact they'd had, that idiotic psycho had her locked up somewhere. That could be anywhere. Glasgow was a big place.

'What am I even doing out here?' Sinead whispered again, stopping at the Cameron Memorial Fountain at the bottom of Woodside Crescent. She glanced up at the clock and saw the time. Ten thirty at night.

She was never going to find Molly Rose and if she tried to ask around, she'd likely bump into her old crowd. That could result in a relapse. But Sinead just stood there, staring at the clock as the seconds ticked away. These past few weeks that Molly Rose had been gone and Sinead had been trying to stay clean had felt longer than the thirty-eight years she'd been wondering where and who her mother was. Now, everything was happening at once. Janey was here, Molly Rose wasn't and everything was a mess.

Sinead decided she couldn't just stand there and stare at a clock and not try to help Molly Rose, just so that she wouldn't have to say no to an old street accomplice and a bag of heroin. Turning her back on the fountain, Sinead stared up Sauchiehall Street and started to walk towards the nightclub-heavy part of the area. From there, she took a left turn and headed up Garnet Street towards the derelict building that was a drug den for junkies. A drug den that Sinead had frequented many a night, which held so many bad highs, physical fights over drugs and money, food and a spot on the floor where she could sleep when she had run out of Orla's money for a bed in a hostel.

Reaching the brow of the hill, Sinead felt her stomach lurch as the building came into view. It looked out of place, especially as it was situated across the road from a primary school. From the outside, the windows were boarded up and the walls blackened with soot from a fire long ago.

Crossing over, Sinead went around the back of the building to the basement entrance and stood at the top of the stairs, which led down to a metal door. She could already hear the thumping of music from inside. Someone was always blasting rock music and no one seemed to know who it belonged to or where it was coming from.

Staring down at it, so much of her recent past came flooding back. She might well be recovering from her addiction, but being back here made it feel like she would easily slip back into her old ways.

Making her way down the stairs, she pulled on the metal door and squeezed through the gap. Immediately, the smell of unwashed bodies hit her. A scent that often came from Sinead herself in those times. Guns N' Roses' "Welcome to the Jungle" blared out from inside. *Fitting*, Sinead thought. It *was* like a fucking jungle in that hellhole and, yes, there were times she really did think she was going to die. Thankfully, so far, she hadn't, although at times she wondered how.

Looking into the space, Sinead saw her old spot in the corner where she would try to sleep while holding on to whatever belongings she had with her at the time. There was always something to be stolen and sold for drugs, no matter how miniscule that item might be.

Pulling Molly Rose's picture out of her pocket, she glanced around the room. Bodies lay on the floor, asleep or high as kites. She raised the picture above her and said as loud as she could: 'Has anyone seen this girl?'

A young woman, about twenty years old – it was hard to tell – looked up at Sinead and squinted in the dark. 'Wit's it worth?'

Sinead sighed. Of course, she was bribing her. It was something Sinead herself would have done in the situation. 'Twenty quid.'

'Double and I'll have a look,' the girl replied, squinting more as she looked at the picture. 'A cannae see it fae here, bring it closer, eh?'

Sinead took a step closer, her keys gripped tightly in her hand in the other pocket, ready to defend if this girl would mug her. It was possible, Sinead had been on that side of things herself.

She stood above the girl as she leaned in and studied the picture. 'Aye,' the word was long and drawn out. 'I hink a dae know her. She's pals wae Kassy. But she never came back efter a job waw a punter an a no seen this lassie in the photae since either. That wis a few days ago, a hink.'

Sinead crouched down in front of the girl and looked at her through narrowed eyes, surprised she hadn't asked for cash before giving up such information.

'Kassy?'

The girl nodded. 'Aye. Pal ae mine; well, no really a pal. More a colleague. We worked Blythswood Square taegether. She hudnae been in the game long. A taught her aw she needed tae know. Watched her get in this guy's motor, that lassie in the photae wis wae her but didnae get in. She walked doon, as if she wis gawn doon tae the Kelvingrove end ae the city. Like a said, a huvnae seen her since.'

Sinead took a breath through her mouth and tried to remember if she recognised this girl she was talking to. And the name, Kassy: it sounded familiar, but then, there were so many prostitutes and junkies around that Sinead had mixed with, even if she had come across her, she probably wouldn't remember her even if she'd been sober at the time.

'Can you remember what the car looked like?' Sinead pressed.

The girl pursed her lips and shook her head. 'It wis dark and a wiz just aboot tae take on a client maself. I didnae pay much attention.'

Sinead sighed loudly and nodded. 'The colour? Size? Anything?'

'It wiz an auld banger, that's aw a remember. Sorry, hen,' she said. 'A hink it wiz a mad, green colour.'

'Mad green?' Sinead questioned. 'Mad as in you were off your face when you saw it? Or what?'

The girl sniggered. 'Nah, a don't get aff ma tits when am on the game. A just mean, like, the kinda auld army green, like camouflage, if ye get me?'

'Long car, short car? Boot, no boot?'

The girl sighed in annoyance. 'A said a don't know. If a did, a'd tell ye. A don't like it when lassies go missin' efter a job. Only really means wan hing and let's face it, it's been happening a lot roon here.'

Sinead closed her eyes and placed her hands on her knees before standing. 'Thanks for your help.'

The girl looked up at her and it seemed like she was going to ask Sinead something.

'Ye clean?' she finally said.

Sinead nodded. 'Trying to be.'

'How'd ye dae it without gawn mental? I cannae go a few oors without wantin a hit.'

Sinead remembered the feeling well. In fact, it felt like that for her right now. 'It's not without difficulty. But I need to get my life back on track. There's more out there than this shithole.'

The girl shrugged. 'Is there? I dunno as much.'

'That's the addiction talking. Telling you it's easier to stay here and keep using. And in some ways, it is. Getting clean is hard.'

'How long ye been aff the smack then?' the girl asked, looking at Sinead's bare forearms and eyeing the needle scars.

'Two weeks.'

'Fuck, an yer back here? Ye no hink it's a bit stupid coming here in case ye end up back on it?'

It was like the girl had read Sinead's mind. 'It's worth it if I can get some information on my missing niece.'

'I wish I shared yer optimism,' she said, pulling a bag out from the back pocket of her dirty jeans, opening a cigarette tin that lay on the floor in front of her. Sinead turned her back on the girl and looked around. She didn't want to see someone shooting up in front of her. It made her feel sick and excited at the same time.

It seemed there was no one else to talk to about Molly Rose's picture. She got lucky with this girl being somewhat *compos mentis*.

'Oi, wit aboot the money?' the girl suddenly remembered.

Sinead sighed. If she gave it to her, she'd be feeding the habit; contributing to her inability to get clean. But if she didn't, all hell could break loose. Sinead reached into her pocket and counted out forty pounds. She dropped it on the floor at the girl's feet and said, 'Do yourself a favour, eh? Use that to buy yourself some food. You look like you've not eaten in weeks.'

The girl ignored the comment and stuffed the money into her own pocket. 'I hope ye find yer niece.'

Sinead headed for the metal door and opened it. As she turned back, the girl she'd spoken with was in the process of finding a vein in her arm. By the looks of her, it wouldn't be long before she'd be injecting into her toes.

Stepping outside and closing the door behind her, she climbed the stairs and took in a huge lungful of fresh air. She never wanted to smell the scent of a drug den ever again.

Chapter 39

He waited until that time of night when no one was out other than the homeless. The streets were dead still. Darkness covered the city as it slept. This was his chance to dump the girl before he got in touch with the Hunter family.

He'd parked the car at the furthest point in the car park, right beside the road bridge over the River Kelvin. This part of the car park wasn't lit, so there was no light to illuminate what he was doing.

He got out of the car and went around to the boot. The smell was unbearable, but he knew that it was now or never.

It had been tricky to undress the dead girl. He'd considered cutting the clothes off her, but he needed them intact. Redressing her had been equally difficult. Her limbs were so stiff they wouldn't move. And she was heavy. But he'd somehow managed to dress her in Molly Rose's clothes. He'd made sure to get this part done quickly before her internal organs started to leak out of her. He'd done his research to keep mess to a minimum.

Next to his car was a tall, metal fence with a few spokes missing. Behind that was a large bush, where he had planned to dump Kassy. It wouldn't be easy, but he'd reversed the car up to the fence, so all he had to do was drag her out and lay her in there. In theory.

Bending his knees, Charlie pulled Kassy out of the boot and dumped her on the ground by the fence. His back felt like it was going to snap with the weight of her.

He took a breath and managed to find the strength to manoeuvre her into the bush, so only her black trainers were sticking out. In the dark, they'd be hard to spot. He'd had his eye on this area of the car park for a few days. No one seemed to use it so it was the perfect spot. She wouldn't be found by anyone other than those he intended.

He took the envelope out of the car and placed it inside her jacket. He'd send the text when he was back at the lockup from the pay-as-you-go mobile phone he had in his backpack. He couldn't wait to see Janey's reaction when she found the body. It would give him great pleasure to see the look on her face – to see her looking around for him.

He'd already typed out the text. All he had to do was press send.

Chapter 40

Staring up at the ceiling as she lay in bed next to Oliver, she wondered how he could sleep through what was going on. This wasn't a usual missing person case. The person claiming to have Molly Rose had demanded a million pounds in cash from Janey, who said she could sort it. Orla had questioned Janey, and gone over and over it in her head. What the hell was it that Janey did to warrant being able to come up with that kind of money? And why was it the police were seemingly doing nothing other than putting out missing-person notices on their websites and social media?

Now, Janey hadn't been in touch since she'd dropped the bag. It was the next morning and there had been nothing. Something had gone wrong, Orla was sure of it.

Glancing at her phone and still seeing no messages from Janey, she threw the duvet off her and headed downstairs. As she walked into the kitchen, she jumped when she saw Sinead at the table.

'Jesus,' she hissed, placing her hand on her chest.

'Sorry,' Sinead replied. 'I couldn't sleep.'

Composing herself. Orla flicked the kettle on and sat down at the table in front of her sister. 'I didn't hear you come in. Were you out all night looking for Molly Rose?'

'Well, not all night.'

'Was Janey with you?'

Sinead shook her head. 'No. Have you heard from her since yesterday?'

'Not since she said she'd done the drop. I think something's gone wrong, Sinead. Why would she not get in contact after that?'

'I don't know,' Sinead said, sipping at a mug of coffee. 'But I'm sure there's an explanation.'

'*She's* the reason Molly Rose is gone. Why aren't you angry about that, Sinead? Why are you hellbent on giving her a chance?'

Sinead looked deflated. 'I'm hellbent on finding your daughter, Orla. And I got some information last night. It's not much, but it could help.'

Orla blinked. 'And?'

'I went to one of my old… hang-outs,' Sinead started. 'I spoke to a young girl. She looked at the picture of Molly Rose and said she recognised her as a mate of a girl called Kassy. The thing is, she hasn't seen Kassy in a few days. Apparently, the last time she saw her, she was getting into a client's car.'

Orla frowned. 'A client?'

Sinead raised a brow. 'This Kassy, she was a prostitute up at Blysthwood.'

Orla felt like her heart was about to stop. 'Oh my god.'

'Right, don't automatically think that Molly Rose was doing the same. It's not like it's in her nature to do something so reckless.'

Orla sat down before she fell. 'Not in her nature? Sinead, she disappeared for two weeks because I wouldn't allow you back in the house. I think she was looking for any excuse if I'm honest. She was still so hung up on Dean, I think she just wanted an out. So to rebel in *that* way…'

'No,' Sinead said with force. 'She wouldn't. She couldn't.'

'How do you know that? We didn't think she'd ever just up and leave. And now we learn she's been hanging around with a prostitute who hasn't been seen since she got into a man's car? What did this girl say about Molly Rose?'

Sinead breathed slowly. 'That she didn't get into the car and instead headed in the direction of Kelvingrove, which is where you said she asked to be picked up?'

Orla nodded, thinking back to that moment. 'Yeah, that's right.'

'The girl I spoke to said that the car was old and the colour was army green.'

Orla pictured the car in her head. 'Army green isn't a standard colour for a car these days, is it? We could get the police to do a search?'

Sinead nodded. 'Definitely could. I know it's not much to go on, sorry I couldn't get more out of her.'

Orla looked at her twin sister who was sat across the table from her and, for the first time in years, she felt sorry for her. They'd been close the way twins are supposed to be up until the point they were separated. It wasn't Sinead's fault she'd been sent to a shitty family who didn't care about the kids in their care. It was a wonder that social services hadn't been called.

'I'm sorry,' Orla said as guilt began to creep in.

'What are you sorry about?' Sinead asked.

'For not helping you when you needed it the most. The experiences we both had have led us to this point. I should have been there for you.'

A look of disbelief crossed Sinead's face. 'I stole from you. I lied to your face over and over, and I took drugs when Molly Rose was in the house. That's not something I'm proud of, or something I even understand myself if I'm honest. I get why you distanced yourself. You were protecting your family.'

'I could have done more to help you get clean instead of giving you money and trying to forget that you exist. I basically enabled you to stay addicted to heroin.'

It was the first time that Orla had actually looked at Sinead as her sister and not a problem.

'I could have tried to get clean. I could have walked away at any point and asked for real help, but I didn't. I should have spoken to our social worker back then, made them aware of what was going on.'

'We were still kids, Sinead. You were let down by the system. We were let down by Janey.' Orla felt emotionally drained going over it all while trying to hope she would get to see Molly Rose again. 'I was trying to do the right thing but instead, I let you down just like everyone else did. You realise none of this would be happening right now if Janey hadn't given us away like some old, unwanted clothes.'

Sinead shook her head. 'No, I don't think that's how she saw it.'

'And what makes you think that?'

'Think about it. Do you believe she would have given us up if she had any other choice? Under what circumstances would you choose to give Molly Rose away as a baby? You'd have to be at rock bottom, wouldn't you?'

'I'm there now,' Orla scoffed.

'Exactly. So, I don't think she wanted to give us up. I think she wanted to keep us. Why else would she come back? Why would she be here now?'

'Yeah, but why didn't she come before all this? She could have come and found us, Sinead. She could have made an effort. But she didn't. And who knows, maybe you could have had a different life?'

Sinead shook her head. She looked exhausted. 'You make it sound as though it was someone else's fault that I became a junkie, Orla. No one twisted my arm. I pierced my own skin with that first needle. And it felt fucking brilliant. That's why I kept going back for more and why I'm here in this state now. It's not your fault. It's not Janey's fault. It's not that fucking couple who called themselves foster carers' fault. It's down to me.'

Reaching across the table, Sinead took Orla's hand in her own and held on to her. A lump formed in Orla's throat. She felt a sliver of pride as, finally, Sinead was beginning to take responsibility and show some remorse for her actions. But with that pride came shame. For so long, Orla hadn't taken *any* responsibility for caring for Sinead. What kind of person did that make her? What kind of *sister* did that make her?

The flick of the kettle switch echoed loudly and broke the momentary silence between them and Orla blinked away the tears. She got up and pulled a mug out of the cupboard.

'Want another?'

Sinead shook her head and gave a gentle laugh. 'No thanks. Don't want to swap one addiction for another.'

Orla smiled a little and made a strong coffee. Just as she was about to sit back down, her mobile buzzed on the table.

She glanced down at the screen and her heart froze.

'Oh my god. Sinead, it's an unknown number.'

Sinead got up and moved around to the other side of the table. She glanced down at the phone over Orla's shoulder as she opened the text.

> Mum, it's me. You need to come.
> He's going to kill me. Please hurry.
> Bring Janey. He wants Janey.
> Bunhouse Road.
> Now. No police.

'Jesus Christ,' Orla whispered. Sinead was already running up the stairs and shouting to Oliver.

Orla couldn't breathe as she read the text over and over again.

Before she could think, Orla was being pulled to her feet by Sinead. Oliver was pacing the floor, with Orla's phone in her hand.

'How do we know it's even her? It could be a trap,' Oliver said.

'That's a risk I'm willing to take,' Orla said, snapping out of her haze of panic. Sinead had her phone to her ear and Orla watched.

'Janey, it's me, Sinead. We've had a message from someone claiming to be Molly Rose. She said you've to come with us. Now.'

Sinead disappeared out of the kitchen and was back quickly with Orla's coat. Orla caught it when it was thrown to her.

'We need to go, right now.'

'We need to phone the police,' Oliver said.

'No!' both Orla and Sinead shouted.

'This is *clearly* a trap,' Oliver said, placing his hands on Orla's shoulders. 'You need to think about this logically.

Enough is enough, Orla. Janey clearly hasn't done what she said she could otherwise she'd be with us now. If you go there, he could kill you.'

'He could kill Molly Rose if I don't do what the text message says. You don't have to come. But if there's a chance that I can save our daughter, especially after everything we've been through lately, then I will.'

Chapter 41

'Kristo said he'll meet us there,' Janey said as she drove along the A82 from their house in Rhu. Ciaran was sat next to her in the passenger seat.

'I wish you'd have let me drive, Janey,' he said.

'I can drive faster than you can,' Janey replied.

'Yeah, that's my point. You're going to kill us both before we even get there.'

Janey bit her bottom lip as she shot out on to the Stoneymollan roundabout, having seen that there was nothing coming from her right. The Defender handled well and she was confident that she'd get them there in one piece. She had to, to help Molly Rose.

'You're so dramatic,' Janey said as she got the car up to a hundred miles per hour. The town of Renton was a blur on the left-hand side and, before she knew it, she'd slowed the car down to thirty as she passed Police Scotland Dumbarton division.

'You're going to get us pulled over,' Ciaran said.

'No, I'm not. And even if they do pull us, it's likely they'll be one of ours and let us go on our way.'

Having failed to catch Charlie picking up the bag the previous day, Janey hadn't been able to face Orla or Sinead. She'd promised she wouldn't fuck this up and she had. Instead of going to Orla and telling her what had happened, she'd gone home, switched off her phone and buried her face into a pillow. Something she didn't often do when things went wrong. But this wasn't just any little thing. This was the life of her granddaughter. Now, Janey was going to have to face more questions. Where had she been? What had she been doing? She'd had Kristo and the team scouring the city looking for Charlie, but it was like he'd vanished. Ciaran had tried to make Janey see sense and go to Orla, but she just couldn't face it. She'd been a letdown to the girls their entire life. Now this.

The journey on Google Maps told them it would take forty-nine minutes to get from the house in Rhu to Bunhouse Road where Orla had been instructed to go. They'd left the house twenty minutes earlier and the map said it would only take a further fifteen to get there based on the speed she was driving at.

She took a breath and tried not to see the unimaginable images going through her mind. What Charlie could do to Molly Rose didn't bear thinking about.

'You think he's worked out that it's counterfeit cash?' Ciaran asked.

'Aye,' she said. 'I do and that's why he's luring us all there. Ciaran, he's either already killed her or he's about to. But I'm prepared for that.'

Janey had her pistol in the inside pocket of her coat, ready to take Charlie's head off when they came face to face – *if* they came face to face.

'Me too,' Ciaran said.

'I'm surprised Orla called me,' Janey said. 'Especially since I went AWOL last night.'

'Considering what might go down today, I don't think that will even cross her mind,' Ciaran said.

Passing through Clydebank, they approached the sign indicating that they'd crossed from West Dunbartonshire to Glasgow City and Janey knew they were close.

She pulled Orla's number up on the screen and she answered after the first ring.

'Are you close?' Orla asked.

'I'm five minutes away. Listen, Orla. Don't approach that street without me. He wants *me*. Not you. Do you understand?'

'Oliver has locked the car doors. He won't let me out until you get here,' Orla replied. 'If he's hurt a single hair on her head, Janey, I'll personally hold you responsible. And where the fuck have you been? You just went off the radar after you told me you'd done that drop-off. Did something happen?'

A rage boiled deep in the pit of her stomach, but not with Orla. With Charlie. Wherever he was, he'd be laughing at Janey's misery.

'He won't have hurt her, Orla. He doesn't want Molly Rose. He only has her to get to me.' Although Janey knew what evil lurked inside Charlie, so she knew that wasn't strictly true.

Orla fell silent on the other end of the line.

'An employee of mine is going to meet us there,' Janey continued.

'An employee? This isn't a fucking job interview,' Orla spat.

'He's more like security. He'll be there before me. When we arrive, wait for my instructions. Do you understand that, Orla? It's very important you don't rush in. We don't even know what we're looking for yet.'

'She's *my* daughter, Janey. I'll do what is best.'

Ciaran sat forward and placed a hand on the dashboard. 'No, Orla. Listen to her. I don't have to reiterate that this guy is dangerous. He has your daughter and, really, he could be capable of doing anything because he already has that money. I'm sorry, Orla, but there's a strong possibility that Molly Rose might already have come to harm. He has no use for her now and if he lets her go, she could go to the police. He's not going to risk that. Is he? And we don't even know that it was Molly Rose who sent that text. It could have been him, luring you into a trap of some kind. You need to do what we tell you.'

'We will.' Sinead's voice came from the background. 'Orla, you need to try to stay calm. We don't want Molly Rose to come to more harm. If Janey says to wait for her instructions, we should do that.'

Janey's phone screen flashed up a message from Kristo that he'd arrived at Bunhouse Road.

'My security guard is there,' Janey said. 'I'll be there soon. Do not get out of the car until I arrive.'

Janey ended the call and looked at Ciaran. 'He might be planning to kill all of us.'

'I'd like to see him fucking try,' Ciaran growled.

Janey's phone rang again and Kristo's name again flashed across the screen.

'Janey, I'm here. Bunhouse Road is a car park at the back of the old transport museum. I can see Orla in her car with Sinead and her husband, they're just at the entrance. What do you want me to do?'

Janey glanced over at Ciaran as she moved on to the express way from Crow Road. 'Do a perimeter check of the car park and the building. We'll be there in five minutes. Do *not* allow Orla to go looking for Molly Rose.

I don't think she or Charlie will even be there, if I'm honest. I think this is a trick.'

'Okay. I'll see you when you get here,' Kristo said, before hanging up.

'If Molly Rose isn't here, what do you think he has planned?' Ciaran asked.

Janey shook her head and sighed loudly as she pulled the car on to the B808 past the West Village student accommodation building. 'It's all about money, Ciaran. He's sick in the head. You can trust me on that one.'

Ciaran licked his tongue over his teeth and tutted. 'If he thinks he can mess with you and get away with it, he's fucking delusional.'

Janey felt a smile raise the corners of her mouth, but she suppressed it. Ciaran was always one for sitting back and letting Janey do her thing because he knew she could handle herself in any situation. This was different. This wasn't a business issue; this was personal and Ciaran was slowly starting to get annoyed.

She kept her eyes on the road as she turned onto Benalder Street. The crossed the bridge, turned on to Old Dumbarton Road and then Bunhouse Road.

'That's Orla's car,' Janey said, pulling into the car park. She switched off the ignition and got out of the car, with Ciaran climbing out of the passenger side and walking around to be next to her.

'Janey? Ciaran?' Kristo said, walking towards them from the Argyle Street end of the road. 'I've done a quick check around the area. There's something down at the very end of the car park where the bridge goes over the river. I couldn't quite make it out but I think we should take a look.'

Janey nodded. 'Thanks, Kristo.'

Turning to go to Orla's car, the window was already down, and Orla had a look of anger and despair on her face.

'I'll climb out of the fucking window if you don't unlock this door, Oliver,' she said.

Janey bent down a little and took Orla's face in her hands. Orla looked up at her, and she could see the same eyes staring back at her that she had when Orla had first been born. The eyes never change.

'Orla. Listen to me. And *really* listen. This is *not* a game. Charlie isn't some two-bit chancer trying to fuck with your head. He's dangerous and you can trust me on that. I've witnessed first-hand just how dangerous.'

Janey felt Ciaran's eyes on her and, when she stole a glance, he looked confused.

Orla pulled away and said: 'I know he's fucking dangerous. I heard that man there—' she pointed at Kristo '—tell you that he saw something down there. She's *my* daughter. I'm going with you.'

Janey stood up straight and took a deep breath. There was no way she was going to change Orla's mind.

'Okay. There's one condition. You stay by my side the entire time and if anything happens you do exactly as I say. I mean it, Orla. If you can't agree, then you're not coming with me.'

Orla nodded and the car unlocked. She got out of the car, and Sinead and Oliver got out with her.

'We'll all go. Molly Rose would want us all to do this together, whatever *this* is,' Oliver said.

Janey nodded. 'Right, get behind me. All of you. Kristo will lead us down to the bridge at the end of the car park. If you see anything, or anyone, unusual, tell me or Ciaran, who will be behind you.'

Orla's expression had changed. She wasn't angry any more. She was terrified. Janey shared the same fear.

Kristo nodded, turned and led them to the far end of the car park.

Chapter 42

Charlie stood in one of the top-floor apartments at the luxury apartment building and watched as Janey and her pathetic little tribe walked along the road toward where he'd dumped her body. Even though the Metropolitan Lofts, as it was named, had its own lobby with a reception desk and supposed security guard, the security itself was next to zero and his ability to force his way into the building and into one of the unoccupied apartments at the top which he knew would overlook the perfect spot had been easy.

His breath was laboured as the excitement began to build the closer they got to the site where he'd dumped the body. He'd watched the man who seemed to be working for Janey discover the site first, although he'd done so from up on the bridge above the car park. If he knew it was a body, he wouldn't have led all of them to it.

The inched closer and Charlie opened the window. He wanted to hear their reaction. He'd stick his head out of the window if he had to or, better, climb out onto the roof terrace and listen from there.

He had the untraceable pay-as-you-go phone in his hand, waiting for the call he knew would come. The mobile he'd text Orla Hunter from, pretending to be Molly Rose, was in the pocket of the prostitute he'd killed to show Janey that he was deadly serious about his plan.

They all stopped, the man at the front held up his hand to indicate for everyone to remain still. But Janey didn't. She stepped forward. Slow, steady steps.

She bent and stared down at Kassy. Then she looked back, and a feeling of euphoria filled his chest as Orla started screaming.

Chapter 43

Janey watched as Sinead wrapped her arms around Orla from behind and tried to hold her up.

Orla crumpled in Sinead's arms and fell to the ground. Oliver had turned his back at the sight of the body lying partially behind the fence and into the bush.

Janey edged closer and peered down at the body of the female who'd been dumped, seemingly by Charlie, and studied her carefully. She'd seen enough dead bodies to last her a lifetime. In some ways, she'd become desensitised to the sight.

She breathed a sigh of relief. 'It's okay,' Janey said. 'It's *not* Molly Rose. It's not her.'

Sinead closed her eyes and took a breath. A sob escaped her. 'Are you sure?'

'It's not her. I promise.'

'But the clothes. The trainers. They all belong to Molly Rose,' Orla sobbed. 'The skull stamp on the bottom… she always did that when she bought new shoes.'

Janey looked back down at the partially covered face of the girl in the bushes and was certain it wasn't her granddaughter. The hair wasn't the same colour. This girl's hair was black, Molly Rose had blonde hair.

'Oliver,' Orla said, 'go and look. Please.'

Oliver glanced down at Orla and nodded. He walked over to where Janey was crouched over the body and looked down at the girl. He let out a sound Janey had never heard in a man before. It was similar to the sound she'd made when she watched her babies being taken away to a new life.

'Molly Rose didn't have any tattoos. This person does. See that,' Oliver said after recovering, pointing down at the left wrist. 'Molly Rose didn't have that. It's not Molly Rose.' The words floated on laboured breaths. 'It's not our girl.'

'Did you just say Kassy?' Sinead asked, staring at Oliver as he moved away from the body.

'That's what the tattoo says,' he replied.

Sinead stared up at the sky and let out a long breath. 'That's the name of the girl Molly Rose was hanging around with. I spoke to someone last night who'd seen Molly Rose with this girl who's a prostitute up at Blysthwood. She said she hasn't seen Kassy in a couple of days.'

Janey got up and moved towards Sinead who was still down on the ground with Orla in her arms, holding on as if they were hanging off the edge of a cliff.

'Who told you this?' Janey pressed.

'I don't know her name. When you were MIA last night, I went out to see if I could find anyone who knew where Molly Rose might be and I went to one of my old haunts. Spoke to a girl and that's what she told me.'

Janey closed her eyes. 'He's murdered this girl and tried to make it look like Molly Rose.'

Sinead frowned and Orla seemed like she was away on her own planet. 'Why would he do that?'

'Because he's sick in the head,' Janey replied.

'So that girl over there must be Kassy if that's what the tattoo says on her wrist,' Sinead suggested.

'It would be too much of a coincidence, wouldn't it? Question now is, where is Molly Rose?' Janey replied.

Orla sobbed and Janey felt like her heart was being pulled from her chest.

'It's okay, Orla. It's not her,' Janey said, moving Orla's hair out of her face.

'So where is she, then? And why would this person lead us to a dead body who isn't Molly Rose?'

Janey raised her eyes and found Sinead's. 'I don't know, but I'm going to find out. I'll find her, Orla. And I'll bring her back to you. I'll die before I let anything happen to her.'

Janey stood up and felt tears pool in her eyes. Ciaran saw this and took hold of her lower arm. 'Janey, why don't the girls go home? We can contact the police about this and then keep looking for Molly Rose.'

Janey looked at her husband and, for the first time since the girls were taken from her, she let a tear fall.

'Yes,' she said, wiping it away quickly and composing herself. Crying was a waste of time – it wouldn't get them anywhere. She had to be the strong one in all of this. It was her fault they were all in this state in the first place. Her fault that a young girl who had nothing to do with any of them had lost her life directly because of Janey. The guilt she felt was staggering.

'Oliver, take Orla and Sinead home. I'll phone the police about the body, about the text. Someone will likely come out to the house to take a statement and then we can get back to focusing on Molly Rose. Okay?'

Oliver nodded. He'd already composed himself and lifted Orla off the ground of the car park. Sinead let go and they walked together back to the car. Janey had expected Orla to protest, to tell Janey that she didn't trust her or the police given everything that had gone on. But she didn't, she was too busy crying and by the look of it, she was in shock.

As they got into the car, Janey waited for them to disappear out of sight before heading back to the body.

She bent down over the girl and gritted her teeth. 'Another senseless, brutal murder of an innocent girl. By another senseless fuck who calls himself a man.'

Her attention was drawn to something poking out from under the girl's jacket. It looked like the corner of an envelope.

'Kristo, get my gloves, please,' she said. Kristo handed her a pair of surgical gloves. She snapped them on and pulled the envelope out. It was addressed to her.

She stood up and opened it carefully, tipping it upside down, and allowing the paper inside to slide out and fall onto her hand.

Janey carefully unfolded the paper and began to read aloud.

Chapter 44

Janey

You thought I didn't know, didn't you? You thought that when Finn sent me away, I'd disappeared from your life and you'd never have to think about me or see me ever again. Well, you were fucking wrong. I know everything. I know about the girls, that I'm their real dad.

I bet you're wondering how I found out about them. I've always known, Janey. After Finn chucked me out, I kept an eye on you. I didn't want you muddying my name like the rest of those lying little bitches. I watched you grow bigger. I watched you pretend you were fine after you gave them away. I could have intervened, but why would I do that? The last thing I ever wanted was to be a dad. Sprogs are a pain in the arse, an inconvenience.

You should have got rid of the fucking sprogs while you were pregnant, you stupid fucking bitch. Maybe I should have come back and shoved you down a set of stairs myself.

But I'm glad I didn't, because now I have fucking leverage. I can use them against you, hurt them if I want and there is nothing you can do about it unless you do what I say.

I can't wait to watch you suffer. You deserve everything that's coming to you, Janey. And when they're all dead, I'm coming for you and the rest of my money I was due back then.

There is a mobile phone in the pocket of the girl's jacket. Take it out and ring the number logged in the contacts. And I'll be watching to make sure you do it. If you don't do it, I'll kill Molly Rose right now.

Charlie.

Chapter 45

She crushed the paper in her hand and looked up at the sky. Janey tried to breathe, tried to remain as calm as possible. She'd had no choice but to be calm while reading it out aloud; going into a fit of panic or rage wasn't going to help anyone. The idea that it was all out in the open now made her feel sick and relieved in equal measures. She'd been holding on to this for so long. She hadn't hesitated when she reached the part that Charlie revealed he was the girl's biological father. What would be the point?

'Janey?' Ciaran said, but his voice sounded like an echo in the distance. She felt his hand on her shoulder and she turned to face him. 'Janey? He's the girl's dad?'

She felt sick. All these years she'd kept it a secret. No one knew. Not even Finn. She hadn't put him on the birth certificate, he wasn't mentioned to anyone. But that didn't matter now, because he'd known all along.

She could barely get her voice above a whisper. 'Yes.'

'But…' Ciaran said, seemingly unable to say another word.

'I don't have time for questions, Ciaran. Not yet.'

She crouched down and carefully took the mobile phone from inside the girl's pocket like the letter instructed and stood up again. She walked into the centre of the car park and looked up at the student buildings in front of her, on the other side of the River Kelvin. It was the only place he could be that he'd have a clear view of them.

Holding the phone up in the air, she spun slowly. If he was watching her, then he could see exactly what she was doing.

She opened the contacts in the phone and selected the number saved. She started to type out a text.

> Fuck you, Charlie. It's not Molly Rose you
> want to kill. It's me. So, come and get me.

She hit send and slid the phone into her pocket.

'What are you doing?' Ciaran asked.

'I'm swapping places with Molly Rose. He's using her to get to me and I'm not having it, Ciaran.'

Ciaran scoffed and shook his head. 'No way. That's not happening.'

'Ciaran's right, Janey. You cannot put yourself at risk like that,' Kristo said.

'And what's the alternative?' Janey asked. 'I continue to play his games? No, he's not doing this anymore. This stops, now!'

The phone buzzed in her pocket. It buzzed again. He was calling her. She took it out, pressed answer and placed it to her ear.

'Charlie?'

'That wasn't a very nice way to start a text to your brother who you haven't seen for years,' Charlie said.

'It was necessary. And just to make things clear, you're not my brother. You never were. Brothers don't do what *you* did to me.'

There was a stretch of silence. And then: 'And what was that?'

Her voice was calm, calmer than she'd expected. The last time Janey had been with Charlie, things had been chaotic. Traumatic. She thought that would all come flooding back when she heard his voice. Ignoring his question, because he knew the answer, she said: 'Let her go, Charlie. It's me you're angry with, not Molly Rose.'

'I could, but I don't want to.'

Janey looked at each of the windows in the building in front of her. From where she was standing, she could see at least a hundred sets of windows. He could be in any of those rooms, overlooking the car park.

'Let me take her place.'

Ciaran tried to grab the phone from her, but she snatched her hand away and gave him a warning glance. Kristo looked just as frustrated.

'Oh, your husband didn't like that, did he?' Charlie laughed loudly. 'Or is he your security guard? I can't tell which is which.'

'So, you *can* see me?' Janey replied. 'You never used to be scared of me, Charlie.'

'What makes you think I am?'

'Well,' Janey said, beginning to pace slowly, her heels clicking on the concrete. 'If you weren't, you'd be face to face with me right now, wouldn't you? And you'd be quite happy for me to swap places with Molly Rose.'

The sound of his laughter on the other end of the line riled her, but she kept it beneath the surface.

'No, you've got it wrong. I'm not scared. I'm in control. You have no cards to play, Janey. I *have* Molly Rose.'

Janey stopped pacing and nodded. 'Yes, you do. But you also have a million pounds in cash. You could go anywhere you wanted, change your identity and no one would find you.'

Charlie gave a sarcastic laugh. 'Ha, aye, like you'd ever let that happen. You'd have your men go to the ends of the earth to find me.'

'If I was going to do that, I'd have done it thirty-eight years ago after you raped me.'

Ciaran's face fell and Kristo turned away just slightly.

'Tell me, Charlie, if Finn gave you so much back then to disappear with, why have you come back now? Why do you feel like you need to take my granddaughter hostage to up your funds now?'

Charlie was quiet. She'd hit a nerve and she didn't know which one. The rape comment or the mention of funds.

'Did you piss it all up the wall, Charlie? I remember the state you were in before you left. Drinking all the time, aggressive with everyone. In fact, that's what you always were, wasn't it? An aggressive, nasty little boy who thought he was a man because he'd been taken in by Finn Hallahan.'

'Finn *pushed* me to be that person.'

'Are you sure it's not because it's in your blood? I mean, your own dad battered you so much I'm surprised you don't have some kind of lasting brain damage. Or maybe that's why you're the way you are. Or are you a monster because you're the product of rape yourself? I mean, I never wanted to give those girls up, but maybe it's a good thing I did. If I hadn't, maybe they'd have turned into monsters just like you.' She didn't mean what she said about the girls – of course she didn't. But antagonising him was her only weapon now.

Charlie grunted and said: 'I'll fucking kill you, *bitch.*'

It was Janey's turn to laugh, although it was forced. In truth, she felt sick.

'No, you won't. How could you get your hands on my fortunes if you did that? A million is a drop in the ocean to someone like me, Charlie. Finn taught me well. I have assets, shares and interests all over the place. I mean, I didn't even want to take over the Hallahan business. But knowing that you would never get your hands on it was enough for me, so I did what I had to do.'

Janey thought back to that time. Getting to take over the business wasn't what she wanted. She'd wanted her babies, but that was never an option for her. Charlie was never in line to take the reins, but he didn't have to know that, did he?

'But it's not my money you want; not really. See the two men I'm with? They're not the only men I have working for me. I have employees up and down the country, Charlie. All men who would tear you to pieces if they were stood face to face with you now. If anything happens to Molly Rose, you won't get a penny more out of me. But you would be signing your own death certificate. So, tell me where Molly Rose is. I'll come and pick her up. Then we can discuss more cash.'

'No.'

Janey was beginning to lose patience. 'Okay then. Why don't you come down here and meet me. I mean, you're up there in one of those flats, watching me, aren't you? It's the only place you can see us from. I could arrange for the building to be stormed and have you brought to me. Or we could do this amicably. It's your call.'

Ciaran was making a call now. Kristo hadn't left her side. He was quiet. Trying to listen.

'Is that what your husband is doing now? Arranging for your men to come and get me? It's too late, Janey. I'm already gone. And by the time you figure out where I am, Molly Rose will already be dead.'

Janey covered the mouthpiece and quietly said to Kristo, 'Get over to that building and get their CCTV pulled. We need to follow him and get my granddaughter back.'

Kristo ran back to his car and Ciaran was still on his phone arranging for every single one of her employees to be out looking for Charlie.

'We'll see about that, Charlie.'

'Oh, we will, don't you worry about that.'

Janey gripped the phone tightly in her hand and started to walk back to the Defender. Ciaran followed her and she got into the driver seat with the phone still at her ear.

'Oh, I always wondered this, Janey. Maybe you could enlighten me on something I've been asking myself for years now.'

'What's that?'

'Do the *girls* know where they came from?'

Janey kept her expression neutral. If he was still watching her, she wanted to make him think that she wasn't fazed by his question. She felt Ciaran's eyes on her and, when she looked up, his face asked a thousand questions.

'No, they do not. And they never will.'

'Funny you should say that. Because I've sent an email to the business email address that Orla is the owner of, detailing *exactly* where they're from. I think they should know what went on between us, don't you? I've tagged it as urgent. She and Sinead have a right to know who their dad is.'

Janey felt the colour drain from her face as the line went dead.

'Janey?' Ciaran said. 'Why didn't you tell me what happened to you?'

She opened the door and began to heave bile from her stomach. The adrenaline coursing through her made her body tremble and shake.

'*Janey*, are you okay?'

'I didn't tell anyone. Not even Finn. I never wanted to be chained for the rest of my life to what he did to me. And it had worked, until now.'

'Fuck,' Ciaran whispered. 'I'll fucking kill him.'

Janey shook her head. 'No, you won't. That's my job and I should have done it years ago. Christ knows how many women he's abused over the years. I mean, look at that girl he dumped back there. And he has Molly Rose. I couldn't bear the idea that he...'

Ciaran took Janey's hand. 'It won't come to that. Kristo is on it. I have a team of men out there right now on his case. They're on their way to the student building to get the CCTV to track his movements. This is it, Janey. He's done. We'll get him today.'

Janey nodded and swallowed back the growing lump in her throat.

'I have every faith our team will get him. But I want you to put the message out there that when he's found, no one touches him until I've spoken with him.'

Ciaran closed his eyes and took a breath. When he opened them, he looked straight at her and replied: 'I don't think that's a good idea, Janey.'

'I said *no one* touches him until I've spoken to him. Get that out to the team. Understood?'

Janey didn't blink as she watched Ciaran process her direct instructions.

He was hesitant, but nodded slowly and said: 'Okay. But I have one condition before I do this.'

Janey looked at him, wondering what he was going to say.

'I'm there when you come face to face with him.'

'There are things I want to say to him about what happened between us, Ciaran. Things you might not want to hear.'

'Hey.' He softened his voice, leaned across and placed his hand over hers. 'There's nothing he can say that can disturb me any more than what he's put you through. And if I'm there, he can't hurt you.'

Janey felt her stomach flip. There was no one in the world she was frightened of. She wasn't even frightened of Charlie. But the fact he'd tried to get involved in demolishing the already fragile relationship she had with the girls scared her. He didn't give two shits about them. All he wanted was to hurt Janey – have that last bit of control over her.

'You can wait outside the door. This is between him and me. I will not bow down to him, Ciaran. I'm Finn Hallahan's daughter. He raised me to stand up for myself and it's something I've always done in my life except for on that day. I should have done that back then. I owe it to Finn to do that now.'

Her own words echoed in her mind. There were two days back then she should have stood up for herself. The day Charlie raped her and the day her babies were taken away. She should have been stronger against Charle. She should have been the one to raise the girls. And she'd have done a good job. Now, she had to get this right, if she had a smidgen of hope of making amends with them.

A look of sadness crossed Ciaran's face then. 'No, Janey. You don't owe it to Finn, or any other man for that matter. You owe it to yourself.'

Chapter 46

Molly Rose sat in silence as she waited for her captor to come back. Each time she heard or felt his presence, she braced herself for death. She hoped it would be quick and painless, but from the knowledge she'd gathered about this man who called himself Charlie, she doubted he'd be so caring in his delivery.

A noise that sounded like a football being hit off a shutter outside made her freeze. And then came the sound of laughing, joking and loud chatter. Male voices. They were close.

The gag was still in her mouth and, as much as she tried to scream and shout, she couldn't get her voice loud enough to make an impact. She began bouncing the chair up and down on the floor, using her body to raise the legs off the concrete and allow it to fall with as much force as possible.

'Help!' she screamed from the back of her throat, barely forming the word at all. She jutted the chair toward the door, hoping that the closer to the exit she became, the more chance she had of being heard.

'Oi,' another male voice came from outside. Aggressive, angry. 'Oi, get that fucking ball away from my car.'

It was Charlie. The sound of the ball being launched against the shutter stopped.

She stopped moving. Held her breath. Listened.

'Who the fuck ye talkin' tae, ye Irish dobber?' one of the voices replied. He sounded just like some of the boys in school back in the day.

The others laughed and Molly Rose jumped when the sound of the shutter rattled in its place.

'Get to fuck, the lot of you, before I—'

'Before ye whit, auld man?' another asked. Or rather, goaded.

Silence followed and Molly Rose's heart pounded as she let out a breath. She needed to get the chair back to its original place. Now.

'You don't want to know. Now move away from my car.'

'Whit, that auld heap ae rusty green shite? It's a fucking banger. Ha ha, a banger fae Bangor!'

The boys outside burst into shrieks of laughter and it gave Molly Rose time to think. She could throw herself at the other side of the door, make as much noise with her body and try to alert the people outside that she was being held against her will.

She jutted the chair closer to the door and threw herself against it before she started screaming. Silence fell over the people outside the lockup. It was as if they were listening.

'Did ye hear that in there?' one of them said.

Molly started making noises as loud as she could, banging her shoulder against the door while strapped to the chair. Pain shot through her, but she didn't care.

'Is that yer lockup? Ye got someone in there?'

'I said get the fuck away from here,' Charlie replied. His voice was closer to the door now. She heard a jangling of keys and felt sick. But if he was going to open the door now, the boys would see her. They'd know she was in there and they'd help her. Wouldn't they?

'Nah, I don't hink so. Whit de ye hink, boys?'

'I hink he's got somethin' tae hide in there.'

'Aye, me tae. Sounds like a wumin.'

The jangling of keys ceased and she heard slow steps move away from the lockup.

'You boys have got five seconds to move away from my car and my property, or I won't hesitate to cut your fucking throats.'

There was a pause, and then more laughter. 'Aye, so ye will.'

'Yer a fuckin' tramp, look at ye. Ye couldnae cut yer way oot a wet paper bag, ye fuckin' dobber.'

'Is that right?' Charlie replied.

Molly Rose threw herself against the door one more time, with as much force as she could conjure up. So much so that the chair bounced back and fell onto the floor. A pain shot through her skull as it struck the concrete. Dazed, she tried to take a deep breath and listened to the commotion outside as she felt herself slip out of consciousness.

Chapter 47

'Is that right?' Charlie said, pulling a knife from the side pocket of his rucksack and holding it down by his side. One of the lads caught sight of it and laughed.

'There's no way he's gonnae use that on us. He's an auld fuckin' codger,' one of the lads said.

The door to the lockup rattled in its frame and they all turned.

'I definitely hink he's got a wumin in there. Sounds like she wants out.'

Charlie took a breath and tried to think quickly. He just needed these lads to piss off away from the lockup and leave him to get on with moving Molly Rose. They were going to fuck up his plan and ruin his shot at getting his life back on track.

'Whit are ye, a fuckin' pervert? Keepin wumin locked up fur yer own pleasure, ye sick fuck!' the tallest lad shouted.

Charlie shot his arm out and held the knife up in front of him. The lads drew back but only slightly. There were five of them. He stood no chance if they jumped him.

'Stooby,' one of the them said, looking at the tallest boy there. 'You've got a knife tae.'

'Aye, an it's better than that heap of shite.'

The lad let the blade slip down and out of the sleeve of his hoodie. He wasn't wrong. It was far bigger than Charlie's. He needed to defuse this situation right now.

'Look, you're right. I am a tramp. I've not got money or anything valuable.'

'That's bollocks,' the tall lad said. 'You said this motor was yours. A heap ae shite, maybe, but it's worth something tae you.'

Then he reached down and began slashing the tyres while his mates cackled like hyenas. Charlie didn't care – he just needed them away from the lockup.

'Ye cannae go far in that noo, can ye?' the slasher said.

Charlie felt humiliated. Back in his day, if this had happened, he'd have floored all five of them by now.

'Are you lot happy now?'

He noticed one of the lads looking at the door behind him.

'What wiz all that noise going on in there?'

Charlie shrugged. 'I don't know. I just came back for my motor.'

The tall lad who slashed his tyres shook his head. 'Nah, yer lying. Why would you park it here if that wisnae your lockup?'

He watched one of the lads approach the shutter covering the window and lean in as if he was listening. 'The noise has stopped. It was probably just the wind,' he said.

The tall boy raised a brow. 'I say we give him a fuckin' kickin'.'

The boy standing at the shutter shook his head. 'Nae point, Stooby. He's no got any money.'

'Search his rucksack,' Stooby said.

The other lad tutted. 'Am no stickin ma hand in that boggin bag. You fuckin' dae it if yer that bothered. Am bored ae this. Am away up the park fur a bevy.'

The other three, who hadn't said a lot, followed him along the road to the end of the arches. Stooby on the other hand, stood there staring at Charlie.

'You not going with your mates?'

Stooby stuck his knife into the back tyre one more time, pulled it out and smirked at Charlie. 'Aye. See ye later, ye fuckin' prick.'

Before he walked away, he took one last look at the lockup and then slowly followed the other four lads down the road. Charlie waited for them to be out of sight before he opened the door to the lockup and slipped inside.

Looking down at his feet, he saw Molly Rose, still tied to the chair and out cold.

'Fucking bitch.' He kicked her legs. 'You nearly ruined everything.'

Molly Rose stirred and then opened her eyes. She looked up at him and he saw the fear on her face.

'Get up. We're moving.'

Chapter 48

Pulling into the car park of the address that Kristo had sent to her, she stopped at the end of the road, killed the engine and Janey got out of the car. She saw Kristo and his team standing at the entrance to a row of lockups and suddenly, her skin began to prickle.

'How do you know he's in here?' Janey asked.

'I don't,' Kristo said. 'Call it instinct. But we tracked him as far as we could based on the CCTV from the student accommodation building. As far as we can tell, this is the only place around here that's semi-abandoned – the perfect place for Charlie to hide out. The only other thing down here is a warehouse, which is used as a nightclub but only for bookings.'

Janey peered down the road and then back to Kristo. 'Okay. I trust your instinct – you've never been wrong before. Let's go.'

'You're *not* going with him,' Ciaran said.

Janey raised a brow and gave him a questioning look. 'Since when did you tell me what I could and couldn't do?'

'I'm not *telling* you what to do. It's just…' he trailed off. She could tell that he didn't want to say anything else in front of Kristo and the rest of the men on the team. And she was glad that he stopped himself. She knew what he was thinking. After having to tell the truth about what Charlie did to her when she was just a child herself, Ciaran wouldn't want Janey going anywhere near him. She understood why. Ciaran would want to protect her. But she could protect herself. She wasn't a child any more. She was a grown woman, with far more sense than Charlie could ever dream of; and she had years of experience of dealing with rats just like him. Danny McInroy being one of them. She could have imagined Danny becoming just like Charlie. The potential was there – in all men who thought they possessed power. Well, not now. Janey wasn't going to let Charlie Hallahan go any further with his plan.

'Right, let's do this,' Janey said as Kristo led the way down the road.

There were about fifteen unoccupied lockups on East-vale Place; Janey read the sign on the wall at the beginning of the road. She looked back and saw a group of youths heading towards them.

'Oi, big man,' one of them said as they approached Kristo. 'Any spare fags?'

Kristo stopped with the other men at his side. The lad looked past him at Janey and then back to Kristo. 'Did you hear me? I said huv ye got any spare fags?'

'No,' Kristo replied. 'Excuse us.'

As Kristo tried to go around them, the tallest of the five boys stood in front of him and stared into his eyes. Janey shook her head, walked up to him and got between them.

'I'm looking for my granddaughter. Have you seen her?' She showed him the same picture from the missing person leaflets and images online. The boy glanced down at it uninterested and then back to Janey before shrugging his shoulders.

'She's missing and she's with a man who is *very* dangerous. It would be helpful if you could all get out of the way so we can carry on our search for her.'

'Stooby?' one of the other boys said. The lad's expression flickered and he blinked. 'We thought there wiz someone in that lockup doon there. We heard aw that bangin'.'

'Aye,' the tall lad said. 'There wiz a creepy auld guy, pulled a knife on us.'

Janey glanced back at Kristo and then rested her eyes on the group again.

'Which lockup?' Janey asked.

'It'll cost ye a pack ae fags or the cash fur them,' Stooby said.

Janey sighed and reached into her coat pocket. 'Here,' she said, handing the lad a twenty-pound note. 'Now, which lockup?'

The lad named Stooby smirked and said, 'A cannae mind.'

Kristo reached around and grabbed him by the throat. Janey saw him push his pistol into the lad's stomach. 'Don't *fuck* with me, boy. Which fucking lockup?'

'Fuck's sake, Stooby, just tell him,' one of the other boys said, panicked.

Stooby didn't answer and Janey wasn't sure if it was out of fear or blatant ignorance to the idea that Kristo would actually shoot him.

'The one wae the motor ootside it wae the slashed tyres. A just slashed them. Wae ma *knife*.'

There was an exchange between the lad and Kristo, before Kristo nodded and the two men next to him removed the knife from the lad's possession. Janey watched as Stooby's colour drained. He was the type to be the hardman if he was tooled up. Not so much if he was faced with someone like Kristo and unable to threaten him with a blade.

'Give the lady her money back and fuck off before I put an end to you, skinny boy,' Kristo said quietly.

Stooby held the money out to Janey but she shook her head. 'No. Keep it. But listen to me. If you want to get by in this world, you're not going to get very far by carrying a shitty little blade like that.'

The other lads had done a runner. But Kristo still held this Stooby lad by the wrist.

'Take us to the car,' he said, turning Stooby and pushing him down the road with the pistol in his back.

'Look, I don't wan any trouble. I wiz only kiddin on,' he said.

'Funny,' Janey replied. 'If that's your comedy sketch then you'll not get very far in life with that either.'

As they headed down the road, a rusty-looking green car came into sight at the far end. 'Is that the car you claim to have slashed the tyres of?' Kristo asked.

'Aye,' Stooby said. 'We heard bangin comin fae inside the lockup it's parked next tae.'

'And you said there was an older man with a knife?' Janey asked.

'Aye. He had an Irish accent. Just looked like an auld tramp, but he wiz ragin we were hingin aboot the motor. Ma pals wur bangin the ball aff the shutters and he went mental. That's when we heard a noise fae inside. Ma pal said he thought there wis a wumin in there, but a thought he wiz just jokin.'

Janey felt sick. 'Why did he think there was a woman inside?'

'Said he thought he heard a lassie screaming, but wisnae sure.'

They stopped outside the lockup. The car was there. Rusted at the wheel arches. Dirty. The tyres were slashed like Stooby had claimed.

Kristo let one of the other men take over holding Stooby and tried the door to the lockup. It opened. Janey felt like her heart was going to come up and out of her mouth.

'Charlie?' Kristo called before pushing the door open wider before stepping inside, pointing the gun into the lockup.

'He won't be here now,' Stooby said. 'He just threatened a teenager wae a knife and got his car done fur it. He's long gone, especially if he did have someone in there. He's no gawnae hing aboot if there's a chance the polis will show up.'

The police were the least of Charlie's worries, Janey thought.

'Any sign?' Janey stepped into what appeared to be an empty lockup.

Kristo sighed and shook his head. 'No. He's not here and neither is Molly Rose. But I think they were. Or at least, someone was.'

Bowing her head, Janey took a breath and turned to Stooby. 'If you know what's good for you, you'll fuck off back to your mates and keep this quiet. And if I see you around again, acting the hard man with your fucking blade, I won't hesitate to pull you apart.'

She saw Stooby's Adam's apple move in his throat as he swallowed.

'Get the fuck out my sight. I've got my men keeping an eye on you, Stooby. One foot out of line and you've had it. You have no idea who you're messing with here.'

Stooby nodded slightly. 'These lockups have two doors, usually.'

'How do you know that?' Kristo asked.

'A've hung aboot here aw ma days. Used to break in when a wiz younger. They've usually got a back door. Some ae them are boarded up, but some urny. It wiz only aboot fifteen minutes since we met the guy. An he husnae passed us on the way oot. So he must ae used another door.'

Janey sighed. 'That's what I'm talking about, Stooby,' she said. 'Keep that attitude up and you'll go places.'

Janey followed Kristo into the lockup and she tried to flick the switch by the door. The light above them didn't come on, but Kristo used the light on his phone to illuminate the back wall.

'He was right. There is another door. It leads out to the expressway.'

Janey rushed to the door and pulled on it. It was locked.

'He's moved her,' she shouted. 'He can't have gone far if his car is still here. Get out on to that expressway now!' she shouted. 'Two of you head towards the city centre, two of you back towards Partick. Ciaran, you and I will take the pedestrian bridge over to the Tall Ship. If Charlie thinks he's fucked this, he could chuck Molly Rose in the Clyde.'

The thought of having to tell Orla that Molly Rose was dead because Janey was too late getting to her made her stomach heave.

'It's broad fucking daylight,' Ciaran said. 'We'll find him and if we don't, someone will see him and clock

Molly Rose. She'll struggle against him, try to fight him off.'

Janey shook her head. 'Not if she's terrified and thinks that co-operating will save her life.' That was exactly what she'd thought herself that day when she was just a teenager. She'd trusted Charlie. He was her stepbrother; practically family. 'Remember, that Stooby lad said he had a knife on him.'

Janey ran along the road and came to the open archway at the foot of the pedestrian bridge. She glanced up to see if she could see Charlie or Molly Rose.

'Fifteen minutes that Stooby lad said. If he's taking Molly Rose somewhere against her will, he'll want to look as inconspicuous as possible. So, he'll be going slower than he would like. He won't want to draw any attention to them. Keep your eyes peeled, Ciaran. When we get across, you take the road to the right and I'll go to the left. The Clydeside is likely where he'll take her. The threat of throwing her in will keep her in check.'

She felt her husband at her back as they ascended the foot bridge. As they crossed over the expressway towards the distillery at the opposite side, Janey felt herself praying that she could get her granddaughter back in one piece. The poor girl would be terrified in the clutches of Charlie and his evil ways. Janey knew just how that felt and knew the fear that she would be feeling in this moment.

Chapter 49

'Remember, Molly Rose, just because I've untied you doesn't mean you can just run off. I've only let you free to stop people from looking at us. One step out of line, and I will slice your throat right here and leave you to die in the middle of this bridge,' he said as they stopped. 'Just think, you lying here, your blood dripping into that water and you becoming at one with the river. You don't want that idea to become a reality, do you?'

Molly Rose didn't dare step a foot out of line. She would do exactly what he said because he'd told her if she did that she'd survive.

'You really shouldn't have tried to get their attention, you stupid, *silly* little girl,' he said into her ear, his lips touching her skin. The sensation made her feel physically sick.

'I'm sorry,' she whimpered. She glanced up at him as he stared out across the Clyde. There were people everywhere, crossing the bridge by foot, by bike. There were boats on the water. She could cry out for help, but what if he really did kill her there and then? He said that, in this moment, he had nothing to lose. Nothing at all. But keeping her alive was what he wanted to get what he deserved. She was just a pawn in his game. He didn't care about what happened to her.

'You're not sorry or you wouldn't have done it,' Charlie said through gritted teeth.

'Where are you taking me now?' Molly Rose asked, trying to hide the fact she was looking for an opportunity to escape.

'I don't know yet. But your grandmother sure as hell has fucked up my plans. And so did those stupid little fucking boys.'

Molly Rose held back the tears and looked down into the water. A small boat was heading towards them. If she got the timing right, she could jump and hope that she'd land on the boat. But that was only if she could get out of Charlie's grip first.

'Charlie?' a voice called. Both Molly Rose and Charlie spun around to face the west side of the bridge.

'Don't come any closer,' Charlie said, pressing the knife into Molly Rose's back. 'I'll fucking kill her, Janey. I swear to fucking God.'

Molly Rose looked at the woman approaching. So, this was Janey, her supposed grandmother.

'We both know that's not true,' she said. 'Let her go.'

Molly Rose felt Charlie's breath on her neck and the sensation made her skin crawl.

'She looks like you,' he said. 'Sounds like you did when you were younger. She even smells like you.'

The look on the woman's face soured. And then the sound of another voice from behind Janey, a male voice, made Charlie loosen his grip slightly.

'Let her go or I'll fucking shoot you,' the man said.

'Ah, Ciaran Hallahan. I always wondered, why did you take the Hallahan name? Isn't it tradition for the woman to take the husband's name?'

'Charlie, let her go. Take me instead and then we can talk about getting you more money,' Janey said. Her tone was firm, her words clear.

'Fuck you. The second I let her go, he'll fucking shoot me. Nah, she's staying with me.'

'No, I can't let you walk away with her, Charlie. She's sixteen, for Christ's sake, just a young girl. She's nothing to do with this. Just let her go and we can talk.'

'She's older than you were when—' Charlie said, but the gun in the other man's hand clicked and Molly Rose saw him point the gun at her, although it was obviously aimed at Charlie.

'Shut your fucking mouth,' the man said.

Molly Rose felt panic start rise in her chest. They were antagonising him. His grip was looser, but the knifepoint was still at the base of her back.

'I'll count to three and, if you've not let her go, I'll put a bullet in your head,' the man standing behind Janey said. 'In fact, make that two.'

'By the time you've finished counting, I'll have sliced through her spinal cord and, while you're trying to save her, I'll be gone with this bag of cash you so kindly donated. Your call.'

Janey shook her head and raised a hand up in a gesture – Molly Rose read it that she was going to take a step closer.

'No one is going to shoot, or *stab* anyone, Charlie. You're safe if you just let Molly Rose come to me. You can turn around, walk away with that cash and start an entirely new life.'

People were starting to take notice of what was going on.

She heard voices, saying they were phoning the police, to let her go, asking what was happening. People gasped when they saw the gun. It was like being in the midst of a crime drama on TV, only this was real life. Molly Rose's life. And it was as real as it got.

'Everyone's watching, Charlie. Your face is going to be all over the news, on people's phones, on social media. Molly Rose is terrified. She *doesn't* deserve this. Let her go, now. And this can all be forgotten.'

Molly Rose kept her eyes on Janey. She concentrated on studying her face, her eyes, the way her mouth moved when she spoke. She looked a lot like Orla.

Sirens in the distance made Charlie stiffen up behind her. 'Fuck,' he growled into her ear. 'You're a lucky little bitch, Molly Rose.'

The point of the knife released from her back and his presence behind her was gone. She didn't move, just froze on the spot in the centre of the bridge. The boat that she'd had her eye on passed beneath her and she felt the bridge vibrate under her. The man who was standing next to Janey with a gun in his hand rushed past her, but she didn't follow him with her eyes. Janey was moving towards her with caution, her arms outstretched.

'Molly Rose, are you all right?' she asked. Her accent was strong, just like Charlie's.

She nodded, as the woman took both her hands. 'Did he hurt you?'

'No. I don't know. Not really. He tied me to a chair. He killed my friend, Kassy.' That was when the enormity of what had happened in the past few days hit her and she felt her knees buckle beneath her. Janey caught her before she hit the bridge floor.

'The team are on it. We'll track him down as soon as possible,' the man said, standing over them.

Molly Rose looked up at Janey and then at the man above them. 'Are you the police?'

Janey moved Molly Rose's hair out of her face and smiled gently. 'Something like that,' she said. 'Come on. Let's get you home.'

Molly Rose got to her feet and allowed Janey to help her walk across the bridge. The man who'd taken her had simply let her go. But she knew this wasn't the end of it.

Chapter 50

Sitting at her desk, Orla swung gently on the chair and stared at the computer screen. She'd locked herself in her office, ready to block out what was happening and throw herself into the depths of her work. There was no other way she could get what was going on out of her head and even that wasn't working because she'd been calling Janey's phone constantly for updates, but had been unable to get through. This caused so much worry and anxiety. They said no news was good news, but not in Orla's head. What if it was bad news and Janey was working her way up to telling her?

Switching on the computer, Orla couldn't get the images of the dead girl out of her head. Who was she? And why would this person make them all think it was Molly Rose? He was sick in the head and it made Orla's skin crawl to think someone could have such a depraved mind.

A gentle tap on the office door made her look up from the computer screen. 'I'm busy,' she called out.

'Can I come in?' Sinead asked from behind the door.

Orla sighed, got up from the chair and unlocked the office door. Her sister's face was pale and a dark shadow lay under her eyes.

'Anything I can help you with?' Sinead asked.

Orla walked back around to the chair and sat back down. 'Not really. I'm just going to check some work emails, bury my head in the sand.'

Sinead stood in the doorway and fiddled with the bottom of her T-shirt. 'My head is fucked after that, and let me tell you, I've seen some horrible shit from my time on the streets and in hostels. Nothing compares to that.'

'It was awful. But not as awful as it could have been if it had been my daughter lying there instead,' Orla replied, opening her work email inbox. She stared at the screen as she waited for the messages to load. There were always at least fifty a day. Owning a company that ran so many early years centres up and down Scotland meant she was inundated with emails from centre and area managers, other companies selling goods for the centres, Care Inspectorate, SSSC. It would be good to get her head into those and away from the hell that was her life right now.

'Orla, you seem like you're not bothered that a girl has been murdered. Aren't you sick with what just happened?'

'Yes, I was, but now I know it wasn't Molly Rose, I can focus on getting her home.'

She looked up and saw the frown on Sinead's face.

'But you're *not* focusing on that, are you? You're focusing on your businesses, which are run for you by area managers. You don't have to be doing any of this. Do I have to remind you that a young girl has been murdered? You should show some compassion, Orla, instead of throwing yourself into your work.'

Orla shot her a look and sighed. 'You think I don't know a girl is dead? It's all I think about. And the idea that the same could happen to my own daughter makes me feel psychically sick.'

Sinead's expression softened. 'I know. But you should be downstairs, with Oliver and me, waiting for the police to give us an update or—'

'There *is* no update, though, Sinead. Is there? If there was, we'd know where Molly Rose is and we don't. And I'm sorry, but it seems as though Janey has more authority than the police, which sounds ridiculous. But why else would she be out there, running around, handing out bags stuffed with cash? So, until I get given new information, I'm going to do this.'

Sinead didn't move from the doorway and Orla didn't care. Her eyes fell on to the screen and an email flashed up in the main inbox as urgent. She didn't recognise the address but, as she read it, her heart began to thump inside her chest.

Sinead must have seen the look on Orla's face because she moved across the room and stood in front of her on the other side of the computer.

'What's wrong?' Sinead asked.

Orla stared at the email address. Surely this had to be a joke. But there it was, in front of her as much as Sinead was stood in front of her. She read it to herself.

ifyouwanttoknowwheremollyroseisthenopenthisemail
@googlemail.com

'Oh my god,' Orla whispered. Sinead made her way around and crouched beside Orla.

'What the actual fuck?' Sinead said loudly. 'Open it.'

Orla shook her head. 'No. There's an attachment. What if it's something sinister, Sinead? It was bad enough seeing that dead girl. What if he'd killed Molly Rose and...'

'Orla, it's obvious that dead girl died at the hands of this fucking nut job. You need to open the email. Look, we'll read it together.'

Orla felt her head begin to swim. 'What if it's a scam?'

'Better to open it and find out,' Sinead said. 'I can do it, if you want?'

Orla hovered over the email and then clicked on it. It opened and filled the screen. Orla took hold of Sinead's hand. It trembled beneath her touch and, for a moment, Orla had completely forgotten about her sister's addiction.

For the attention of Orla Hunter and Sinead Coyle,

First off, let me introduce myself. I'm Charlie Hallahan. I'm glad the email address got your attention. I want to start by saying that as much as the email address states, you won't come to the end of this email with any new information about Molly Rose's whereabouts. But I did want to catch your attention for another matter.

I'm not just anyone. I'm your father. The one who wasn't put on your birth certificate or had a say in what happened to you both.

Janey Hallahan is nothing but a self-centred, heartless bitch. She didn't give a shit about you back then and she doesn't give a shit about you now. You're probably thinking the same about me. Let me be clear, I don't. But I do believe people have a right to know how they were brought into this world. And you girls didn't have that. So… here it is. I'm your dad. And yes, you'll hate me for what I'm doing. But that's just life. It's tough, unfair.

The one thing I will say is this: don't let Janey sway you about what happened between us. I'm not that kind of man. Janey wanted it as much as I did – more, in fact. I won't have her say that about me just to get one over on me. Do you understand?

Anyway, sorry about Molly Rose. But I just can't let her go yet. I'm still owed far too much.

Orla and Sinead were both silent as they stared at the screen, and Orla heard the rush of blood in her ears. This wasn't happening. This *couldn't* be happening.

'Oh my god,' Orla said. 'What, I mean, how…' She couldn't form a sentence as she read over the last words. 'The bastard didn't even sign off the email. He literally created that email address to get our attention. Jesus Christ.'

Sinead was quiet as she stared at the screen. Her breathing was shallow by Orla's left ear. 'He's insinuating that Janey is claiming he raped her and that's how we were created.'

Orla read over the words again and shivered. 'Sinead, what if…?' She couldn't let the words leave her mouth. A wave of nausea took over and she started to panic. 'Fuck, fuck, fuck. Sinead, what are we going to do? He's going to… he might already have—'

'Don't think it. Don't picture it. You need to stay focused,' Sinead said as she pulled her phone out of her pocket and stared tapping on the screen. Holding it to her ear, the silence was deafening in the room as Orla continued to read the last line of the email. He wasn't going to let Molly Rose go.

'I can't get hold of Janey,' Sinead said, breaking the silence. 'She's not picking up. I'm phoning the police. They can trace where the email came from.'

Orla opened her mouth to speak when the bell at the front door rang twice in quick succession. Orla and Sinead glanced at one another and got to their feet. Orla ran down the stairs to the front door but Oliver was already there. He opened it and Orla gasped as she took in the scene in front of her.

'Oh my god, Molly *Rose*,' she said, rushing towards her daughter, who was clinging to Janey.

'I'm okay,' she said. 'Really, I promise you I'm okay.'

Orla and Oliver took their daughter from Janey, who was standing at the front door with her husband, Ciaran. They held on to her tightly. Orla kissed the top of her head and began to cry.

'Where did you find her?' Orla asked, locking eyes with Janey.

Janey slid her hands into the pockets of her coat and said, 'There's a lot to talk about. Can I come in?'

'Of course,' Oliver replied.

Orla watched Janey step into her family home and the email, which hadn't actually left her thoughts, came back to the front of her mind again.

'We need to talk to you about something,' Orla said. 'Just me and Sinead. But let me get Molly Rose settled first.'

Janey nodded. Orla noted that her expression was pained. Things were about to get worse.

She held Molly Rose away from her and looked into her eyes. 'Come on. I'm going to run you a bath and get some food into you.'

Molly Rose didn't blink. Instead, she glanced from Orla, to Janey, then back to Orla. 'Is she my grand-mother?'

Orla closed her eyes for a second. This was never in her plan. She didn't want to have to go over any of this with her daughter. It was too dark, now more than ever after receiving that email.

'She is,' Orla replied.

'She saved me,' Molly Rose replied. 'If it wasn't for her, I would be dead.'

If it wasn't for her, you'd never would have been taken, Orla wanted to respond. But for once, she kept her mouth shut, smiled gently and led her daughter upstairs.

'Olly,' Orla said. 'Make us all some tea.'

Reaching the top of the stairs, she led Molly Rose to her bedroom. Once inside, she watched her daughter lay slowly down on the bed and bury her face into the pillow.

'He murdered my friend,' she said, her words muffled by the material surrounding her mouth.

It was like a stab to the chest, hearing the pain in her voice.

'Which friend?'

Molly Rose sat up and wiped tears from her eyes. Other than the fact she was crying, she seemed fine. It would be the shock, Orla thought. She's been through a traumatic time. She wouldn't have processed any of it yet.

'Kassy. She took me under her wing when I...' her voice trailed off. 'When I left home.'

Orla fell silent. Kassy. The dead girl.

'She was your friend?' Orla asked, gently.

Molly Rose sobbed and nodded her head.

She knew she had to give her daughter time to speak. The whole reason she left in the first place was because Orla refused to acknowledge her thoughts and feelings, was always disregarding her. She wouldn't make that mistake again.

'What happened?' Orla asked, not wishing to tell Molly Rose about how they found Kassy and were made to believe it was her.

Molly Rose took a breath, composed herself, sat up straight and placed her hands on her knees. She tapped her fingers gently on her knees in a rhythmic motion. Orla realised it was something she also did when she was stressed. She was trying to regulate herself.

'Don't kick off or freak out when I tell you. I just need you to listen, Mum. Can you do that?'

Orla smiled softly. She knew she had to give her daughter time to speak without being judgemental or getting upset. She hadn't listened to her daughter. She wouldn't make that mistake again. 'Of course I can do that.'

'Kassy was a prostitute who I became friends with when she stopped me from being mugged on my first night away from home. Anyway, she was stopped by a guy for business the night I was kidnapped; I don't even know how long I've been gone for. Anyway, it was the same guy who took me.'

Orla took a breath to steady her anger and listened carefully as Molly Rose told her story. As the words left her daughter's mouth, Orla felt a mix of anger and fear.

This poor girl, Kassy, had been murdered by someone because of Janey. It could very well have been Molly Rose who had been killed and dumped like a bag of rubbish. But at the same time, Janey was the one who found her. If she hadn't, who knows what could have happened to her.

Once Molly Rose got into it, there was no stopping her. Her story came in waves, along with the tears, and

Orla vowed, even if it killed her, that she would never let her daughter come to harm ever again.

Chapter 51

He dropped the duffle bag on the ground and placed both hands on the wall, bent his head low and let out a growl, which in turn became a scream. The fury running through his body, his veins, was overwhelming. He'd let her go – had become weak. Even if the sirens hadn't made Charlie panic and let go of that little bitch, Molly Rose, he'd had no doubt that Ciaran Hallahan would have shot him. And he would have got away with it because the fucking Hallahan firm had police in their pockets in every major town and city up and down the fucking country.

'Fucking bitch,' he spat, as he stood up straight inside the abandoned, roofless building on the disused Govan docks.

He'd been chased down by Janey's men, but they'd been unsuccessful, even while carrying a very heavy bag of cash. Charlie had scouted the city of Glasgow for hideouts in case things didn't go according to his plan. And they hadn't. Leaving Molly Rose on the Millennium Bridge hadn't been part of his plan. He'd planned to bring her here. No one would look for her in this place. It was silent, out of the way of people and police. Now, he was here alone. And his face would now be known to every fucking gangster working for Janey Hallahan. However, he did have a million pounds. He could do what Janey said – disappear and start a new life. With that amount of cash, he could buy a new identity and still have plenty leftover. He'd have to forget about buying back his house. He just hoped that his secrets remained buried there. A thought entered his mind then. Finn had paid him off almost forty years ago, to never return. It seemed Janey had taken a leaf out of Finn's book. Was that the best she could come up with? The idea made him snigger.

Sitting down on the ground next to the duffle bag, he unzipped it and pulled out bundles of cash. As he counted the piles, he noticed something. The texture of some of the notes was different to the others.

He studied them carefully, one bundle at a time, flicking through each note.

'You've got to be fucking kidding,' he said, running his thumb across the wording at the top of the notes.

He stood and stared down at the money. About ninety per cent of the bundles were counterfeit notes. She'd tricked him; fucked him over in true Janey Hallahan style. 'Ah, no. No fucking way. I'll kill her. I'll fucking kill all of them.'

Charlie balled his hands into fists and began banging them off his forehead.

He couldn't let her get away with this. He might be a lot of things, but he wasn't a fucking doormat.

Charlie put up his hood, zipped up his jacket and shoved his hands in his pockets before stepping out from behind the walls of the building on the dock. He looked across the Clyde towards the West End of the city. A ball of anger sat heavy on his chest. He knew what he had to do to take his final revenge on Janey. She thought she'd got one up on him. He'd never let her win so long as he was breathing.

Chapter 52

She sat on the top step and listened to what Molly Rose told her mum about what happened to her that first night Charlie had taken her. How she'd tried to run from him. She'd gone through the park, through the trees and the bushes, scratching and scraping her skin as she attempted to conceal herself from him. It hadn't worked. He'd bundled her into the boot of his car, along with her friend who he'd murdered earlier. Janey knew what was likely to have happened before the murder took place. Charlie had always had a sinister side to him, even when they were younger. He'd been obsessed with catching mice out in the horse fields and breaking their necks when they were kids. She'd always been wary of him. But as she'd grown older and wiser to how the world worked, Janey's assumption was that he was just training to be like his stepdad. He'd need to have a hardened heart to run things. Thanks to Charlie, Janey was the one who had an ice-cold attitude when it was needed.

'Janey?' Sinead said, standing on the middle of the staircase and looking up at her. 'Can I ask you something?'

'Of course,' Janey replied.

Sinead looked down the stairs and through to the kitchen where Oliver and Ciaran were. They'd poured everyone tea. It would be cold by now.

Sinead nodded, and tears sprung to her eyes. 'Is it true?'

'Is what true?' Janey asked, although based on Sinead's expression, she was worried that she was about to ask a question about Charlie. Had he really sent that email? Had the girls already read it?

'The man who took Molly Rose – he's claiming to be our biological dad. And given what the email said, he's suggesting we should take what you say about what happened between you with a pinch of salt. That you consented?'

Janey looked down at her feet and took a steadying breath, although if the ground could open up and swallow her whole, she'd welcome it.

'*Is* he our biological dad?' Sinead asked again.

Janey looked up and blinked before nodding. 'I'm sorry. I didn't mean for you to find out about any of this.'

'Oh God,' Sinead whispered, sitting down on the middle stair and holding on to one of the spindles. 'He said he believed that people should know how they were brought into the world, that he isn't *that* kind of man and that he was born out of that kind of evil.'

Janey puffed out her cheeks and exhaled loudly. 'Jesus Christ. He's trying so hard to turn you against me before I've even had the chance to get to know either of you.'

Sinead stared at Janey, unblinking. '*Did* he rape you? Is that how you got pregnant with us?'

Janey wished Ciaran had shot Charlie on that bridge. She wished she could have watched the light go out of his eyes. Knowing that he was no longer walking this earth would be the only punishment for him, given what he'd done to Molly Rose. She should have killed him, or had him killed, a long time ago. It would have prevented all this mess.

Molly Rose's bedroom door opened and Orla came out, closing it quietly behind her. Janey and Sinead looked up and Janey was glad of the distraction, even if it didn't last long.

'Is she okay?' Janey whispered.

Orla nodded. 'She said she's okay. But then, she was in the boot of his car next to her friend's dead body – you know, the girl we found? Would you be okay with that? I know I wouldn't.'

Janey thought about what it must have been like. How terrifying it would have been. 'No, I don't think I would have been.'

Janey got to her feet as Orla descended the staircase. Sinead's question hung in the air and the girls deserved to know the truth, since Janey's past was the reason they were all together now.

'Girls,' Janey said, exchanging a glance with each of them. 'We need to talk.'

'I got an email,' Orla said bluntly.

'I know. Sinead told me. And we've chatted briefly and I think you two deserve some answers.'

Orla hovered by the top of the stairs as Janey made her way down. Sinead and Orla slowly followed her through. 'Is there somewhere we can chat?' Janey asked.

Orla led them all through to the large lounge at the front of the house.

When all three were sat down on the sofa, Janey felt the burn of both her daughters' eyes bore into her.

'Sinead told me what the email said. She asked me if it was true, if Charlie is your biological father. And sadly, yes. He is. And it wasn't through choice, let me assure you. The man isn't human. He's utterly evil. I'm sure I don't have to tell you that.'

Orla stared at Janey and tears sprung to her eyes. 'We're the product of rape?' Her words didn't come from a place of anger but more sadness.

'I'm sorry, Orla. He had no right to do this.'

'Are you okay?' Sinead asked, tears slowly dropping from her eyes.

'Me?' Janey asked. 'It was almost forty years ago. A lot has happened since then. I've come to terms with it, accepted what happened and that it wasn't my fault. And it wasn't your fault either.'

Sinead and Orla were silent for a moment. Being told you were conceived through such an act would have been a hard hit.

'Janey, I'm sorry. If talking about this makes you uncomfortable, we don't have to,' Sinead said.

'No,' Janey said, holding her hand up. 'It's okay. He wanted you to know the truth, but his truth isn't real. It's a figment of his reality. He's the type of man who could never face up to what he did and who he really is as a person. My truth is what's real. I may have given you up, but you need to know that I never actually had a choice, for various reasons. If it was up to me, I'd have kept you. But with what happened, I couldn't risk him coming back and finding out about you or trying to have a part in your lives. With the business that I was born into, it wasn't a safe place for little ones to be around.'

Janey thought about the conversations she'd had with her dad about the pregnancy and the girls back then. There was no way she could tell them that he refused to let her keep them. As much as it pained Janey that he didn't support her right to be a mother to them, she didn't want Orla and Sinead thinking badly of Finn. He was still her dad and, if it wasn't for him, she wouldn't be the successful, strong woman that she was. And the idea of someone thinking badly of Finn upset her. She still loved and missed him so much.

'I thought I did the right thing. I hope you can understand. When I thought of you both, my mind didn't automatically go to him. It went to each of you: what you were doing; what you looked like. As much as what happened was horrifying for me, you two were a gift I didn't get to keep. I never stopped loving or thinking about you both. You crossed my mind every single day.'

Orla and Sinead glanced at one another and then back at Janey and she felt a tear fall. It was the first time she'd cried in years.

Chapter 53

Janey watched as Orla got up from the couch and left the room. Janey and Sinead were silent. Orla quickly returned with a wine bottle and three glasses. She placed them on the coffee table and filled them.

'I think we all deserve a drink,' she said, sniffing loudly and pouring wine into each glass, filling them almost to the top.

Sinead waved her hands and said, 'None for me, Orla. I'm not in a place to be putting anything other than food and water into my body right now.'

Orla glanced at Sinead and raised a brow. 'I didn't even think. Sorry.'

'It's fine,' Sinead replied. She looked at Janey and smiled gently. 'I'm recovering from… well, everything really.'

Orla downed the wine in her glass and poured another.

'I had thought, but didn't want to assume,' Janey replied.

'Yeah, I'm on methadone once a day for the heroin. But I was careering towards alcoholism too. I mean, binging, blacking out, not really feeling the hangover. Or maybe the heroin withdrawal masked it. I'm even trying to come off the cigarettes, although if I'm honest, I'm finding that the hardest. I haven't even tried to stop that,' Sinead said.

'We all have our vices,' Janey replied, glad and surprised that they all seemed to be opening up and getting along in the face of such traumatic experiences.

'Shit, sorry. Here's me talking shit about all my problems when you've just told us about... well, you know.'

'It's okay. I don't need you to tread carefully around me.'

Orla was quiet as she drank from the wine glass and Janey noticed how she stared at the back wall of the lounge. She wasn't blinking and her silence spoke a thousand words.

'Orla, are you okay?' Janey asked.

Orla blinked, held the glass down by her side and said, 'Am *I* okay? I should be asking you that. I feel like such a bitch for being so horrible, so blunt.'

'You didn't know. And I'm sure you were just protecting yourself. Trust me, I know how to do that better than anyone.'

A noise out in the hallway made them turn to the door. Orla got to her feet and went to the door. Janey peered around her to see Molly Rose sitting on the bottom step.

'Have you been listening?' Orla asked, sounding deflated.

Molly Rose stood up and entered the living room. She walked across the plush carpet that looked like it was either freshly laid or had never really been walked on and stood next to Janey.

'Did you hear our conversation?' Janey asked, hoping to God that she hadn't. She'd already endured so much.

Molly Rose nodded. 'I can't believe it. Are you okay?'

Janey smiled down at her granddaughter and sighed. 'I am. Now. But this isn't about me. It's about you.' She looked up at her daughters and said, 'It's about all of you.

Your safety. Charlie isn't the type to just walk away because Molly Rose is back home. My men have already been assigned their positions outside, to make sure you're safe.'

Orla's face contorted. 'Your *men*? I'm sorry, but the *police* should be out there, guarding our door. In fact, since you turned up, the police haven't been around as much.'

Janey pulled her lips into a thin line and considered how to explain things. The girls had been hit with so many shocking revelations and there were more to come from Janey.

'Yeah, I know. About that, there's something else you should know about me. Something you're probably not going to like, but I think if we're going to have any kind of relationship going forward, I need to be transparent and have you all know the truth.'

'What is it?' Sinead asked. 'Are you involved in some kind of organisation that runs the police?'

Janey simply nodded. 'Not in so many words. But in short, yes, I'm the head of an organisation that sometimes has the police working for me.'

Everyone stared at her in confusion, disbelief. Orla laughed incredulously.

'So that's how you got the money together so fast?' Sinead asked.

'The money's not real,' Janey replied. 'Charlie has a bag of counterfeit cash. Well, most of it is.'

Orla's mouth dropped open and Molly Rose raised a brow.

'What if he'd found out before I got away?'

'He's not bright enough to check immediately. And he had other thoughts in his head. It's likely that he'll have discovered it by now. And he'll not be happy about it, which is one of the reasons I'm having some of my employees posted to stand guard at the house, just until Charlie is found and dealt with effectively,' Janey replied.

'Effectively?' Orla asked. 'As in… dead?'

'Like I said, there's a lot about me you don't know and probably won't like. There's no better place for someone like him. Allowing him to carry on in life could result in more murders.'

Molly Rose wrapped her arms around Janey's waist and held on tightly. It shocked Janey to the point where it almost brought on tears.

'Thank you for saving me. There's nothing you could do that could stop me from thinking about you as anything other than my hero,' Molly Rose said. 'You're right about him. He's a monster, he deserves to die. If I had the balls to do it, I'd kill him myself.'

'Molly Rose!' Orla shot her a look.

'What?' she shrugged. 'He murdered my best friend, took me hostage and was going to kill me. He deserves to be six feet under, or a pile of ashes. I mean, what the hell happens to a person to turn them into someone like Charlie?'

Orla sighed. 'Many things, but it usually goes back to early childhood trauma, doesn't it? That nature versus nurture discussion. It was either because he was subjected to something himself, or it's in his blood.'

Janey knew what had happened to Charlie, and how it had influenced his behaviour. 'It was both,' she said. 'But that's not an excuse for what he does to people. He still deserves punishment. And he'll get it.'

Chapter 54

The next morning, as everyone was still in bed asleep, Molly Rose's stomach rumbled. She had barely eaten anything since Janey had brought her home. She couldn't stomach the thought of food, even though all she'd pretty much eaten in the past two weeks were a few slices of bread. Charlie might have kept her alive, but he'd kept her weak.

Now, as she lay in bed, staring up at the ceiling, her stomach growled so loudly that she got up and went downstairs. The sight of croissants, bagels and muffins on the kitchen counter set off her saliva glands.

As she made her way across the kitchen towards the kettle, something caught her eye outside the window. A man, dressed in black, stood with his hands clasped together at his back. She could only see the back of his head. He was one of Janey's men, stationed outside in case Charlie turned up. And she knew it was a very strong possibility. Of everyone, Molly Rose knew what the man was capable of. The image of Kassy's body in the boot next to her when she was first taken was memory enough.

Molly Rose set about making as much food as she could fit on one plate and a mug of very strong coffee. She sat down at the kitchen table and noticed that yesterday's newspaper was folded up and sitting on the seat next to her. Pulling it out, she opened it and browsed the pages.

Any news other than what was going on in her family would be a good enough distraction.

As she took a bite of the blueberry muffin, its taste and texture transported her back to that night when she was taken by Charlie. It was the last thing she'd eaten while walking back to the hostel to wait for Kassy.

Placing the muffin back down on the plate, she swallowed hard and took a large mouthful of coffee. Suddenly, she'd lost her appetite again. The bastard was impacting everything, even down to what she wanted to eat.

Sighing loudly, Molly Rose glanced down at the pages of the newspaper but didn't read any of the reports, just the headlines. All to do with scandals in Westminster, the cost-of-living crisis, even protests happening at sports events. Then, when she turned the page, the eyes of the person staring back at her made her gasp out loud.

'Jesus,' she said, staring down at her ex-boyfriend.

And as she started to read the report, her stomach dropped, her skin prickled. She knew, in that moment, that Charlie Hallahan was nothing compared to what could have happened to her.

Chapter 55

MAN WITH 'LINKS TO EUROPEAN GANG' FOUND DEAD

A man has been found brutally murdered following a suspected feud with a European human trafficking gang.

Dean Davidson, 20, was under police surveillance, due to intel that he was part of a trafficking operation with links to the European gang, when he went missing last year.

Mr Davidson, who police suspect was responsible for the recruitment of women and the production of counterfeit passports, was found dead by the owner of a scrapyard in the Parkhead area of Glasgow a few days ago.

Investigators from Police Scotland are working with Interpol with regards to the dealings between Davidson and the European gang.

Chief Superintendent Walter Clarke, said: 'The people in charge of this operation are highly skilled individuals, with dealings in counterfeit passports that are extremely sophisticated and hard to spot. Dean Davidson was believed to be in charge of the production of said passports, alongside the act of luring victims into being trafficked.

'His murder is being investigated and the European gang we believe he had links with has a part to play in that. We are working with Interpol to find the people responsible for this organisation and put a stop to it.

'As well as people being sent across the continent, we believe that there are people being sent to Scotland too.

'We would ask the public to be vigilant. If you believe that there is something going on in your community that could be a trafficking-related situation, please get in touch with Police Scotland. An example of this could be large groups of women living together in small flats, these women might change regularly as the traffickers often move them around. You might find that there are sex workers in your community who weren't there before. Again, if you suspect anything at all, get in touch with us.'

A police spokesperson asked that if anyone has a loved one who has gone missing within the past year, who they believe could have been victim to trafficking, to contact Police Scotland.

Chapter 56

Staring down at the words on the page, the bite of blueberry muffin threatened to come back up. She swallowed hard, read the report again and again, before looking at Dean's face with an open mouth.

How could this be right? He was her boyfriend once. A nice guy. Older, yes, which her mum had disapproved of so much that she'd made him break up with her. If he was the criminal the paper was depicting, would he have given up that easily?

'Morning, lovely,' Orla said, her voice making Molly Rose jump. She turned in her seat to see her mother standing in the kitchen doorway.

'Have you seen this?' Molly Rose asked, turning back to look down at Dean's face.

'The paper? No, I don't usually read it when it comes through. And with everything that's happened, I've not bothered,' Orla replied. She crossed the kitchen and kissed Molly Rose on the top of her head.

'Dean's in the paper,' Molly Rose said as Orla looked at it. She grabbed the paper from the table.

'What the fuck?' Orla said loudly.

Molly Rose kept thinking about the word "trafficking". He was a monster.

'I knew there was something off about that little shit. Jesus Christ,' Orla said, sitting next to Molly Rose. Orla turned to her, took Molly Rose's hands in hers and said: 'Did he ever do or say anything about going away together?'

Molly Rose shook her head and started to cry. 'Mum, I could have ended up away, anywhere. Being made to do things… awful things. Did you know? Is that why you made him end it?'

Orla breathed slowly, shook her head. 'No sweetheart, I didn't know he was this. Christ Almighty, I can't believe he actually did what I said. He could have…' She stopped, blinked.

'It seems the universe is dead set on making me disappear,' Molly Rose cried. 'What the hell is wrong with people?'

Orla wrapped her arms around her daughter and pulled her in close. 'You're safe now, darling. You're home. There are men here, keeping all of us safe.' She glanced out of the window. 'But I do think we should tell the police that you were involved with Dean. It's important for the safety of others, don't you think?'

Molly Rose pulled away from Orla, before wiping a tear away with the back of her hand. 'I mean, what's the point? He's dead. I'm here, like you say. I'm safe.'

Orla's expression was pained, but she didn't speak against Molly Rose.

'I threatened him, you know.'

'What did you say?'

'I told him that if he didn't leave you, I'd kill him.'

Molly Rose's eyes widened in shock. 'You said that?'

'Mm hmm, I did. I was bluffing, obviously. I'd never have done it. But what if the police suspect me?'

'Mum, if they did, they'd have come knocking by now.'

'They might still,' Orla said. 'He was only discovered a few days ago. And I'm sorry to say this, sweetheart, but if you were an intended victim, he might have information on you somewhere. If the police find that, then they might suspect me.'

Molly Rose stared at her mum in disbelief.

'Molly Rose is right, they'd have come knocking before now,' Janey's voice interrupted them as she stepped into the kitchen. She stared at her new gran – the one she didn't know even existed up until two weeks ago – and slumped on her chair in defeat.

'I'm done with *everything*,' Molly Rose said. 'Charlie, now this. It's like I'm a target or something. Someone is hellbent on putting an end to me. I don't know what's worse: being captured by that madman Charlie, seeing my murdered best friend in the boot of that car, or the idea of what Dean *could* have done to me if my mum hadn't forced him away. I mean, it doesn't bear thinking about.'

Janey glanced down at Molly Rose and sat down at the table. She'd stayed the night at the house, insisting that her presence would be extra protection. Orla had argued that it might be extra danger, but in the end agreed to Janey's presence.

'No, it doesn't. So don't, because you don't have to go to that place,' Janey said, looking at the paper. 'Is this him? Dean?'

Molly Rose nodded. 'How could he do that? He seemed so… nice.'

Janey reached across the table and took her hand. 'They do, at first, Molly Rose. Charlie seemed nice too, until he wasn't. But not all men are bad. Look at your dad. Look at Ciaran. Don't let this influence your future. You're a bright girl with a bright future ahead of you. You only have to look at your mum to know that you've come from good stock. And no, you're not a Hallahan by name, but it's in your blood to be strong. You might not feel it right now, but you are. Otherwise, you wouldn't have survived everything that you've gone through.'

The three of them sat around the table. Gran, mother, daughter. It seemed surreal. Molly Rose looked down at Dean's face. Picking up the page he stared up at her from, she went to the sink and tossed it in before pulling a box of matches from the drawer next to the sink. She struck one, studied the small flame before dropping it directly onto his face.

'Burn in hell.'

Chapter 57

It had all got too much for Orla. The revelation of Dean, the discovery of his body. The fact Molly Rose was struggling was like a dagger to the heart because there was nothing Orla could do about it.

As a mother, Orla should have seen this coming, she thought. She should have been more observant when it came to Dean. But how was she to know that he was part of a wider organisation? It wasn't something any of them expected.

Seeing Molly Rose get up and burn the picture of his face in the sink while hearing Janey tell her she was strong because she had Hallahan blood in her veins had pushed her over the edge. She'd slipped out of the house and quietly got into her car. She had no plans as to where she was going, but soon she was pulling up outside one of her early years centres. Her work was always an escape for her and she decided it would be the best place to hide away from everything.

Management wouldn't be expecting her, but she knew she needed to be doing something that didn't involve thinking about her daughter's near-murder, or her almost trafficked daughter, or the fact she was the result of a rape.

Orla got out of the car and went to the front door of the nursery. The sounds of happily screaming children in the large garden at the back of the building rang out as the manager opened the door before Orla had the chance to pull out her keys.

'Don't worry,' Orla said. 'I'm not here to inspect that you're doing your job properly. I'm just here just to be here.'

The manager smiled. 'You don't have to explain. Come and go as you please, obviously.'

Orla stepped into the building and went into the office. She pulled out one of the finance files and flicked through it, not really bothering to take in any of the information from the pages. Even if she wanted to, she couldn't concentrate.

'So, how are you? What's happening with Molly Rose?' the manager asked. 'Sorry, you probably don't want to talk about it.'

Orla looked at her, confused. 'How do you know about Molly Rose?'

'I follow the Police Scotland missing people's page on Facebook. Sorry, I shouldn't have asked. I haven't told anyone, by the way. It's none of my business.'

Orla waved a dismissive hand. If anything, she was glad someone had noticed the posts. It meant Molly Rose hadn't just been another blank face on the missing list.

'She's home,' Orla replied. Then she looked up at the woman and smiled. She couldn't remember her name. *Shit*, she thought. Glancing up at the office door, which was still open, she looked at the sign. Lauren Green – Nursery Manager. How the hell had she managed to forget that? Yes, she'd only worked there for a month, and yes Orla had only met her twice in that time, but to forget her name entirely?

'Oh, that's such good news. Is she okay?'

'Yeah, she's okay. I'd rather not discuss it, if I'm honest.'

Lauren nodded. 'Of course. Sorry. I've got some emails to get on with. I'll leave you in peace,' she said, sitting down at the computer.

Orla glanced around the office. She owned so many of these nurseries, anything could be happening in them and she wouldn't know a thing. That was what managers were for, she supposed. They were there to run the place and protect it.

Orla sat at the second desk in the office and took her phone out of her pocket. Looking down at the screensaver, she felt a sadness wash over her at the sight of the faces staring back at her. A family picture of the three of them on holiday in Lanzarote when Molly Rose was just fourteen. An image capturing happiness, before everything went to shit.

'I've got a show round coming in just a few minutes. Just going to pop to the loo before they get here,' Lauren said, getting up from behind the desk and leaving the office.

Orla smiled in acknowledgement and watched as Lauren headed along the long corridor past the preschool classroom. Then the buzzer for the front door rang. Orla got up and put on her best smile. As she left the office, she saw a couple with a baby standing at the door.

'Hi, welcome to the nursery,' Orla said.

'We're here for a show round for our wee one,' the woman replied.

Orla opened the door and allowed the couple to enter. 'Lauren will be with you in a moment.' As Orla reached out to pull the door closed, she looked across the road to the entrance of the small green space the children often played in for their forest school sessions and saw a figure standing under one of the trees. He was staring at her and a chill ran up her spine.

Closing the door quickly, she showed the couple into the office and sat them down. Lauren appeared seconds later and began the rehearsed speech about the nursery and what it offered.

Orla quietly excused herself and went back to the front door. The man was still standing there, staring into the nursery. And then he waved. In that instant, she wondered if calling the police would be the smartest thing to do. But curiosity got the better of her. She had an idea of who this man was and if she was right, which deep down she knew she was, she wanted to look him in the eye; not to confront him, or to challenge him, but simply see his face. Orla was unable to believe that pure evil like him truly did exist, and the only way to believe it was to see it for herself. There was no thought to how dangerous that might be for her and she didn't feel fear like she knew she should.

Opening the door, she crossed the road and cautiously approached him.

'How's Molly Rose doing since she got home?'

His voice made her feel sick.

'Charlie,' Orla said. She wasn't asking. She *knew* it was him.

He nodded. 'Orla, it's a pleasure to finally meet one of my daughters.'

'It's actually the fucking opposite,' she said quietly, pulling her phone out of her pocket. 'And I'm not your daughter.' Before she dialled, she looked him in the eye, for a few seconds more than initially intended. There was a glint there, right in the centre as he glared at her. Jesus, she thought. He really is evil. She glanced down at her phone again, ready to dial.

'Ah,' he said. Holding his hand up, he tutted and shook his head slowly from left to right. 'I wouldn't do that if I were you, unless you ever want to see your family again.'

'Fuck you,' she said, dialling for the police. But he quickly reached out and grabbed the phone from her hand. Orla gasped and realised the street was empty. It was just the two of them.

'Now, you're going to drive that lovely car of yours, with me as your passenger, to where I tell you to go. And then we're going to get in contact with your mother.'

'No, we're fucking not.'

Charlie laughed. 'You sound just like her, without the accent.'

Orla turned her back on him and stepped off the curb.

'Don't think I won't kill you right now if you don't do what I say, Orla. Daughter or not.'

Nausea forced the bile in her stomach to rise but she swallowed hard and stopped on the road. She turned back and blinked. What the hell had she been thinking, coming out here on her own when her gut told her who he was? She should have just called the police.

'Is that how you get off? Attacking women? Terrorising them? You raped Janey, you murdered Kassy and you took Molly Rose. Now you're threatening me?'

Charlie frowned. '*Raped?*'

'Don't treat me like I'm stupid, Charlie. You think I'd believe your version of events over Janey's?'

Charlie closed his eyes and sighed. 'I didn't *rape* anyone.'

'Of course you didn't. Janey just had us because she *wanted* to be pregnant at fifteen. And then changed her mind at the last minute and decided to give us away.'

Charlie shrugged. 'She's selfish that way. If it doesn't suit her, then she doesn't do it.'

She looked down at her phone still in his hands and realised she didn't care. She didn't need the phone. 'You won't live to see the end of the day,' Orla said. It wasn't the first empty threat she'd made to a monster. She'd threatened Dean too and he did end up dead, though not because of her. Janey had told them all that he'd get his punishment and Orla believed her.

She turned her back on him once more and, as she went to walk away, she felt him pull her back. His hand gripped tightly around her throat from behind and a sharp pressure pressed into her back.

'Get into the fucking car, Orla. I won't tell you again.'

'My keys are inside the nursery.'

'You don't need them. I can start it without them. Just get into the car and don't do anything stupid or the knife I have at your back will pierce through and into your lung, just like I almost did to your precious Molly Rose. You don't want that to happen to you, do you? I mean, you've only just got her back and then you die? It's quite poetic, really.'

Charlie forced her round to the passenger side of the car. 'Open the door.'

'I said the keys are in the nursery.'

She felt his hand release its grip from her neck and move down to the handle. He pressed the button on the door and the car unlocked.

'You're a liar, just like your mother,' Charlie said. 'Now *get* in.'

Orla breathed through the panic and slipped into the car. He closed the door and stood outside for a few seconds. Once he moved around to the driver side, she could get out and run. But if she did that, she could lead him into a nursery full of children. That was something she just couldn't risk happening.

Charlie climbed into the driver seat and used the start-stop button to start the car.

'Where are we going?' Orla asked.

'That's for me to know and you to find out. But don't worry. I'm not going to hurt you. Well, not unless Janey doesn't do what I say.'

Chapter 58

Charlie drove along the road towards the disused docks where he'd been hiding out since Molly Rose's escape and where he'd kept the duffle bag of fake cash. The fake cash he was going to use as leverage for Orla's freedom.

Orla hadn't said a word to him since they'd driven away from her business premises. One of many, he thought. If Janey wasn't going to cough up, then maybe Orla would. If she thought it would take her daughter and herself out of danger then it was possible. The only thing was, Orla wouldn't have as much revenue as Janey. Nursery owners would never make as much money as the head of an Irish drug cartel. Never.

'Why have you brought me here?' Orla asked, looking down towards the roofless building and interrupting Charlie's thoughts.

'You'll see.'

He drove the car along Govan Road and then turned down on to Stag Street. He'd left the gate open so that he could get as close to the building as possible without having to walk.

'What the hell is this place?'

Charlie frowned. 'I don't know. All I know is, no one will find us here unless I want them to.'

He drove down the old, cobbled road and the car juddered under them, before he stopped outside the building.

'Right,' he said. 'Out.'

Orla glanced at Charlie and turned in her seat. For some reason she didn't seem frightened. She was more like Janey than he could have ever imagined.

'Doesn't it bother you?' Orla asked.

'What?'

'That you're a heartless piece of shit who could do this to his own flesh and blood?'

Charlie raised a brow. 'It's not something I struggle with, no. Now, I said get out.'

Orla exhaled loudly and got out of the car as Charlie moved around to be next to her. He took her by the elbow and led her inside the derelict, roofless building.

Once inside the confines of the heavily graffitied walls, Orla looked around before her eyes fell upon Charlie.

'Now what? You're going to kill me?'

Charlie shook his head. 'No. And I won't have to if Janey does what she's told.'

'And what makes you think she won't find me before you get what you want? I mean, she managed to get Molly Rose away from you, didn't she?'

Charlie looked down at his feet. The grass and weeds snaked up around his ankles. The holes in the soles of his shoes allowed the cold soil to creep inside.

'You know, you'd never believe me if I told you I was once a wealthy man.'

Orla rolled her eyes. 'Yeah, you definitely look like it.'

Charlie laughed. 'Yeah, I get why you wouldn't believe me. But it's true.'

'Charlie, I'm not fucking interested in anything to do with your life. Just do what you brought me here to do, eh? Get on with it.'

The sudden sharpness to her tone made him take a step back. 'Woah, calm down, girl. I was only going to give you some background because it's necessary. But if you're going to get arsey with me, then I'm going to have to do this the hard way.'

Charlie raised his arm quickly and struck Orla over the face with the back of his hand. She let out a yelp like an old dog and fell to the ground. He stood over her, looked down at her now swollen cheek and smiled. 'Maybe the hard way will be more fun.'

He pulled up his leg and stomped down on her ribs, two, three, four times. Orla rolled over and was now face down on the ground. Leaning down, he pulled at the back of her hair and lifted her head up. Putting his lips to her ear, he whispered, 'Are you fucking listening now?'

Chapter 59

As soon as she knew she was awake and remembered what had happened, she refused to open her eyes. It wasn't the fear of seeing his face, the sick fuck that he was. It was the fear that his would be the last face she saw. Because after what he'd just done to her, she didn't doubt that he would kill her, daughter or not. That meant nothing to him.

Pain seared through her entire body as she tried to remain as perfectly still as she could, but her body shifted as she tried to ease the pain.

'Ah, she's awake,' Charlie said, somewhere nearby.

Slowly peeling one eye open, Orla looked around. It had rained in the time she'd been unconscious. She didn't know how long she'd been out for, but the place was soaking, the ground beneath her cold as the rain and soil seeped through her clothes.

Her right arm ached from the shoulder. She turned her head slowly to find that she'd been chained to a metal fence, which surrounded the outside of the building, but peeked up from the space that used to be a window.

'Okay, so I wasn't successful with Molly Rose, but let me tell you something, I will get what I want *this* time. Janey, this is your daughter. Are you really going to let her die because of a stupid decision to put fake cash in the bag and the fact you refuse to give me what is rightfully mine? I doubt that very much.'

Orla opened the other eye and looked across the derelict space to see Charlie standing in front of the opposite wall. He was holding her phone up in his hand, the light from the camera on and shining in her face. He was filming her.

'Let me fucking go,' she said, or at least attempted to say behind her swollen lips.

'When the *real* money is with me, you're free to go.'

Orla pushed herself up so that her back was against the concrete wall. One hand was still free. That was strange to her. Why would he only half tie her up? Why wouldn't he make sure she was completely secure so that she couldn't escape?

'Right,' he said, lowering the phone, before tapping on the screen. 'And… sent.'

Orla imagined the look of terror on Molly Rose and Oliver's faces when they saw the footage.

'You're not going to get away with this,' she said, pulling at her chain as much as she could.

'Oh, but I will, Orla. I've got away with every single crime I've ever committed. The prostitutes, their deaths, the robberies. This one won't be any different.'

'You're nothing but a sick bastard!' she shouted. And then she started to scream, opening her mouth as wide as she could and screaming loudly until her throat scratched.

Charlie rushed towards her, shoved a rag in her mouth and clamped her jaw shut with his hand. 'Shut the fuck up, Orla.'

Panic began to rise in her as she thought about what Janey had told her. About what he'd done to Janey, his stepsister, from when they were young. If he could do that to her, then…

'Why are you looking at me that way?' Charlie said, tying another piece of material at the back of her head to hold the rag in place. 'You're scared of me, aren't you?'

Orla tore her eyes away from his. She'd rather die than let him touch her.

'Good, you fucking well should be. But don't worry, once Janey gets your message, she'll be here, ready to save you, like any good mother would. But then, she's *not* a good mother, is she? I mean, she abandoned you and your sister, Sinead. Didn't she?'

He stood over her and looked out at the world outside the derelict building he was holding her in. 'Ah, Sinead. What I wouldn't give for you both to be here. But it was difficult to get close to her. She's not really left Janey's side in a while, has she? Seems she's more accepting of her than you are. I don't know why, though. Isn't Janey the reason Sinead's an addict, being a big-time drug boss? Funny that.'

Orla kicked out at Charlie and, as he jumped back, she raised her foot and caught him in the groin as hard as she could from the position she was in.

He cried out and fell to his knees, and again, she raised her foot and the toe of her stiletto caught him in the mouth. Blood exploded all over her shoe as he raised both hands to his face.

What she'd done could have cost her her life. But if he was desperate for the money, like he seemed, then he would only punish her with another beating. That, she could take.

'You feisty little bitch,' he said, wiping the blood away with the sleeve of his manky old coat. Orla stared up at him, hoping that he'd have a sudden, quick change of heart and realise that what he was doing was wrong. She was his daughter. Surely that would mean something to him.

Fear and terror gripped Orla as an evil, black rage clouded Charlie's eyes.

'You'll pay for that,' he said as he raised his hand.

Chapter 60

Sat in her bedroom, away from the chat downstairs about what had happened to her and to Janey, Molly Rose couldn't help but travel back in her head to that time when she thought Dean was the only person in the world she could trust. How much of an idiot was she? Seeing that report in the paper... it was unbelievable. Her mum had seen something in him that Molly Rose hadn't. Being a young teenager, blinded by what she thought was love, had completely skewed her vision and understanding of the situation.

Sinead popped her head around the bedroom door.

'Hey,' she said. Molly Rose looked at her aunt. Her expression appeared pained. 'Can I come in?'

Molly Rose nodded and shifted position on the bed. 'Are you okay?'

Sinead smiled. 'I'm coping. But what about you?'

Molly Rose didn't want to tell her aunt that she looked like shit, but she had no colour in her cheeks and she practically heard her bones rattling inside her as she climbed the stairs.

'Janey told me about what you found in the paper. About Dean. How you feeling about it all?'

'I don't want to talk about it,' Molly Rose said. 'If you don't mind.'

'Of course,' Sinead replied. 'Just wanted you to know I'm here, you know, as a punch bag if you need one.'

Molly Rose sighed. 'I didn't think I could feel any sadder than I did after Dean. Then I met Kassy and now she's dead. My heart's in pieces. I miss her. And I know I didn't know her for that long, but she was a real friend, you know? The kind who stuck up for me when I had no one else. She took me under her wing...' Molly Rose swallowed the lump in her throat. 'She was unique. I doubt I'll ever find anyone like her again.'

Sinead's expression was awash with empathy. 'I get it, Molly Rose. It doesn't matter how long you were friends for. The fact is, she was there for you when you felt you had nowhere else to turn. You'll have that forever. You were so lucky to have found a friend like that.'

'Luck doesn't come into it. If anything, I'm bad luck. And I'm sick of that, you know? Dean leaving, Kassy dying, Charlie trying to kill me. It's just all... too much. And thinking about it is hard enough, never mind talking about it.'

'I get that. No more chat,' Sinead said, quickly, and then changed the subject to what she had come in to talk about. 'I can't get through to your mum on the phone. Have you heard from her?'

Molly Rose shook her head and looked down at her phone. 'Not since this morning when I decided to burn the paper in the sink.'

'Ah, so that's what the smell was,' Sinead joked, offering a gentle smile.

Molly Rose pulled up WhatsApp and opened the chat with her mum.

'It's saying she's online. Do you want me to phone her?'

Sinead nodded. 'Yeah, I want to ask her something about my methadone programme.'

Molly Rose hit the call icon on the screen, but the call was rejected. Frowning, Molly Rose glanced up at Sinead. 'That's weird. She hung up on me.'

Sinead sat down on the bed and took the phone from Molly Rose.

'What's wrong?'

'I don't know, but I have this gut feeling that something isn't right,' Sinead replied. 'Call it a twin thing.'

Molly Rose frowned. 'Do you guys have that? I didn't think you would, given how distant you've both been with each other over the years.'

Sinead called Orla again. 'Maybe it's not a twin thing. But something has unsettled me. Call it instinct or the fact we have security men posted outside the house and Orla's not here.'

The call was rejected again. But when Molly Rose looked down at the screen, it stated that Orla was typing.

Then, a message appeared.

> Are you all sitting together like a nice big happy family? If you're not, I suggest you do it because a very special video is about to come through. I'll give you all five minutes.

She held the phone up to Sinead to show her the message.

'Shit,' Sinead said, getting up and moving towards the door.

Molly Rose got up and followed, panic consuming her. 'What? What's wrong?'

Sinead was running down the stairs, calling out to Janey and Oliver.

Janey appeared at the bottom of the stairs, concern on her face.

Sinead showed her the phone and said: 'Something's wrong. I know it. That's not Orla, it's not.'

Janey took the phone from Sinead's hand and glanced up at Molly Rose.

'Have you spoken to my mum?'

Janey nodded. 'Not since this morning in the kitchen with you.'

'Did she say if she was planning to leave the house today?' Oliver asked.

'She said she was going into work for a while, to help clear her head,' Janey replied.

'Which work?' Oliver asked.

'I'm sorry, I don't know. She didn't specify. I said she could have a security man with her but she point-blank refused.'

Molly Rose felt sick. 'Dad, phone round all the four nurseries in the West End. See if she was there?'

Oliver took out his mobile but as he was about to call, every single one of their phones pinged at the same time.

Molly Rose froze as Janey took out her own mobile.

'It's a video message,' Janey said.

She hit play and Molly Rose immediately recognised the voice. It was Charlie Hallahan. She stared down at the screen as Janey held the phone in her hand and what she saw made her gasp out loud. Her mum, Orla, was tied to a fence as Charlie filmed her while he spoke. She looked like she'd been badly beaten. Tears pooled in Molly Rose's eyes.

'Good afternoon to you all. Hope you don't mind the message, but I thought it would be best to let you all know what I'm going to do next. Firstly, as you can see here, your beloved wife, mum, sister, daughter, is in a bad way. She got a tad cheeky with me, so I took her down a peg or two. Sorry about that.

'Secondly, as you've probably already guessed it, I have Orla. You can blame your beloved Janey for that one. Giving me fake money wasn't your smartest move, Janey. I want what's owed to me. And if you don't give me what is rightfully mine, then I will put an end to her. I'm fed up of waiting now.'

His voice stopped, and then he laughed. 'Ah, she's awake. Okay, so I wasn't successful with Molly Rose, but let me tell you something, I will get what I want *this* time. Janey, this is your daughter. Are you really going to let her die because of a stupid decision to put fake cash in the bag and the fact you refuse to give me what is rightfully mine? I doubt that very much.'

Orla's voice slurred in the background before the video came to an end.

'Jesus Christ,' Oliver said. 'Janey, what are you going to do about this?'

Janey was quiet for a moment. And then she started tapping on the screen on her own phone.

'Gran,' Molly Rose said. Everyone looked up at her as she stood on the middle step. Janey stared at her, through glistening eyes. 'You need to do something. He'll kill her if you don't.'

Janey nodded. 'I will. You don't have to worry.'

Sinead sat down on the bottom step and buried her head into her knees. 'Don't have to worry? We don't even know where they fucking are.'

'This is all my fault. If I'd just stayed with him, if I hadn't made such a fuss then…'

Janey rushed up to Molly Rose and took her face in her hands. 'No. None of this is down to any of you except me. This mess was started because of me and I intend to finish it.'

Chapter 61

'I've forwarded the video to you both,' Janey said as she spoke on a joint video call with Ciaran and Kristo. She was sat in the car outside Orla and Oliver's home, and trying her best not to lose it. The thought of Orla being alone with Charlie, injured because of him, brought back raw and terrifying memories.

'Do you think you could find out where he is?' Janey asked.

'I recognise this place,' Kristo replied.

'Seriously?'

Kristo nodded. 'Yeah. It's sometimes used by junkies. I've often been down there to pick up debts.'

Janey sighed. 'And you're absolutely sure?'

Kristo was typing something into his laptop and was silent for a moment. Janey let him do his thing.

'Janey, are you okay?' Ciaran asked.

'I'm fine.'

'You're not going there, *are* you? You're going to let us deal with this?'

Janey laughed incredulously. 'He only wants me, Ciaran.'

'Sorry, Janey. I know you're my boss, but I won't take orders to allow you to do this on your own. We'll be there. But he won't know it,' Kristo said.

Janey couldn't argue. She didn't want to.

'Okay,' Kristo continued. 'The wall markings were what gave it away. The graffiti. It's definitely the place I thought.'

'Where?'

'The old Govan Graving Docks. They're abandoned, and used, like I said, by local junkies, sometimes youths, late at night. I'm sending you the address now.'

Janey nodded, closed her eyes and tried not to think the worst.

Just as she was about to start the car, the passenger door opened.

'I'm coming with you.'

Janey locked eyes with Sinead and shook her head. 'Absolutely not.'

'She's my sister. I'm not just going to sit in the house while she's going through this. We've only just started to make amends. I can't lose her to that fucker. If you don't take me, I'll just follow you.'

Janey hesitated and then sighed loudly. 'Fine.'

'You're taking all of us,' Oliver said, appearing behind Sinead. 'We're a family and she *needs* all of us.'

Janey got out of the car and walked around to the passenger side. 'Molly Rose, you're not coming. It's too dangerous. In fact, it's too dangerous for all of you.'

Molly Rose raised a brow, opened the back door and said: 'Try stopping me.'

Janey watched as they all climbed into the Defender; Sinead into the passenger seat, Molly Rose and Oliver the back. She couldn't help but smile. After all this time, she had the family she wanted but this wasn't the way she'd imagined it. Not the way the girls found out and certainly not how she would have wanted to meet her granddaughter. If anything, Janey felt more like a mother now than she did the day she gave birth to Orla and Sinead. Now, she had to do what any other woman would do to save their child. She would throw herself in front of Charlie's knife for Orla. And that scenario was very possible. Having the rest of the family there wasn't a good idea and certainly not safe for any of them. But, as she stared at them as they put on their seatbelts, it seemed like she didn't have much of a choice.

Against her better judgement, Janey got back into the car and put on her own seatbelt. 'Okay, *rules*. When we get there, you will all *stay* in the car. I have people meeting me there to deal with this.'

'No way. I'm coming in with you,' Sinead started. 'I want this bastard to look me in the eye and tell me why he's such—'

Janey turned sharply. 'Sinead, this isn't a game. Charlie is dangerous. There's nothing he won't do to get his money and he's even angrier now that I tried to trick him into taking fake cash. An angry, betrayed man like Charlie isn't someone to be messed with.'

'Then give him what he wants?' Oliver suggested. 'If it means getting Orla back.'

Janey glared at him. 'Are you really that naïve? If I do that, then what does he do next? He's a poisonous leech, Oliver. He'll come after you all if I don't put an end to this now. So, like I said, when we get there, stay in the car. I'm not kidding.'

They all fell silent as Janey started the engine and typed the address into the sat nav.

'I know that place,' Sinead said, staring down at the screen.

'You've been there?'

Janey raised a brow, wondering how.

'I used to go there with some of my mates back in the early days… It's like hell on earth.'

Chapter 62

Janey stopped the car at the gate and got out. Kristo and Ciaran were standing at the entrance to the disused, cobbled road and on the corner was a car with blacked-out windows. More of Janey's employees were ready and waiting.

'Please, Janey,' Kristo said. 'Don't go down there. Let us go. We can take him out from a distance. You can get Orla back. But if you do it your way, you run the risk of him killing her and you.'

Janey glanced down the road and saw the roofless building in the distance. 'Is that it?'

She looked back at Kristo and then Ciaran. They both nodded.

'Right,' she said, slipping her hand into the inside pocket of her coat and checking for the gun, even though she knew it was there. She'd checked it a million times already. 'Cover me.'

Ciaran moved forward and stepped in front of Janey. He shook his head. 'No. Janey, I've never, *ever*, stopped you from doing anything. But you're *not* doing this. He's a fucking—'

'Rapist? Murderer? Kidnapper? Yeah, I know. But he's also a drunk, desperate for cash. If you go in all guns blazing, he's already got nothing to lose. He'll kill her. If he sees me, he'll think he stands a chance of getting what he wants. I need to be the one who faces up to him. Like I said, cover me. And do not—' she gestured to the Defender '—let them out of your sight.'

'I'm not moving,' Ciaran said.

Janey smiled at her husband, leaned in and kissed him on the lips. 'You will, sweetheart. You've never stood in my way. It's why *you* took *my* name.'

Taking a breath, she glanced at Kristo, nodded and then sidestepped around Ciaran. 'Don't follow me. If he thinks I have an entourage, he might react and do something drastic.'

Passing through the entrance, Janey began walking down the cobbled road towards the building. She noticed the burned-out car down in the hill, the graffiti all around her, on the ground, on the walls surrounding the docks. The click of her heels on the cobbles seemed louder than they actually were. She kept her eyes on the building, the old pumphouse. Her daughter was being held in there, by the man who'd left Janey mentally scarred for life after what he did to her. He could do the same to Orla. Christ only knew how he hadn't done the same to Molly Rose.

The road turned to the right and Janey followed it. The cobbles were overgrown with moss and weeds, and as she approached the house, she held her breath. She could hear Charlie's voice. She could hear him talking. She heard every single word.

Chapter 63

Orla had been quiet since Charlie had sent the video of her to her entire family, including Janey. It was satisfying, seeing the double blue ticks appear on the message, knowing they'd all seen it. Knowing that Orla was being held in an unknown location.

'I'll be sending details on to Janey now, to let her know how and where to transfer my money. Once I know it's there, you get to go home. I think.'

Orla looked up at him and then blinked.

'What happened to you as a child to make you like this?' Orla asked.

'Excuse me?'

'I mean, you must've gone through some kind of trauma for you to have turned into someone this nasty and evil.'

Charlie thought about it, then nodded before sitting down in front of her. He looked her over as she winced in pain.

'You think I'm evil?'

'You think you're not? You kidnapped a sixteen-year-old girl, murdered her best friend, then your plan went to shit and you forced me to come here to protect my daughter. Not to mention that you're a rapist. What the hell happened to you?'

308

Charlie closed his eyes and cast his mind back to the day his stepfather, Finn, disowned him. He'd never forgotten that day. *That* conversation.

-

The punch to the back of his head sent him flying across the gravel. He lost his balance and fell forward, splaying his hands out in front of him to break his fall.

'What the fuck?' Charlie said as he flipped onto his back and looked up at the man who'd attacked him from behind. 'Da, what the fuck are you doing?'

'I'm not your da. No son of mine would behave the way you have.' Finn reached down and gripped Charlie by the throat, his fingers squeezing tightly as Charlie was pulled to his feet.

'Tell me it's not true?' Finn said, with fire in his eyes. Charlie had never seen Finn this angry before. Not even in his line of work.

'What the hell are you on about?' he gasped, trying to peel Finn's fingers away.

'You know what I'm talking about. The rape!' he growled.

Charlie felt his stomach lurch, as if it was going to fall out his arsehole. Had Janey told him?

'What the hell? Rape? Who?' The words struggled to leave his mouth behind Finn's strong grip.

Finn let go of Charlie and stepped back, coughing and spluttering.

'If you're asking who, does that mean there was more than one?'

Charlie thought about that night with Janey. He'd indirectly warned her not to breathe a word. 'More than one what?'

Finn began to pace in front of Charlie, shaking his head as he looked down at the gravel on the ground. He stopped, looked up at him through narrowed eyes.

'Don't play me for a fucking fool, Charlie. You know what I'm talking about,' Finn said, reaching into his pocket. Charlie watched as his stepdad pulled out a gun and pointed it at his face.

Charlie raised his hands and felt fear creep through him.

'I've been approached by someone who claims their daughter was raped. By you. That you drugged her? He has a security camera on the side of his house and, when he showed it to me, I clearly saw you walking away from the building. So, what the fuck have you got to say for yourself?'

Charlie thought about it, quickly. This man could have been any one of the girls' dads. He had to be careful not to incriminate himself.

'It wasn't me,' Charlie said, staring down the barrel of the gun.

'You're saying my eyes deceived me? You're calling me a liar?'

Charlie shook his head. 'No. I'm simply saying it wasn't me. Whoever this girl is, she's the liar.'

Finn laughed incredulously. 'Get inside.'

Charlie stared at him wearily. With that gun pointed at him, Finn could shoot him and there would be nothing Charlie could do about it. 'Why?'

'You're packing your bags. I don't want you near me, or Janey. You're bad for business, for my reputation. In fact, you're a disgrace to the Hallahan name and you're not even blood.' Finn gestured with the gun for Charlie to move. He turned, headed to the house. He had no other choice. He had no doubt that Finn would shoot him.

Charlie walked towards his bedroom and went inside.

'After everything I've done for you, took you on as my own after what happened to you as a child. Your ma leaving, your da beating seven shades of shit out of you. He was a rapist too, you do remember that, don't you? That's why your ma left. She couldn't face you every day, the reminder of what Gerry had done

310

to her and what he continued to do most nights. I felt sorry for you. The night I took you, after I found out what he did, Gerry told me I'd never get away with taking his boy. So, I arranged for him to be run over while he was walking home from the pub, pissed out his head. I fucking trusted that bastard. He was my friend, my business partner. You and Janey would have got equal shares when the time came. But he went and fucked that up. And then you go and do the same thing he did. Nah, you're not staying here and dragging my family name through the mud. Pack. Now.'

Charlie stared at him in disbelief. 'You had my da killed?'

'Aye, I did.'

For some reason, something deep inside him felt like it was going to erupt. 'You're a prick.'

'Aye, and you're a rapist. So, like I said, get packing.'

Charlie thought about everything Finn had said. The fact that he would have had an equal part in the business when Gerry and Finn retired, but now he was going to be left with nothing. It wasn't right. 'But where will I go?'

'I don't give a shit. But you're not staying here. I'm disowning you. You don't get to use the Hallahan name any more. And I mean that literally. Get your name changed back. You're nothing to do with this family any more.'

Charlie stared at his stepdad with wide eyes. 'You can't be serious? You haven't even heard my side of the story yet.'

'Thought there wasn't a story to tell?' Finn raised a brow, the gun still pointed at Charlie's face.

'What about my inheritance? Surely there's still money owed to me given my da's part in the business.'

Finn laughed loudly. 'You don't have an inheritance. And Gerry's shares dissolved a long time ago. And that was all it was, Charlie. Shares. I took over this business from my own father many years ago. Did you really think I was going to hand over the Hallahan business to anyone who isn't a Hallahan by blood? And anyway, you've had everything owed to you already. I raised you as my own. Janey treated you like a brother. And even after all that, you still managed to fuck it up with what you did to that girl.'

'But I didn't do anything.'

Rushing forward, Finn pressed the gun into Charlie's forehead. 'Don't stand there and fucking lie to me, boy. You're nothing but scum, just like Gerry was.'

He lowered the gun and took a breath. Charlie watched as he tried to calm himself. He wouldn't want to shoot Charlie in his own house, surely?

'Fine. If that's what you think of me, I will go. I wouldn't want to hang around somewhere I'm not wanted. But no matter what you think of me, Finn, I'm entitled. And I will not leave here without what I'm owed.'

Finn's jaw tensed and Charlie watched as he left the room. A few moments later, he was back. He threw a cheque at him and it floated on the air to the floor.

'Take that, you piece of scum. And you better fuck off. And I mean far away from here. You've got enough money to start a new life. I never want to see your face again.'

'If I'm that much of a scumbag to you, why don't you just kill me?'

Finn eyed him and closed his eyes. 'Because I used to think of you as the son I never had. I really should hand you into the police. But that's not in my nature either. So, you'll take that cheque and you'll go.'

Charlie bent down and picked the cheque up. He looked at the amount and whistled loudly. 'Fine, I'll go to Belfast. Start a new life with this money.'

'Ha,' Finn laughed loudly. 'You wouldn't last five minutes on your own in Belfast. Not with everything that's happening.

And, if I remember, I said you were to go somewhere far away. Does twenty miles sound far to you?'

Charlie fell quiet. He was right. Belfast wasn't the best idea he'd come up with. And with all the trouble going on, it wasn't exactly somewhere he could set up a new and comfortable life.

'You're dead to me,' Finn replied. 'Now pack. I'll drive you to the airport myself. Pick a flight. Get on it and don't come back.'

That was exactly what Charlie would do. Because he knew that, one day, Finn would find out about Janey, one way or another. And for that he knew he couldn't be around. Because the moral rule that Finn lived by about not hurting family would dissolve immediately.

—

'Nothing,' Charlie replied, bringing his thoughts back to the present.

'I don't believe you,' she said. It was like she was picking at an old wound that had never properly healed.

'I don't give a fuck if you don't believe me, I said nothing happened. This is just me. I'm not a bad person. I just want what's mine.'

Orla shifted her position, wincing and gasping as she did so. 'And to get what you wanted, you murdered someone and then took my daughter off the street while she waited for us. Oh yeah, you're a fucking angel.'

'Do you want another tanking? Cos I'll give you one if you don't shut your mouth,' Charlie said through gritted teeth.

Orla looked away.

'My stepdad, your grandad…' Charlie started, getting to his feet and looking out of the building above Orla's head. 'He was like a real dad to me. Better than the one I was born from. I was brought up, or rather, dragged up, by Gerry, thinking that I was unlikeable. No one wanted me. I was just there, in the way.'

He looked down at Orla to see if she was paying attention. She wasn't watching him, but he could tell she was taking it in.

'Anyway, I was the product of rape.'

Charlie began pacing back and forth, slowly. Steady.

'So, you became just like your own father?' Orla piped up. Charlie ignored her. He refused to think of himself like that. 'That explains a lot.'

'I did *not* rape anyone. Janey was a willing participant.'

'You're a monster. A predator.'

Turning, he looked at her and shook his head. 'I always wondered if either of you would turn out like me. But you're just like her. Janey. You're too feisty for your own good.'

Charlie let the blade up his sleeve slip down into his grip. Orla looked at it and then fixed her eyes on him.

Chapter 64

'Willing participants are usually conscious, Charlie. They're usually able to use their voice to consent to what is happening. Only, that's not what happened, was it?' Janey said, stepping into the building with the gun pointed at Charlie's face.

Charlie turned and smiled as he saw Janey.

'Ah, you found us. Your little team help with that, did they?'

Janey eyed the blade in Charlie's hand and then glanced down to see Orla chained to the fence by her wrist. She looked in a bad way, blood running down her nose, one eye almost completely swollen shut. He was stood right next to her.

'Unchain her,' Janey said.

Charlie sighed and shook his head. 'Not until you pay me with the real cash you owe me.'

'Pay you? I'll fucking shoot you dead right now.'

'Then why don't you?' Charlie challenged.

'Because I want to ask you something.'

She always promised herself she'd never do this. She'd never put herself in a position where she came face to face with the monster that was her stepbrother. But she just couldn't walk away from this. He'd put her through too much.

'What's that?'

'You knew what your own mother had gone through. What Gerry did to her. So why become like him?'

'I'm *not* like him.'

Janey frowned. '*Of course you're not.* I mean, this really does prove it, doesn't it. You're a good man. With a good heart. You've never hurt anyone in your life. Except me. Except the girl in the pub who you raped after me. Except Kassy, who you murdered and kept in the boot of your car. Except when you kidnapped Molly Rose and held her hostage. Except when you brought Orla here, and beat the fucking shit out of her, chained her to the fucking fence and threatened to finish her off if I didn't give you money you think you're owed.'

'I'm. Not. A. Rapist.'

Janey stared at him in disbelief. 'Is that how you get by each day? By lying to yourself?'

'Shut up,' Charlie said, reaching down quickly and holding the knife to Orla's throat.

Janey squeezed gently on the trigger and took a step forward. She felt her footing go beneath her and, as she fell forward, the gun slipped from her hand and skittered across the ground.

'Fuck!' she shouted.

'Bad luck, Janey.'

The sound of Orla's blood-curdling screams coursed through Janey's entire body as Charlie plunged the knife into her daughter's neck. Janey tried to reach for the gun.

With it back in her grip, she rolled round and shot at Charlie. He pulled the knife away from Orla and blood spurted from her neck. Janey watched as Charlie fell to the ground, clutching at his leg and screeching in pain. It all happened so quickly, she barely had time to register what had happened.

'Orla!' Janey called, crawling towards her. 'Orla, hold on.'

Janey took in the scene in front of her. The knife by Orla's side, the blood pouring from the side of where her neck met her shoulder. Charlie writhing in pain as blood flowed from his thigh.

He screeched: 'You fucking bitch!'

She took Orla in her arms and applied pressure to the wound. 'Stay with me, Orla.'

The sound of cars rumbling down the cobbled road outside drew closer. *They would have heard the gun shots*, she thought.

Orla looked up at her through the one eye that wasn't swollen shut. She was gasping and spluttering.

'Mum?'

'Don't speak. You're going to be fine. I promise.'

'Fuck, Janey!' Ciaran shouted. She looked up at him and saw him moving to Charlie.

'No. Don't kill him. Phone an ambulance. She's bleeding out.'

Janey blinked and saw Sinead, Molly Rose and Oliver rushing towards her. Molly Rose was silent as she sat down next to Orla. Sinead was screaming. Oliver looked helpless.

'What the hell happened?' Molly Rose said, looking over at Charlie.

'Not now, Molly Rose. Take off that hoodie. Oliver, press it against Orla's neck.'

Molly Rose removed her hoodie and handed it to her dad. Janey sat the gun down by her side and Oliver took over cradling Orla.

'Ambulance is on its way,' Ciaran said.

'Janey, let us deal with him,' Kristo's voice came over the chaos that was unfolding. She shook her head.

'No. Just let me be with her.'

Janey looked down at Orla. She wasn't moving. The sounds of her gasps had stopped.

'Mum?' Molly Rose whispered.

Sinead was sobbing loudly, pulling at Orla's hands. 'Wake up, don't you fucking dare die on us now. Not now. Jesus!'

Everything felt like a blur. It was all her fault. All of it. If she'd just stayed away, Charlie might not have found the girls. They could still be living their lives. Orla wouldn't be—

'Molly Rose, *no!*'

A deafening shot rang out and everything fell silent.

Chapter 65

The power of the gun had thrown her back a foot or so and her shoulder felt like it had popped out. As she lay on the ground, she looked up at the sky through where the roof should be.

A loud ringing sounded in her ears and suddenly she felt lighter than she thought possible. The sound of chaos descending around her brought her back and she sat up slowly.

'Is he dead?' Molly Rose asked, looking at the two men standing over Charlie.

The other man, the one who wasn't Janey's husband, glanced down at her and nodded. 'Yes.'

Molly Rose blinked and looked over at her mum. 'Good.'

Oliver cradled Orla in his arms as Sinead sobbed loudly next to her. Molly Rose got to her feet and slowly moved towards her family. Dropping to her knees in front of her mum, she looked down at her face. Her eyes stared up at the sky. There was nothing in there. No light. No life. Instant grief rose from the pit of her stomach and she let out a scream, which lowered in pitch. Then she cried silent tears. Janey got to her feet and pulled Molly Rose up with her.

Janey picked up the gun and wiped it on her coat. Turning to Ciaran and the other man, she said: 'Here, take this. Take Molly Rose to the house. Get her as far away from here as possible. Do not stop. Take the backroads.'

'Yes,' the other man said.

Janey took Molly Rose's face in her hands and said: 'You say nothing to anyone. You weren't here today. Got it?'

She nodded slowly. Glanced back at her mum.

'No, don't look. Look at me, into my eyes. That's it.'

A wave of nausea came over her and she took a breath. 'That's it. Breathe.'

Molly Rose noticed the blood on Janey's hands. Her mother's blood.

'Is she really dead? Is this just a horrible dream?'

Janey hesitated. She didn't have to say or gesture. Molly Rose knew.

'Then I'm glad I shot him. I hope it fucking hurt.'

Ciaran stepped forward and took Molly Rose's hand. 'Okay, love. Let's get you out of here. Quickly. Come on.'

Molly Rose allowed Ciaran and the other man to lead her out of the building, but not before she stole a glance down at the man who'd murdered her friend and now her mum. He was still. Blood poured from his chest and leg. Had she shot him twice? She wasn't sure.

Before she knew it, she was in the back of a car she didn't recognise. Ciaran was in the passenger seat. The other man was driving.

As she glanced out the window, she heard sirens in the distance. Raising her hands to her ears and leaning forward, she asked Ciaran to turn up the music. She needed to drown out the thoughts in her head.

Ciaran turned on Spotify and the song that came on chilled her to the depths of her soul. It was Orla's favourite; an artist that Molly Rose hated because it was all Orla listened to. "In This World" by Moby. It was the song that was playing just before Molly Rose left home.

Now, as Molly Rose listened to the lyrics, it was almost as though it was written for both of them.

The shock of what had just unfolded caused Molly Rose to shiver and shake in the back of the car. She swallowed hard, tried to stem the screams that wanted to leave her throat. Her mum had just died in the most horrific way, right in front of her. Charlie had stabbed her in the neck.

'Breathe, Molly Rose. Breathe. In and out, in and out,' Ciaran said from the front seat. But she was panicking now. Hyperventilating.

'She's… she's dead. He killed her!' she screamed. 'Oh God, we have to go back. I can't leave her,' Molly Rose unclipped her belt and attempted to get out of the car, but the door was locked.

Ciaran turned and grabbed at her hand. 'Listen to me, Molly Rose. She's dead. She's not there. And you killed Charlie. We can't go back there. You can't be seen anywhere near that place. You have to try to calm down, for your own safety.'

Molly Rose stopped pulling at the handle but kept her hand there while Ciaran kept her other in his grip. She stared at him but could barely see his face through her tears. The man driving was silent.

'Is she really dead?' Molly Rose whispered, the emotion making her throat ache.

Ciaran's expression was pained. 'I'm sorry, sweetheart. She is. But you got her justice. You killed the man who took her life. She would be proud of you for that.'

She let go of the handle and sat back, her stiff body suddenly softening, and she laid down on the back seat.

She let the sobs come in waves and surrendered the shock of what had happened to her mum. The one woman in the world who, despite their differences, had only tried to protect her. She could see that now. But it was too late. She couldn't tell her she understood, or that she forgave her. Orla would never know how *right* she was.

Chapter 66

One month later

Janey got out of the funeral car, alongside Oliver, Sinead and Molly Rose. The family had insisted that she help carry Orla's coffin into the crematorium. She was honoured and broken at the same time. The whole reason the funeral was taking place was because of her.

'Mrs Hallahan,' the funeral director said. 'If you could come to the front and stand at the left, Mr Hunter will be to your right. Sinead and Molly Rose will be in the middle, and two of our pallbearers at the back. Wait for my cue and you will both follow me. Okay?'

Janey nodded and stood where she was told. Her legs felt like jelly beneath her, but she couldn't falter. Not now. She'd never been there for Orla or Sinead in all the years they'd truly needed her. She wasn't about to abandon them now.

The next few moments were like a blur, like she wasn't inside her body for carrying the coffin. It was as though she was up in the corner of the ceiling, watching herself. She heard Sinead breathing deep and steady, Molly Rose was silent, as was Oliver.

Once Orla's coffin was on the catafalque, a name she'd only just learned that day, she sat down next to her family, between Sinead and Molly Rose, and Oliver on the other side of his daughter. They all held hands and Ciaran sat behind Janey, his hand resting on her shoulder.

Listening to the humanist talk about Orla was like a lesson in the life of her daughter. She learned so much about her, from school, to how she built her business. No mentions of negativity, no mentions of her murder. Only good, wholesome things.

Tears streamed down her face, and she felt Sinead and Molly Rose's grip tighten around her fingers as she held in the threatening wails of emotion. The loss was worse than if she'd been in Orla's life, because now she'd never get to experience being any kind of mother to her.

-

Janey sat on the edge of the bed and stared down at her twin babies. She couldn't believe she'd agreed to go through with this. But she didn't have another choice. What kind of life could she give them if she kept them? Finn would throw her out. He'd refused to bring up more children that weren't his. Charlie had been problem enough. Another reason she couldn't tell her dad what had really happened, and who their biological dad was.

The bedroom door opened and two women stood in the doorway, dressed in black suits.

'It's time,' one of them said, stepping into the room.

Janey swallowed hard, but the tears escaped from the corners of her eyes. She slid off the bed and sat on the floor between the girls. Leaning down and kissing them both gently on the forehead, she said: 'I'm sorry I couldn't be the mum you both deserve. I love you both so, so much.'

She couldn't watch them being taken away from her. It was too painful, like a knife repeatedly stabbing her in the heart.

The sound of her babies crying as they were carried from the house made her want to walk in front of a train. Maybe she would. Maybe that was the only way she could rid herself of the pain, the guilt of not having the courage to refuse this.

'They'll be well looked after,' Finn said. But he couldn't look her in the eye.

Things had changed between them. Janey knew it would never be the same. But she would try. Because now, Finn was all she had left.

–

Stood on the terrace outside the hotel where the reception had been held, Janey expelled a plume of blue smoke and swallowed the lump in her throat. She refused to cry here. It was hard enough letting the tears fall during the service.

'Why are you out here on your own?' Ciaran said as he opened the door and stepped out from the hotel.

'I don't know anyone here. They all find out who I am and they just look at me like they don't know what to say. Not that I blame them. They probably all knew Orla without a mother. And now I rock up carrying her coffin. The woman no one has heard of. If they knew the real reason Orla was dead, I doubt I'd be welcome.'

'The real reason she's gone isn't because of you, Janey. You need to understand that.' Sighing, Ciaran handed Janey a glass of gin. 'Here, get that down you.'

Forcing a smile, she took the glass from his hand and drank back, greedily. She could easily drink herself into a coma today. But she wouldn't.

'You were incredibly brave to do what you did. And the fact you were asked speaks volumes about how the family views you, Janey.'

His words were kind, and he was only trying to help her feel better, but it didn't stop the pain and the guilt.

'I feel so empty. I don't know what to do with myself.'

'That's normal. You've endured a lot over the past month. You gained your daughters and lost one. That's bound to take time to set in.'

She took a long draw on the cigarette in her hand and held it in her lungs.

'You're not still thinking about going, are you?' Ciaran asked with caution in his tone.

'I have to,' she said, exhaling loudly.

'Do you really, though? Won't it just make things harder?'

She shook her head. 'No. I need to see that coffin go to the fire. I need to know he's gone. And then I can move on. You know, knowing he was out there, living the fucking high life, I always regretted not telling Dad. I always feared, someday, he'd come back and I'd have to face what he did. Maybe if Finn had known, he'd have killed him and none of this would have happened.'

Ciaran moved closer and pulled her in close. 'You can't torture yourself with what-ifs, Janey.'

'I know,' she said. 'But Orla's dead, Ciaran. She died. Molly Rose became a killer. Oliver became a widower. That entire family lost someone close to them because I was silent.'

It was a thought she would have to live with for the rest of her life. Because there was nothing else to think of in that moment. Nothing at all.

Chapter 67

She stood at the bar and waited for the barmaid to hand the vodka glass to Sinead.

'That'll be a fiver,' said the barmaid.

'And you're going to drink it?' Molly Rose asked.

Sinead pursed her lips and shrugged. 'I don't know. But I wanted to hold the glass in my hand, to be able to smell it to see if I had the strength not to drink it.'

Molly Rose glanced at the barmaid, who was awkwardly waiting to be paid. She slid the fiver across the bar and smiled, before taking the glass in her hand and holding it out for Sinead to take from her.

'Go on then,' she said. 'If getting hammered will make you feel better after being sober for a month and a half, then on you go.'

Sinead hesitated, took the glass and waved it under her nose. Grimacing, she placed it down on the bar. 'That fucking stinks.'

'Yep, as will you when you wake up covered in your own vomit tomorrow. And then what, it's back to Kelvingrove, sleeping rough, back on the junk too?'

Sinead shook her head. 'You're wiser than your years, you know that?'

'Yeah, a wise woman once told me to look after myself. That there was no one else out there who could do it better than ourselves.'

Sinead smiled and turned her back to the bar.

'So, what happens now?' Molly Rose asked.

Sinead shrugged. 'I don't know. I suppose we just… start to get on with things?'

'Will I go to prison?'

Sinead shot her a look. 'No. Janey's already sorted things. You'll never be implicated for what happened.'

Molly Rose remembered the look on Charlie's dead face after she'd shot him. She hadn't felt remorse, fear, worry. Nothing. He deserved it.

'I don't think going to prison would worry me,' Molly Rose said. 'I think after what that bastard put me through, I could face anything.'

Sinead glanced at her. 'Yeah, I don't doubt you could. But you're not going to prison for scum like him. You took what he did. A life for a life. Orla was worth a million souls over him.'

Molly Rose had tried not to think too much about how Orla had died. Brutally, painfully. The idea that she'd wasted so much time being in a teenaged huff about the boyfriend, who'd evidently turned out to be a human trafficker, made her feel sick. As did the guilt for being so awful towards her mother, when all she'd done was try to protect her daughter.

'I miss her,' Molly Rose whispered, looking at the framed picture of Orla on the bar. 'She didn't deserve to die. She was a good mum.'

Sinead was quiet. Molly Rose knew she was struggling with the death of her twin sister while still trying to remain clean and sober. It was a test not even Molly Rose thought she'd pass.

Taking a breath and trying not to cry – it was all she seemed to be doing these days – Molly Rose said: 'Do you think Janey will go to his funeral?'

Sinead shrugged. 'I don't know.'

Molly Rose wanted to go. She wanted to see him burn, even in death. That piece of shit deserved the flames for eternity.

She glanced out the window and on to the terrace outside. Janey was stood with her back to the hotel, staring out at the forest in front of the building.

She wondered what Janey was thinking. How she was feeling.

One thing was for sure: Molly Rose wanted Janey to remain in their lives. She wanted to know more about her grandmother. She fascinated Molly Rose: her lifestyle; her attitude; her lack of fear. All of it. She didn't have her own mother now. But she had Orla's.

Chapter 68

She stood outside the crematorium and looked inside. The place was empty. No mourners, no family, no friends. *Good*, she thought. That was the way it should be. Although she didn't expect anything else. Charlie was a horrific human being. There couldn't possibly be anyone left in the world who cared for him even the tiniest bit. Seeing the empty seats inside proved that, among other reasons.

Janey thought about Charlie lying inside his most basic-of-basic coffins. His lifeless body set to be cremated. Death had been too easy for him. Now, she'd never hear him admit what he'd done, although deep down she knew that would never have happened anyway. He was a coward, unable to face up to his own actions. Never willing to accept he was a bad person, rotten to the very core.

'Are you just going to stand out here and listen, or are you going inside?'

Janey turned and saw Molly Rose standing behind her. She was dressed in jeans, a T-shirt and a bright-pink hoodie. A stark contrast in comparison to Janey, who was wearing all black.

'What the hell are you doing here?'

'I want to make sure that prick goes to the fire.' Molly Rose glanced inside. 'I'll never actually believe he's gone until I see it with my own eyes.'

Janey stared at her in disbelief. 'You can't be here, Molly Rose. And especially not dressed like that.'

Molly Rose frowned and looked down at herself before meeting Janey's eye again. 'Why not? You're here.'

'That's different.'

'Is it? How?'

Janey rolled her eyes. She was still just a young girl, a teenager. She didn't understand the true extent of it all. Not the way Janey had at her age.

'I have years' worth of grief and regret to get rid of when he goes through those curtains, Molly Rose. I need to be here to see him go.'

Molly Rose nodded, pursed her lips and said, 'Go on then, if you're going.'

'You're not coming in with me.'

'And you're going to stop me? That bastard murdered my best friend, almost killed me and then tortured and murdered my mum. Nothing and no one on this planet is going to stop me from watching this. If you don't like it, there's not much you can do about it.'

As Janey was about to argue her point, Molly Rose walked around her and strode inside as if she was going for a leisurely walk. Janey watched after her, wondering where she got her attitude from. Was it Orla, or was it her?

Taking a long, deep breath, Janey walked inside and sat down next to Molly Rose.

'Are you family of the deceased?' the man standing up at the coffin asked.

Janey hesitated. 'Old acquaintances,' she replied.

The man nodded and began reciting some passage about God and Jesus. Janey wasn't listening. She had her eye on the coffin, waiting for the curtains to close. She'd go as far to ask if she could watch the cremation itself happen. But that wouldn't be possible.

Molly Rose nudged her and whispered, 'Are you okay?'

'I will be,' Janey replied. 'You?'

Molly Rose took Janey's hand and said, 'I will be.'

-

Later that day, Molly Rose sat across from Janey in the restaurant and drank from her wine glass. Janey watched her carefully, studied her face, the way she moved. She was like a clone of her mother.

'So,' Molly Rose said, sounding hesitant about what she wanted to say. 'I've been meaning to ask you, after everything that's happened…' The words trailed off and she stared at Janey with wonder in her eyes.

'Go on then, say whatever it is you want to say.'

Molly Rose shifted in her seat and cleared her throat. 'Are you a gangster?'

A laugh burst out of Janey unexpectedly and Molly Rose smiled.

'What? I'm being serious.'

Janey composed herself. 'No, I wouldn't call myself a gangster.'

'But others would?'

Janey shrugged and took a sip from her glass. 'I don't know. Possibly. Probably. But that's how it's glorified by society. You know, how it's reported in the media to draw in its readers.'

Molly Rose raised a brow.

'It's the only way I can explain it to you.'

'So, if you're claiming you're *not* a gangster, what would you call yourself? I mean, what is it you do? And don't lie to me.' Molly Rose turned mildly serious. 'You pretty much erased me from the picture that day down at the docks. You must have some big influence over some high-up people to do that?'

Janey narrowed her eyes. 'You're very curious,' she said.

'Not curious. I'm observant. So, are you going to tell me?'

Janey sighed, put down her glass and said: 'Let's go for a walk.'

They got up and Janey paid the bill quickly before leaving the small restaurant on Byres Road. They headed along Dumbarton Road towards Kelvingrove Art Gallery. A part of the city that would forever be engrained in her memory – in all their memories.

'You know, I thought I wouldn't be able to walk around these parts again, you know, after what happened. But knowing that fucker is nothing but ash now makes it a lot easier.'

Janey didn't say anything. She didn't want to interrupt her granddaughter's thoughts. Speaking about what happened would have been hard enough without someone filling in the moments of silence.

'What happened to Kassy's body?' Molly Rose asked.

Janey cleared her throat. 'The police dealt with that situation. I'm not sure if they ever located any of her family, or if she even had family.'

'I don't know,' Molly Rose said. 'She mentioned a stepdad that had beat her up. I think that's why she was on the street. But I don't know anyone else.'

'I thought you two were best friends?'

Molly Rose stopped in the middle of the Partick bridge and looked over the edge to where Charlie had dumped Kassy's body, and pretended to Orla and Oliver that it was Molly Rose.

'I didn't know her for long, couple weeks maybe. But she took me under her wing when we were on the street together. She looked after me, showed me what was what, you know? I learned more about life in those two weeks than I had in my entire sixteen years. I don't even know if she's had a funeral, where she's buried; nothing. It's like she never existed.'

Something about that made Janey want to cry. Molly Rose had been through too much for only being on the planet for such a short space of time.

'It just goes to show, you can have the best upbringing, with wealth, and so many opportunities to grab at, but when you get out there into the real world, it can swallow you whole. It's how you deal with it that counts.'

Janey leaned back against the bridge wall and looked across at the galleries. She'd never met Kassy, but from what Molly Rose had told her, she sounded like a good girl at heart, even with her issues.

'You're right,' Janey said.

Molly Rose turned and leaned back too. They were now both facing the galleries.

'There's a lot I do. A lot of which is legal and above board. Some of which, not so much.'

Molly Rose faced Janey and smiled. 'Like what?'

Janey shook her head. 'No can do, I'm afraid.'

'Och, come on. I'm your granddaughter.'

'Exactly,' Janey said. 'You've seen too much already for your age.'

'Okay then, tell me about the boring legal stuff.'

Janey laughed, took her cigarette pack out from her pocket, placed one between her lips and lit it. Inhaling loudly, she said, 'I own various businesses up and down the country. Some of which I'm a silent partner.'

They started to walk past the galleries and round towards the park.

'What kind of businesses?' Molly Rose pressed.

'I own holiday parks. A few nightclubs. I've been looking into buying over a company that runs beauty shops.'

Molly Rose laughed. 'You launder money through those?'

Janey shook her head. '*I* don't do anything of the sort.'

'Ha, bet you don't. Seriously, Janey, I want to know where I'd fit in.'

'Fit in?' Janey frowned.

'In your business. You know, like, what I could do? How I could work for you?'

Janey stopped and stared at her granddaughter. 'No. Nope. No way. Not a chance.'

'Thanks.'

'You're young. You don't need to be getting involved in…' Janey trailed off. *In what?*

'If you're not a gangster and you're all above board, then what's the problem?'

'Don't you want to go to university? Study for a degree? Meet new people and build a life for yourself?'

Molly Rose looked up at the sky. 'I want to earn money, not get into student debt for a degree I'll likely never need or use. And I will meet new people. Every day. If you give me a job.'

Janey puffed out her cheeks. There was so much that she didn't want Molly Rose to know. She'd come across so much violence before she even knew who Janey was and that she'd even existed. Getting into that world would expose her to so much more than she could ever imagine.

'The look on your face tells me you don't think I could handle your world.'

'Oh, I think you could handle it. But your mum, she wouldn't want this for you, Molly Rose.'

'Yeah, well, she's dead. I'm not. I have everything to live for, Janey. And I get to do it with you.'

'And what about Sinead? Look at her. She's had to go to rehab because she lived in this world. You really want to be part of the problem?'

'You don't seem to take issue with it? You don't get down to the real nitty-gritty of it all. You've got a team of people doing that for you. You're the one at the top, aren't you?'

Janey raised a brow. 'At the top?'

'Don't treat me like a child, Janey. I might only be sixteen, but I've been through enough in recent weeks to understand what this is all about.'

Janey shook her head. 'Yes, I'm the one at the top.'

'Do you ever worry you'll get caught? That the police have you and your operations under surveillance?' Molly Rose asked.

Janey pursed her lips. She didn't want to tell Molly Rose the integral workings of the Hallahan empire just yet, or that she was virtually untouchable with having some of the highest-ranking officers on her payroll.

'I have a team working hard to make sure that operations run smoothly,' Janey simply replied.

'Like I said, I'm not stupid, Janey. I get how it all works? I mean, the police didn't come looking for me when I went missing, did they? It wasn't them who found me, it was you and your employees. You have them in your pocket, don't you? You took over searching for me so you could keep your operations hush-hush and deal with Charlie yourself.'

Janey couldn't help but smile. Her granddaughter was a smart, switched-on young woman.

'You should get into the psychic business. You'd make a fortune.'

'All I'm saying is, you shouldn't take my age and my once-vulnerability as a sign I can't cope. You should take the fact I fucking ended *him* as a sign that I can do anything. I'm not remorseful. I'm not sorry. He deserved to be wiped off the face of the planet. So merciless, so callous. I was the one who delivered the final shot when none of you could because you were all too distracted by Mum. I was the only one who didn't take my eye off the ball. If Mum's death has taught me anything, it's that, no matter how many people are around you, you can only truly protect yourself. *I* protected all of you when I pulled that trigger.'

Janey stared at Molly Rose in shock.

'What?'

'I thought you were a lot like Orla. Gentle, kind. But you're like me too. I don't know if that's a good thing yet.'

Molly Rose smiled and shook her head. Shoving her hands into her hoodie pocket, she walked towards the park. Just a few steps ahead, Janey called after her to stop.

'You will start off small. Just to see how you feel, how you fit in. I've got a new business opening up very soon. And I have just employed someone for the management position. Her name is Cheryl. She's lovely, very experienced in her field.'

'What's the business?' Molly Rose asked.

'I'm launching a beauty and wellness salon. It's something I've always wanted to add to the list and I thought that Glasgow would be the best place to do it now that I've got family here.'

Molly Rose nodded. 'And this woman you've employed to be the manager; is she family?'

'No. She's just very experienced. Has worked in the industry for a long time. Knows the suppliers, the clients. I'm just the owner. In fact, she'd be a great mentor to you. Would you like a job there? You could maybe do an apprenticeship? Work your way up?'

Molly Rose shrugged. 'Would I get to run the place one day?'

'Maybe. But you'd have to work hard, Molly Rose. You won't just have it all handed to you. There's no point being in charge when you don't know what you're doing.'

'Yeah,' Molly Rose said. 'All right. I'll give it a go. Might be fun to work as a Hallahan cartel boss.'

Janey raised a brow and the look on Molly Rose's face told her she was joking. 'Haha. Very funny. I'll assess things after a month, see how you're getting on. I'll ask Cheryl to observe you, give you jobs to do. Her CV said that she's a qualified trainer, so we can arrange for her to teach you how to do certain treatments, and how to run the shop properly, and we'll go from there. All legit, all legal. Nothing dodgy.'

Raising a brow, Molly Rose's mouth raised at the corner. 'Aye, for now.'

Chapter 69

Endrick Castle Estate sounded so much posher than it was. From the outside, it looked like a castle that had been forgotten about. On the inside, they'd tried to make the place look like a home, but it still felt clinical. It also made Sinead's cravings far worse than they would be on the outside because being there felt like prison. But she had no choice. At least here, she couldn't just go out and buy heroin and booze. Here, she had to check in every single day. She had to talk about her feelings: how she was coping and facing up to things.

'So, you're enjoying it here then?' Janey asked.

Sinead looked around her small room with ensuite bathroom and rolled her eyes. 'Enjoying is a bit of an overstatement. Now, if you'd said tolerating, then yes, I'd agree with that.'

Janey fell silent and Sinead worried how she'd react. Janey, her mum, was paying for this after all. And it hadn't been forced. It was accepted gratefully. That didn't make it any easier though because facing up to things had been the hardest part. It meant realising that as much as she wanted a mother in her life, Janey wasn't exactly the best person for her to be around, given her line of work.

'It's hard, I get it,' Janey said.

Sinead wasn't sure she agreed. In all honesty, it was Janey's type of business that put drugs on the streets and now she was paying for rehab. It was out of guilt. Janey wasn't responsible for the heroin supplying Glasgow drug addicts, but she was still part of the problem.

'Yeah, it's hard,' Sinead said. She didn't want to get into it with Janey right now. After everything that happened, she just wanted to focus on getting clean.

'You'll get there. Endrick Castle Estate has an incredible track record in successful rehabilitation.'

Sinead took a breath. Rehabilitation wouldn't change things though. The addiction would always be there, wouldn't it? Clawing to get back in. And Sinead knew herself: the slightest blip and she'd cave. Orla's traumatic death was one of the triggers and, every night, Orla's bloodied face was all she could see. Molly Rose taking Charlie out was one of the best and worst things to have come from that day. Now, Molly Rose was left out there, on her own with Janey to shape her. Oliver had had a breakdown and decided to go to America to visit his brother. Molly Rose had insisted she'd be fine on her own, that she could look after herself. Oliver should never have left her; Orla would be turning in her grave.

But Molly Rose would be far from fine. She'd either end up like Sinead or she'd end up like Janey. She'd be the victim of Janey's work, or a cog in the machine. Neither option was good. However, Sinead discharging herself wasn't an option. If she left rehab before completing her course here, she would be no use to Molly Rose either. Sinead had no doubt she'd fall back into her own ways to block out the trauma of the past month and a half.

'Yeah,' Sinead said. 'I know.'

Sinead listened as Janey made small talk. But all she could think about was how torn she was. On one hand, she had her birth mother back in her life – something that she'd always wanted. But on the other, Janey was the cause of so many problems. Sinead's drug use wasn't the issue – that was something she could handle on her own. It was that, since she'd been in rehab, she'd realised Orla's barrier against Janey had been spot on. Yes, of course it wasn't her fault what had happened all those years ago. But all Sinead wanted was a mother figure. Instead, she had a crime boss. Someone who was responsible for putting drugs on the streets. The drugs Sinead was addicted to.

'So, when are you allowed visitors?' Janey asked, her words penetrating Sinead's thoughts.

'Oh,' Sinead said. 'Actually, I don't think I'm strong enough for any visitors yet. I need to break my connection to the outside world and my association with people I know being able to bring me... well, you know. So, I think I'm going to do my full twelve weeks without visitors. And then I have twenty-four weeks outside to get through.'

Janey hesitated, then replied, 'Yes. Of course.'

'So, how's Molly Rose?'

'Oh, she's fine.'

'Really? She's fine, after everything?'

'Yes. She seems to be coping very, very well. I'm surprised, actually, considering what she's gone through.'

Sinead was doubtful. Molly Rose was good at masking her feelings. She'd call her later, double-check for herself how she was getting on.

'Right,' Janey said. 'I need to get going. I've got a ferry to catch.'

'You're heading home?' Sinead asked.

'Yes. Got some business to attend to. Molly Rose is coming with me.'

It was like a punch in the gut when she heard the words. 'She's going to Belfast with you?'

'Yeah, she insisted. Wants to find out where her ancestors were from. Wants to see where I grew up.'

Sinead closed her eyes. 'Right. Well, look after her.'

'I will. Don't sound so worried, Sinead. She's my granddaughter. I won't let anything happen to her. Not after everything that's happened.'

'Make sure you don't, Janey. She's been through enough.'

Silence hung between them before Sinead said goodbye and ended the call.

The thought of Molly Rose being sucked into that world made Sinead want to throw up. It triggered her addiction. Drinking away the thoughts in her head would be the easiest solution. Going out and injecting heroin would be her preferred method of coping. But she couldn't. And what would be the point. It wouldn't change anything.

There was a gentle tap on the door and Sinead looked up to see one of the councillors standing by the open door.

'Are you joining us for the art therapy session this afternoon? It starts in ten minutes.'

Sinead glanced down at the phone in her hand and then back up at the councillor. 'Yeah,' she said. 'I'll be right down.'

Because what else could she do? She couldn't leave and tell Molly Rose not to go with Janey. Of course, Sinead knew that Molly Rose would be safe with Janey, in theory. Janey would never intentionally hurt Molly Rose. She wouldn't intentionally hurt any of them. But she was in a world that only Sinead had scratched the surface of. She knew it went a lot deeper than she'd experienced herself. With drug trafficking and dealing came violence and death.

When Sinead got out, she'd do what she could to convince Molly Rose to stay out of that side of things with Janey. No matter what, it would lead her down the wrong path.

Chapter 70

Molly Rose looked up at the sign which stretched across the top of the entrance and the front window. Orla Wellness and Beauty. Janey had actually named the place after her mum.

Molly Rose stepped into the shop in Glasgow and took it all in. It wasn't like your usual side street sunbed shop. It looked glamourous. It sold smoothies, other healthy drinks and snacks in its health bar. It had white walls, a gloss floor and a chandelier hanging from the ceiling. There was a small gym in the glass room to the side of the building. There was a nail bar at the back, and an inhouse makeup artist. It was for people with money and a decent lifestyle.

'Wow,' Molly Rose said. 'You'll put the rest of the sunbed places in the area out of business.'

'Ha! Well, it is the best of the best. But it costs money to come here. You need a membership and I'm particular about who I let in. So, you need to ensure you go through the procedure for entering new clients into the system.'

Molly Rose frowned. 'Jeezo, it's not like they're applying for a job in a school. You make it sound like a police check.'

Jancy pursed her lips. 'I like to be thorough. After everything that's happened, I want to be sure that the clients I let into this place are legit. This place is going to be used by the super-wealthy, Molly Rose. And they won't want to be mixing with just anyone. It's important to get this right.'

Raising a brow, Molly Rose laughed. 'Sounds a bit stuck-up if you ask me.'

'You don't have to take this job if you don't want it, Molly Rose. But you were the one who wanted in on the family firm. This way, you're on the legit side of things and I keep you safe.'

'Safe?' she asked. 'Why wouldn't I be safe? The worst has already happened to me, Janey. To us. What else could possibly happen that makes the past few months seem like a fucking theme park ride?'

Janey looked at her wide-eyed, before smiling and saying: 'Point taken. But still, you know I'll always want to keep you safe. I owe it to you and your mum. I owe it to all of you.'

Molly Rose moved to the centre of the floor and slowly turned, taking it all in. She glanced back at Janey and said: 'I never thanked you.'

'Thanked me for what?'

'For protecting me. You stopped me from going to prison.'

Janey shrugged. 'There's no need to thank me. It wouldn't have mattered who pulled the trigger, Molly Rose. No one deserved to do time for that piece of shit. Especially not you. And I'm your gran, that's my job. The moment I met you, I knew I would never let anything happen to you. That's why I was so reluctant to let you into the firm. But here we are. You got your own way.'

Molly Rose smiled. 'I always do.'

Janey opened her arms and pulled Molly Rose in for a hug. After a short embrace, Janey let go and walked across to the front desk. 'Now, this place has a manager, you'll be assistant to her. You will do everything she says – no backchat.'

'As if,' Molly Rose scoffed. 'Who is she?'

'Her name is Cheryl. She's very nice, very experienced. She'll show you the ropes.'

Molly Rose nodded as she slipped in behind the desk. 'So, what will I be doing?'

The door to the shop opened and both Janey and Molly Rose turned.

'Janey,' the woman said.

'Cheryl, it's good to see you. Thanks for coming in early on your first day. I know how much of a pain in the arse it can be to add hours on to your day,' Janey said.

Molly Rose took in her new boss's appearance. Dressed in white to match the décor, it seemed. Subtle makeup, hair in a neat bun on top of her head. She was well turned out. Perfect for this kind of place. Molly Rose looked down at herself. Also dressed in white, but definitely less glamorous.

'And you must be Molly Rose?' Cheryl asked. 'Janey's told me all about you.'

'Like we discussed, I'd like for Molly Rose to learn about the business.'

'Excellent,' Cheryl replied. 'So, you can take calls, log appointments. I'll start you off with the basics and when your college classes start, I can support you with that too. I'll go over everything with you. Does that sound okay?'

Molly Rose nodded and took a deep breath. 'I think I can manage that.'

Janey smiled. 'I don't doubt it. Right then, I'll leave you both to it. I've got somewhere I need to be.'

Molly Rose gave her a nervous smile as she walked out of the door. Once out of sight, she turned to Cheryl, who was switching on the computer.

'So, my gran said you've got lots of experience?'

Cheryl nodded. 'I've worked in this industry since I left school. Could run the place with my eyes shut. And by the end of the week, we'll have you doing the same.'

Molly Rose thought of Kassy. It made her sad to think that she never had this chance. They could have done this together had she not fallen foul of Charlie.

'Right then,' Cheryl smiled. 'Let's get started.'

Chapter 71

Janey got out of the car and stared up at the building. Ciaran followed her. The grand house looked like it hadn't been cared for at all. The garden was overgrown, the walls were covered in moss and the drive was cracked.

'Janey,' Kristo said as he walked towards her. 'Ciaran.'

'Are you sure about this, Kristo?'

'Absolutely. Our links with the CID got in touch when you were back in Belfast. It's definitely his. Or was, until the bailiffs chucked him out months ago. He was bankrupt.'

Janey raised a brow but kept an eye on the house. A forensics tent was set up at the front, and forensics officers came and went.

'What the hell is going on?' Ciaran asked.

'The people who bought it at auction decided to renovate. Turn it into luxury flats. When they stared pulling the place apart, human remains were found.'

Janey closed her eyes. 'Remains? How many?'

'They don't know yet. But so far, at least three.'

'Jesus,' she whispered, opening her eyes again and looking back at the house. 'Female?'

'It's likely. One of the officers said that they're hopeful the remains are of three prostitutes who have been on the missing list. Of course, it was off the record.'

'Seems like he used this place like his own personal brothel,' Kristo replied.

Janey nodded. 'I hope the fucker is burning in hell,' she said.

Kristo pulled something out of his pocket and handed it to her. 'I don't know if you want to see it or not, but it's addressed to you. It looks old. Like it was written years ago. But I thought you deserved to know it existed and you can decide what you want to do with it.'

Janey took the envelope from Kristo and glared at the messy handwriting. The old farmhouse address had been scribbled on the centre. By the looks of it, the letter had been returned to him, saying that the addressee was no longer at the place stated on the front of the letter.

'Thank you, Kristo.'

'So, what's happening now?' Ciaran asked.

Kristo glanced back at the house. 'Well, our CID officers said they'd be in touch if they had anything else for us. But it looks likely that the reason Charlie was desperate for the money from you was because he had secrets literally buried in the walls of the house. Looks like he either wanted to get away or buy the house back.'

'Fuck,' Ciaran said.

Janey looked down at the letter and felt sick. Anything could be in there. Did she really want to know what he had to say? Could it be a confession, an admission to what he'd done to her and possibly others? Unlikely, considering how selfish he was.

She folded the envelope in half and shoved it into her pocket.

Janey shook her head. *A horror house*, Janey thought. Whatever anyone could think up, it would be nowhere near as vile and horrific as the truth.

'Good, if they've any sense, they'll burn the place and sell the land on to some farmers.' Sighing loudly, Janey continued, 'I'll leave you to deal with the rest of this. I'm heading home.'

She got back into the passenger seat of the Defender and Ciaran started the car.

'Are you okay?' he asked. 'Are you going to read that?'

She felt the weight of the letter in her pocket. 'I don't know. Whatever is in there isn't going to make me feel better about what's gone on over the years, is it? And it looks like it was written long before I came back to find the girls. So, it's probably got nothing to do with them.'

Ciaran drove down the private road away from the house. The cordon at the bottom was opened by the guarding officer, who gave them a nod on their way out.

'You think you'd regret not reading it?' Ciaran asked, pulling on to the A81 and heading away from Strathblane.

'I don't know. But I know that as soon as I hear his voice in my head when I start reading, I'll wish I hadn't opened it. So, no, I probably won't.'

'Do you want me to read it for you?'

'No, thank you. You don't need to be poisoned with his bullshit any more than the rest of us. He's done enough damage.'

They fell silent and Janey couldn't handle how quiet things were. Silence meant space for intrusive thoughts. She leaned over to turn the radio up when a huge force shunted the car onto its side.

'Fuck!' Ciaran shouted as the car spun several times. Janey raised both her arms to protect her head as the car rolled for what seemed like an eternity.

It came to a bouncing stop and landed on the wheels. Glancing around her, Janey noted that they'd landed in the field, a good hundred yards off the road.

'Ciaran?'

Her eyes were fuzzy, her head throbbed but the adrenaline that coursed through her made her body feel like it was buzzing.

'Ciaran, are you okay?'

She looked at him, slumped over the wheel. Blood trickled down from his nose. His eyes were open.

Janey unclipped her belt and leaned over, placed her fingers on his neck and waited. And waited.

'Ciaran!' she shouted, giving him a shove with her hand.

Nothing.

Janey opened her mouth as uncontrollable sobs and screams escaped her.

Epilogue

'It's done,' Leo Davidson said into the burner phone as he sat on his sofa and watched the video on his mobile phone, over and over again. He rejoiced in the crunching sound as the car was run off the road. The exhilaration he felt as he watched the car flip down into the field was unexpected. But he was glad to feel something other than pain.

'You're sure?' the voice on the other end of the line asked.

'I've seen it with my own eyes. She's dead, there's no way she's survived that.'

'Good,' the voice replied. 'That family cost us hundreds of thousands of pounds, Leo. And don't think I've forgotten the part you played in that. Your son under-estimated that girl's family and I'm sorry to say, you over-estimated your son's capabilities in this line of work. I'm still fucking seething at that.'

Leo closed his eyes. 'I know, boss. I'm sorry. You can be assured that kind of thing *won't* happen again.'

'I'm sorry your son is dead, Leo. But he was a liability and we don't deal in liabilities. He lost us some very good revenue. We do not accept this. You need to focus now, do you understand? Otherwise, you'll be the next one to get his head crushed in a car accident.'

Leo felt his stomach lurch at the threat.

'I'll be in touch; we've got another shipment detail to go over.'

Leo nodded. 'Yes, boss. I'll talk to you later.'

Leo hung up the phone and replayed the video again. The idea that he had to keep working for the people who'd murdered his son because of one slip-up was killing him. Orla Hunter getting involved, telling Dean to break things off with her daughter was a warning. She could have brought unwanted attention to their door. But then, when their Polish boss found out about the mishap – that Dean had lost a sale because he'd not been clever enough in his recruitment – he'd been punished. Not only for that, but for the lack of quality in the passport production. These people didn't take anything lightly and Dean had paid the ultimate price.

The sound of the front door opening made Leo sit up straight. He saw his wife walk into the lounge with an expectant look on her face.

'She's dead?' Leo's wife asked.

He gestured for her to watch the video. She didn't blink as she watched the car flip down into the field. Her expression didn't change. She didn't blink.

'I'll get confirmation soon, but there's no way she'd have survived that,' Leo said, filling the silence. 'You've seen it yourself now. If she's not dead yet, it won't be long.'

'Good. Our son deserves justice. And I won't stop there. An eye for an eye?' she sneered. 'More like an eye for an entire clan. We can't get to the ones who killed our son, but we can destroy the people who caused his death.'

Leo nodded. He didn't tell her what his boss had said about Dean being a liability. It was all still too raw for her. The grief their family had felt when Dean's body had been found had nearly killed them both. But now, revenge was what Leo Davidson lived for. And he wouldn't stop at Janey Hallahan.

'Sweetheart, trust me on this, I'll make sure there isn't a Hallahan left on the planet by the time I'm done.'

He watched his wife let down her neat, blonde bun from the top of her head and step out of her crisp, white uniform.

'I promise you, Cheryl. I'll get the next best thing to justice for Dean. And the next one on my list is that little *bitch* Molly Rose Hunter.'

A letter from Alex

Well, hello there and welcome to my tenth novel. Ten! How did that happen? I feel like I've only just signed my first contract with Hera, which was back in 2018 when they took my book baby, *No Looking Back* and made it the most amazing thing that could have ever happened to me.

So, yeah, book ten. That's a huge achievement for me. I was so close to giving up writing just before Hera signed me. I'm so glad they did and I'm so glad I didn't.

How I've written ten books in five years is insane to me, but here I am.

I want to thank every single one of you, whether you are an eBook, paperback, audio or library reader. You are the reason I can keep coming back with another book and I'm so grateful that you keep coming back to read the next one. If you're new to my work, welcome and thank you. You have no idea how much I appreciate your interest.

Janey Hallahan is by far my very favourite character. I see her everywhere and she's always in my head. What would Janey do/say about this? It's constant and I don't want her to go away and I hope that you feel the same about her, because she has so much more to give.

As always, you can find me on all the socials if you want to contact me, including TikTok.

Alternatively, you can email me directly at alexkaneauthor@gmail.com

Acknowledgments

I couldn't possibly start anywhere else with this: to Hera Books, especially Keshini. You're all amazing. I feel so lucky to have you by my side, cheering me on and encouraging me with each book. Keshini, your editorial skills are second to none. Here's to ten books x

My wonderful agent, Jo Bell. I genuinely don't have words. You're so amazing at what you do, and I can't wait to do the next ten books with you. To all at the agency at Bell Lomax Moreton, thank you.

To you, the reader. You're amazing. Thank you for the purchases and the borrows, the recommendations and the reviews. Without you, I'd just be talking to myself (which I actually still do anyway ☺).

I want to pay a special thank you to Dee Vought Blake, who back in March 2023, entered a competition on my Instagram page to come up with the name for one of my characters. That character became Molly Rose. I did say that whoever came up with the most fitting name would get a mention in the acknowledgements at the end of the book. So, thank you, Dee. The name absolutely fits the character. ☺

To my supportive family and friends, thank you for your words of encouragement.

To my parents. As always, thank you for all you do for me and my wee family, especially during times of illness and stress.

To my daughter. You're the reason I continue to strive to write better books, because being able to do this as my job means we get to spend every day together without living by the clock and I feel so lucky that we can.

To my husband, Chris. Thank you for continually encouraging me to keep going and for reminding me that I can still do this. You're amazing.